DEATH OF A BUTTERFLY

Death of a Butterfly

THAMES RIVER PRESS
An imprint of Wimbledon Publishing Company Limited (WPC)
Another imprint of WPC is Anthem Press (www.anthempress.com)
First published in the United Kingdom in 2013 by
THAMES RIVER PRESS
75–76 Blackfriars Road
London SE1 8HA

www.thamesriverpress.com

All the characters and events described in this novel are imaginary and any similarity with real people or events is purely coincidental.

A CIP record for this book is available from the British Library.

ISBN 978-0-85728-003-9

Cover design by Adrienne Brown.

This title is also available as an eBook

DEATH OF A BUTTERFLY

Simon Brown

THAMES RIVER PRESS

Also by Simon Brown

The Healer (O Books)
Macrobiotics for Life (North Atlantic)
Feng Shui Life Coach (Godsfield Press)
The Secrets of Face Reading (Godsfield Press)
Practical Wabi Sabi (Carroll & Brown)
Modern Day Macrobiotics (Carroll & Brown)
The Feng Shui Bible (Godsfield Press)
The Principles of Feng Shui (HarperCollins)

ACKNOWLEDGEMENTS

Writing can be very personal and subjective. My words can be read in so many ways and the story may provoke an array of responses. During my writing, it is important to me to test the book out and understand how readers are responding. In this I have enjoyed the great help of several wonderful people who have read through various drafts and provided more objective comments. I would like to thank Tine Weis, who read through the whole manuscript and described how she responded to my writing on each page, to Klara LeVine whose attention to detail helped me create a consistent writing style, and Charlotta Andersson who provided insightful comments and suggestions. My agent Darin Jewell also arranged for several readers to make very helpful reviews.

Adrienne Brown gave expression to her amazing artistic talents to create a beautiful image and cover design.

The characters in this novel are created out of a blend of various people who have been influential on my way of living, and these include my mother Patricia, Dragana Brown, my children Christopher, Alexander, Nicholas and Michael, and Greg Johnson, along with all my students, clients and friends.

I would also like to thank my agent Darin Jewell for getting my writing published and everyone at Thames River Press for making this book a reality.

You can find out more about me at www.chienergy.co.uk and get in touch with me at simon@chienergy.co.uk

CATERPILLAR

CHAPTER 1

The adult butterfly lays eggs which hatch in about 3–7 days. The young caterpillars start off eating frantically for 2–3 weeks. They grow quickly and increase their body mass by a few thousand times.

Caterpillars grow so much that they shed their exoskeleton several times, and can change their appearance through this process.

I watch my aunt pour the pearl jasmine tea. Her long fingers clasp the handle whilst her free hand gently touches the lid. I listen to the bubbling sound of the liquid falling into the cup. My eyes stare into the swirling steam. I see the reflection of the window in the surface of the tea. I pick up the cream china in my hands and feel the warmth. I lift the smooth curved handle and touch the rough unglazed surface underneath. I smell the sweet fragrance, letting the steam float across my cheeks. I tip the cup slowly until the liquid touches my lips and seeps into my mouth. The heat spreads across my tongue and gums. I taste the jasmine and slowly return my cup to its saucer.

I am living more of my life as it happens through my senses. I look up to see eyes, set within peaceful faces. My mind interrupts, grabbing an inherited judgement. Instead of beautiful, loving humans, I see a rapist, murderer and the woman my once beloved husband left me for. I wash those thoughts from my consciousness. This is my new family. These are the people I have chosen to explore the next phase of my life with.

I walked up the paved path to my front door. My mind turned to tea and biscuits, before marking Monday's homework. It was late September, and dry brown leaves had blown up against my door forming a small pile. I brushed them to one side with my shoe, letting them spiral into the wind. I fumbled through my bag for my keys.

As I looked up I saw my reflection in the glass. My shoulder length hair had blown to one side creating a lopsided appearance. Long wriggling snakes fought each other. Their blond heads seemed to want to escape their darker roots. A few strands had stuck to my lip-balm. I unlocked the latch and pushed the door open, hearing the familiar sound of the draft strip brushing across the mat.

My new business cards were scattered across the black and white hall tiles. I squatted down to impatiently scoop then up. I held one up to the light. Oh fiddlesticks, the mauve background seemed a little too pale for the white letters.

As I walked into the living room, I was jolted out of my rhythm. I dropped my bag and keys. My eyes slid down Mathew's body and froze on his left ankle. His skin was showing. Mathew hated his trousers being short.

There were small white feathers on our beige carpet.

I knelt and pulled the charcoal grey fabric down to his shoe. I touched his cold hand and straightened it so I could tidy his sleeve. I smelt Mathew's cinnamon fragrance. I started to adjust his tie, and then felt helpless. The end of the tie seemed to have been sucked into a hole in his chest. The maroon silk blended into the wound. The fabric was matted to his shirt and skin by dark coagulated blood. Nausea rose and I instinctively put my hand over my mouth. Slumping back against the side of our blue sofa, a shaking consumed me. Tears ran down my cheeks. I pulled my knees to my chest and rocked back and forth.

The feathers blew around me as I swayed.

I could not trust my senses. The image in front of me was all wrong. There had to be some way back to my normal sensations. I wanted to shout out that there had been a mistake. Yet I was too numb too act, too anaesthetised to feel any emotion. I had been struck dumb.

I still had my old red coat on when I opened the door to a uniformed policeman. I was aware of a peripheral commotion, blue flashing lights, cars pulling up, a large woman opening the gate but it was the constable's face that held my gaze. He held my arm, gently leading me back into my home.

"Is there another room you can sit down in?"

We passed the living room door and I sat at the kitchen table. I looked at a circle of crumbs on the bare wood surface.

The constable put the kettle on.

I looked back down the corridor and could see men and women sealing themselves into zip up protective clothing. Two strode into the living room. Flash, flash, flash. A man knelt to examine the front door. There was banter, organisation and familiarity to their routine.

"Here you are, Mrs Blake." The constable placed a cup of tea in front of me. An orange Bart Simpson stared at me with an inane grin, jolting me into a different reality for a split second before the numbness kicked in again.

A large sky blue, nylon-suited woman spread out on the chair opposite me. Her rose perfume was overwhelming. She took a chocolate bar out of her bag broke it in two and put half in front of me.

"I'm Inspector Pride. How are you?"

"Confused, shocked, disorientated."

Pride looked at me sympathetically.

"I'll find someone to help you. Do you feel ready to just go through the events?" She took a bite of her snack.

I held my half and looked at it.

"Hey ho, life's a box of chocolates."

I immediately regretted saying that. It was a saying my mother used a lot. Dad used to say it completely out of context to make me laugh. Mum's face, lined with a deep frown, made it all the funnier. As I got older I inherited the expression and it would appear in my head whenever life took a difficult turn. My mother explained it as meaning life was full of surprises. Sometimes you bit into a chocolate and enjoyed the filling whilst others tasted disgusting. Dad extended the expression to include random objects. Life's a bowl of fruit, life's a shop full of clothes, life's a cupboard with three pairs of shoes. The more obscure the context, the funnier my silly expression became. Those words had become so ingrained in me that today they flew out of their own volition.

Pride looked at me with a quizzical expression for a moment.

"Yes, well, right now I need to hear what happened when you came home."

I nodded. I wanted to talk. I wanted someone to help me make sense of it all. I hoped the inspector would drag me back to normality. My skin crawled as I considered she might join me in my nightmare.

After I described my homecoming, there was silence. The inspector looked a little confused. She finished her mouthful.

"So you came home from school at four-fifteen, found your husband dead on the floor, but did not call us until six?"

I nodded. I felt a pang of guilt. The thought flashed through me that this made me a suspect. I had a history of feeling nervous around authority. I remember feeling tense around my teacher, the odious Mrs Maddox, as a child. Even as an adult, I am self-conscious when in the presence of the head teacher. Now I felt a need to persuade the policemen and women in my home that I was innocent.

"I just couldn't believe it. I just froze." And then as an afterthought I added, "He doesn't usually come home until six."

I put my hand over my mouth in an attempt to stem the stupidity coming out of it.

"There is no obvious sign of a break in. Do you know anyone who might have done this? Any enemies he has upset?"

I shook my head.

"I keep asking, Why? Why my Mathew?"

"Your husband's wallet was on the table, does he usually keep money in it?"

I nodded.

"It was empty when we checked."

A policewoman took me to our neighbours, Edward and Edwina Edwards. Mathew and I used to laugh about their names trying to imagine Edward's parents snorting with laughter as they wrote Edward on the birth certificate. We later found out that Edward changed it himself, by deed poll. He used to be called Peter. Edwina was her original name. We assumed they got drunk and thought it would be a hilarious wheeze to get married and be Edward and Edwina Edwards. They even shared the same birthday, although Edward was two years older than Edwina's thirty-five.

I used to smirk in their company when they mentioned each other's name, but not today.

Edward stood by the window adopting a martial arts style stance. He looked athletic and rooted to the ground.

"Oh Amanda, you poor thing. You must feel like you're whole world's fallen apart. Who would have thought the grim reaper would visit our quiet street." Edward continued his karate kata with a series of strikes and blocks. Then he took off his glasses and shook his head with a look of resigned disapproval.

"If I get my hands on the culprit, I'll…"

Edward spun round and executed a sidekick, catching the sofa with his foot. He lost balance, hopping on his standing foot until retrieving his striking limb. He must have injured his groin, as he limped back to the window pressing his hand into his hip.

Edwina made a point of ignoring him and sat next to me on their brown leather sofa. She put a glass of red wine in front of me.

"Well, I hope they catch whoever did it."

"Live by the sword, die by the sword," Edward muttered.

Edwina put her arm around me. I felt the softness of her body.

"Don't worry, Amanda, we'll look after you. Eddy can get your things and you can stay the night."

I wobbled emotionally and started sobbing again. I didn't want them to see me like this. Edwina led me to bed and left some sleeping pills on the bedside table.

When I woke, I cried my heart out. Edward came in with some tea and sat on the side of the bed. He put his broad hand on my head and gently moved my tear soaked hair to the sides of my face. His skin felt warm. I smelt orange scented soap. He pulled a tissue from the box on the bedside table and dried my face. Edward sighed.

"Once more unto the breach."

Edward left. I looked at my phone. Tuesday 7.45.

Inspector Pride came round later during the morning. She collapsed into a plump black leather chair opposite me. There was an initial thud followed by a slight wheezing as the fabric of her clothes adapted to the shape of the chair. These small, obscure details occasionally broke through the heavy fog pervading my mind. Edwina offered to make some tea. I began to smell the inspector's fragrance.

"Do you feel ready to talk?"

"No, not really, but if it would help…"

"So far we know your husband died between one and two yesterday afternoon. He had just eaten some salami, salad, bread and water. We think he opened the door to someone and that person came into the living room. It would appear that your husband was kneeling when he was shot, as though he was executed. He was shot three times in the chest from about two metres. The assailant was standing. One bullet pierced his upper left ventricle. He would have died very quickly. The killer used a cushion to help silence the shots."

"I just don't understand why someone would want to kill him."

"Apart from the money in his wallet, have you noticed anything else missing?"

"In the night, I remembered Mathew's watch was missing."

Pride wrote on her pad.

"Can you describe it?"

"Black face, orange hands, chrome body and black leather strap. I bought it for his forty-eighth birthday."

Edwina came in with the teas. Pride looked at the three cups of steaming tea and, I thought, gave a little sigh.

"I think I have a little treat in here." Pride rummaged through her bag and produced a packet of chocolate biscuits. Pride offered me a biscuit and I took one even though I did not particularly like them. I didn't want to offend her.

"Okay, so far we have no motive other than an unknown sum of cash and wristwatch. Let's try and explore some possibilities. What was your husband's work?"

"Mathew ran a men's clothing shop with James Harris in Welwyn Garden City. It's called Stiletto. They had been working together for four years."

Pride looked up from her pad. She frowned and I thought a shadow crossed her face.

"James Harris."

She said the words with a hint of menace as she wrote them down.

"And how did they get on?"

"Fine, I think. They had minor differences, but nothing serious."

"Did your husband have any close friends?"

"He liked social events, parties, dinners and playing his guitar, but apart from James he did not have any close friends."

"Did he go out on his own much?"

"Just up to London to play at various blues jam sessions."

Pride raised an eyebrow.

"He would go to a club with his guitar and they would each get called up to play a couple of songs."

"How long have you lived here?"

"Since we were married five years ago, just after my thirtieth birthday."

"How long did you know Mr Blake before your wedding?"

"About a year. My mother died in a car accident and in an effort to stop moping about the house, I went to tango classes and met Mathew. My father died of a heart attack five years earlier, so Mathew became my new family."

I swallowed hard to contain a rush of sadness that threatened to spill over. I did not want to cry in front of Pride. I certainly did not want her to comfort me.

"Do you feel able to go back to your home? I would like you to see if anything has been disturbed."

My left eye twitched and I pressed my hand against the eyeball to stop it. I looked up at Pride and nodded.

There was blue and white tape marking out an area around the front door. We entered. I felt awkward. It was as though my home and I had been very close, but we had experienced something so awful that just seeing each other conjured up a terrible reminder. I felt an icy crevice between us. I pushed my hands into my pockets and kept myself away from the walls and furniture. My only contact was my tentative steps on the floor. Pride introduced me to Derek Sopwith. Mr Sopwith took my fingerprints to eliminate mine from the crime scene.

"Have you got anything, Derek?" Pride called out.

"Not yet, Inspector. I don't think we will find any DNA here. There's nothing on the wallet. I think the victim must have handed any money over himself. Just a smudge on the front door, made as the attacker left."

Pride took a call and asked whether there was any news from interviews with neighbours.

I started in the living room. A plastic sheet covered the area where Mathew had been shot. I noticed our big orange cushion on the floor with holes in it. There were black marks spreading out from the holes. The feathers had floated out across the room and into the hallway.

I experienced a flash of frustration thinking of cleaning it all up. I took a deep breath and looked at the rest of the room.

Everything seemed to be in place. Mathew was the tidier of the two of us. Sometimes I would find him straightening all the books on the shelf or rearranging the clock, candles and photos on the mantelpiece. He had a piercing eye for detail. I found it slightly intimidating. It felt more like his house than mine.

I remember, after a year or two of living together, starting to experience a discomfort when I finished dressing, and he cast his critical eye over me. He never made any comments, just observed with an intense expression. My friends smiled when they saw Mathew picking a hair off my jumper or flicking a piece of dust off my shoulder.

Recently I had begun to put on a little weight. I had filled out around my hips and my legs were chunkier. I began to feel uncomfortable undressing with Mathew in the room. I felt he would be quick to notice any new bulge, cellulite or wrinkle.

"Where was the wallet when you found it?"

"Derek, can you show Mrs Blake where the wallet was?" Pride called out.

Sopworth came in with a laptop. He squinted as he searched through files until an artificially bright photograph appeared with the brown wallet on the smoked glass living room table. It was placed close to the corner so that the two nearest edges of the wallet were parallel and equidistant to the edges of the table. Only Mathew could position his wallet in such a way after handing over money to someone pointing a gun to his chest.

I tried to look at the room with Mathew's sense of precision. The symmetry of the mantelpiece was unbalanced. I put my hand to my mouth and gasped.

"The photograph of us in Paris is missing."

"Can you describe the photograph and the frame?"

"We were standing on the roof balcony of the Pompidou Centre with Paris behind us. It was in a plain wood frame."

Pride wrote in her pad.

"Can you notice anything else?"

There was a slight gap on the bottom bookshelf. My copy of *Practical Wabi Sabi* was slumped at an angle and pulled out slightly. Our old photograph album should have occupied the empty space. Mathew had made up a printed album of all the best photographs of the two us for our fifth wedding anniversary. I checked the other shelves. Pride encouraged me to search the rest of the house. I looked for the album in all the obvious places but it was not there. I noticed I became slightly frantic, as though finding the photographs would bring some sense of security.

I walked back into the living room and reported that the album was missing. I felt a chill run up through my abdomen to my heart. I began to feel invaded, exposed and vulnerable. The killer had too much information. Pride looked perplexed. Sopworth was the first to speak.

"Mr Blake lets someone into his home having eaten lunch, and they come to the living room. He takes out his wallet and possibly gives the intruder cash, puts his wallet on the table, kneels down here and is shot three times in the chest at close range. The killer removes and takes his wristwatch, grabs a photograph from the mantelpiece and finds and removes the family photo album. Bizarre, don't you think."

"Perhaps Mr Blake gave the intruder the album, Derek. Otherwise it would imply the killer spent time searching for the album after he shot Mr Blake and knew of its existence. Stealing a photo album is unlikely to be a random act, but I can't imagine the killer had murdered for the album."

"Looking at the neatness and precision of Mr Blake's placement of his wallet, I wonder whether he would have held the other books in place as he removed the album."

I swallowed and nodded.

"Yes, I'm sure he would, even if he was about to be shot."

Pride nodded and turned to me.

"Can you retrace your steps and see if you remember anything else unusual when you came home?"

I went back outside, put my key in the door and pushed it open. Then I remembered my cards on the floor. I told the inspector.

"Must have brushed them off the table on the way out. He or she was in a panic."

I continued into the living room. Nothing else stood out.

"I don't think I would be comfortable sleeping here tonight."

Pride put her blotchy, pudgy hand against my arm. I stiffened.

"I can have a PC stay here if you wish."

"I would prefer to stay another night with the Edwards."

CHAPTER 2

I lay on the small bed in the Edwards' home. My feelings alternated between a raw sense of loss to numbness. Earlier, when with Inspector Pride, I could objectively speculate on why Mathew had been shot and then later fall into a deep pit of despair. My heart felt as though it had been bruised, scratched and then repeatedly grazed against cold gravel. Each time I felt my pain was beginning to heal, the scabs were pulled off and I began to bleed with uncontrollable emotions.

I longed to sleep but even with the sleeping pills, my night was filled with cold sweats, anxiety, panic and wild dreams. Part of me was still in my premurder life, thinking Mathew would suddenly appear and slip into bed with me.

When I woke I was disorientated. For a moment I forgot where I was. Edward came in with breakfast. He set the tray down beside my bed. He sat on the side of my bed, resting his hand on my leg. Edward looked into my eyes. His blue eyes looked enlarged through the lenses of his silver rimmed glasses. I thought he wanted to say something but he could not form the words.

"Edward, are you alright?"

He patted my leg and looked flustered.

"I'm fine. I'm just feeling worried about you."

Edward took off his glasses and immediately put them back on again before he got up.

"I'm going for a run."

He took in a deep breath, and then opened the door with a karate style movement as he breathed out strongly.

When I finished my breakfast I had a long bath, dressed and went downstairs. Edwina came into the kitchen whilst I loaded my breakfast dishes into the dishwasher.

"Is Edward alright?"

"Yes, I think so."

"It's just that he seemed kind of speechless and left abruptly when he brought my breakfast up."

"Well, we are both shocked by what has happened and I don't think Eddy really knows what to do when a woman is upset. I don't think his world includes too many emotions."

I felt her last sentence was spoken with an edge of bitterness. It was as though the claim held an emotional charge over her. The words seemed to tighten around her throat causing her jaw to stiffen. I tried to change the subject.

"I didn't realise Edward is so keen on martial arts."

"Oh, don't take any notice. It's just another of his passing phases. Last month it was all yoga postures. He's showing off because you're here."

I spent Wednesday in my home. I cleaned up the feathers and wiped the crumbs off the kitchen table. I spent some time lying on the sofa watching television, I sat by the window watching the clouds go by, then I felt withdrawn and curled up on my bed. I bunched up the pillows, cushions and duvet, creating a nest to hibernate in. Mathew used to be irritated by all the cushions I piled up on our bed, accusing them of being of no possible use and cluttering up the room. Even I did not foresee their later use.

I began to think about Mum and Dad. Many of my memories of doing things with my father had a classical music soundtrack to them. If I ever wanted to be reminded of the sounds of my mother, I only had to listen to BBC Radio Four. When Mum died, I found my father's old Quad amplifier, preamp and turntable in the attic, along with his records. I kept them in my home and when I later showed them to Mathew, near the beginning of our relationship, his face flushed with excitement. He claimed the old valves gave the music more authentic, mellow tones.

I thought music might fill the void I felt inside me. I started with my father's favourites, Beethoven's "Immortal Beloved," then I lifted the needle and listened to Rachmaninoff's second piano concerto. Next, I transferred my musical associations to Mathew. We went through a phase of listening to sixties music. It coincided with my exploration of pop art. I played "Californian Dreamin'" by The Mamas and Papas and then "White Rabbit" by Jefferson Airplane. That reminded me of an instrumental version Mathew played a lot. I searched his collection until I found the George Benson recording. This led me to "The Thrill Has Gone" played by B.B. King, and more tears.

I turned off the music. The silence contributed to an empty sensation. I walked back to the kitchen. My footsteps took on a sinister tone. I stopped abruptly, just to make sure they were mine. I turned the radio on, set it to Radio Four and let my imagine run to my mother being with me.

Still not feeling secure enough to sleep at home, I slept at the Edwards' during the night. On Thursday I could not be bothered to get up at all. Edwina came in to see me. I described my feelings. Edwina gave my hand a squeeze and encouraged me to make a "To Do" list. She got the paper and pen. I sat up in bed and started to write:

Formally identify Mathew's body.

Arrange funeral.

Get death certificate and see solicitor for his will.

Transfer various bills into my name.

See bank manager regarding Mathew's account.

Talk to James about the shop.

Call school and arrange leave.

My visit to the mortuary was a cold formality. I thought I would plunge into further emotional turmoil, but the environment was so stark and clinical that it felt more like a hospital visit. I could smell the disinfectant. The mortician pulled back a light green nylon sheet so I could see Mathew's face, I nodded, and Inspector Pride led me out again.

"Have you had any further thoughts about who might have killed Mathew?"

I shook my head.

"So far, we have very little to work on. We are still appealing for witnesses who might have seen someone enter your house around one. Some kind of description is our best hope. Wait here and I will arrange for a lift home."

I collected Mathew's certificate from the doctor and took it round to the registrar's office to get the death certificate.

Friday became a busy day.

I started by calling the school's head of art and explained Mathew's death. I felt awkward listening to Mrs Howe's expressions of shock and sympathy. I was given a month's compassionate leave.

Next I arranged to meet our solicitor, Graham Parker, who had written our will. Early afternoon I took the death certificate so he could officially read me the will. Mr Parker glanced at me over his reading glasses with a grave expression as he opened the will. It was simply an act of reading back the document we had signed a few years earlier. Mathew left me everything.

On the way home I visited the bank. I asked to see the manager. After a long wait I was shown into the communal office. The manager's badge told me he was Rasneesh Patel, before he could introduce himself.

"How can I help you, Mrs Blake?" he said cheerily, as he stood to shake my hand.

"My husband died on Monday and I thought I should tell you."

Mr Patel looked concerned. He waved me to a seat and we sat down.

"I'm very sorry to hear that. Was it unexpected?"

"He was murdered."

The manager looked genuinely shocked and I immediately regretted being so blunt. Mr Patel looked at the death certificate, will and my driving license. He then tapped details into his computer.

"I will arrange to have all the funds from his personal accounts transferred to yours. There is £1,278.59 in his current account and £7,203.89 in his savings account."

"Are you sure? I was under the impression Mathew was steadily saving."

Mr Patel stared at the screen intently. He pressed his lips with his fingers, looking confused.

"Well, it is quite strange. During the last year he made three large deposits from the North Hertfordshire Building Society, whilst he has withdrawn ten thousand pounds a week in cash."

"Ten thousand pounds a week in cash?"

My voice had become high pitched as I accentuated each word. The numbers rolled around my head like lottery cubes.

Mr Patel swung the screen around so I could see the statements. He scrolled down pointing out the weekly withdrawals and the three large deposits.

"I just don't understand it. I'm sorry but there must be some mistake."

There was a long pause before Mr Patel spoke. He cleared his throat.

"Well, let's see. Your husband would have seen all the statements except this month's. If he checked them, I presume he would have noticed a mistake, especially one as large as this. Was he the type of person who would read his statements?"

"Um, yes, he was meticulous with most things."

I sighed as the realisation that Mathew must have known sunk in.

Mr Patel looked concerned.

"I will, of course, check but I think it is highly unlikely there has been an error." The manager leant forwards and lowered his voice. "You said he had been murdered. Well, this does look a little suspicious to me. It appears that he has taken out mortgages and then withdrawn large sums of cash. I think it would be wise to inform the police."

I searched in my bag for the number Pride had given me. Half an hour later I saw Inspector Pride's bulk enter the bank. She was slightly out of breath. We went back to the office so Pride could see the statements for herself. The inspector searched her bag and I thought she was going to pull out a packet of biscuits but instead she found her notebook. She wrote out the dates and amounts of the deposits from the building society to Mathew's personal account and made notes about the cash withdrawals.

"So every Monday your husband came here and took out ten thousand pounds. And you did not know anything about this?"

I shook my head. I experienced an irrational feeling of guilt, as though I should have had greater control over Mathew and been on top of our family's finances. I swallowed hard and bit my bottom lip. This could not be happening to me. Life had been so predictable. This wasn't part of the script. Suddenly there was no Mathew, no getting up early for school, and now no money. The cliché that I would wake up and find it was all a nightmare, washed around my head. I pinched my forearm, just in case. Pride asked to see the screen again.

"Last Monday he did not make a withdrawal. What time were the other withdrawals made?"

Mr Patel went off to locate the times.

Pride looked at me intently.

"Have you any reason to believe he was being blackmailed?"

"No, of course not."

"Do you mind if we search your home more thoroughly?"

I nodded in acquiescence. My voice felt very weak as I spoke next.

"I thought we had paid off the mortgage. My mother died just over six years ago and I inherited everything. After we were married, we used the money to buy our home with a mortgage. We paid it off last year."

Mr Patel came back to the office. Most of the withdrawals were made between 9 a.m. and 11 a.m. He had an ongoing arrangement to collect the cash in £50 notes."

Pride rubbed her left eye and looked tired.

"So every Monday Mr Blake comes into the bank to collect his money, but last Monday he did not collect the cash and later that same day he is murdered."

"Excuse me, Inspector, but perhaps the reason he did not withdraw the cash was that he did not have the funds," Mr Patel pointed out helpfully.

"He finally runs out of money and his blackmailer strikes. Seems a little impatient, but at least it give us a theory to explore." Pride continued her musings. "I will give that building society a visit."

At home I slumped back into nothingness. Somehow Mathew had created a financial abyss. I certainly did not have the means to pay off a big mortgage on my teacher's salary. What next, I thought. Perhaps I will find I have terminal cancer.

In the evening, Edwina asked how I got on and I told them about my experience at the bank. I noticed that as I was talking I was pressing my fingernail so hard into the flesh of my hand that the knuckle started to bleed. They asked lots of questions I could not answer. Edward leant forward and reassured me that the building society could not have made any loans against our home without my signature. Perhaps it was all a mistake and would be sorted out next week.

"The darkest day," he muttered.

In the morning Edward brought me breakfast in bed. Edwina had gone out for her yoga class. He sat down on the edge of the bed looking awkward. Edward placed his hand on my leg and gave me a squeeze before removing it again.

"How are you this morning, Amanda?"

"I am not sure I can go on. What's the point?"

Edward looked into my eyes. He seemed to be searching for something.

"You never know what is around the corner. Life might seem bleak now. For all you know a wonderful new life might be slowly edging towards you."

Edward looked away and took off his glasses. He cleaned them with a white handkerchief. Then he turned back to me. I looked up from his blue denim shirt to his eyes.

"Can I talk to you confidentially?"

"Sure."

Edward looked down and dropped his glasses. He fumbled around his feet before retrieving them.

"Things are not going well with Edwina. I feel I have fallen out of love. I could probably invent lots of reasons, but the essential truth is that the feeling's gone."

I placed my hand over Edward's.

"Edward, I don't know what to say. Have you told her?"

"No. I don't know how. I can fire people at work, close down businesses, but I cannot tell my wife it's over."

Edward patted my thigh, put his glasses back on and left. His broad shoulders seemed to droop slightly as I watched his back exit through the bedroom door. Then I said "Oh fiddlesticks" aloud. I instinctively looked around just in case someone might have heard. This was another of those ridiculous expressions I had inherited, this time, from my father.

There was something strange about Edward's declaration. Why would he tell me? Was there more to his declaration? Poor Edwina.

CHAPTER 3

A week after my husband's murder I woke in my own bed. Even though I had moved home, I started to view the house as being something temporary. How long would it be mine?

In an effort to cleanse myself of the toxic emotions that contaminated me since learning of Mathew's loans and withdrawals, I packed up all his clothes and took them to a charity shop. Next I got to work packing up his books and sold them to the second-hand bookshop in Hitchin. I created a pile of things to sell on eBay, including his guitar and amplifier. I rearranged the shelves and mantelpiece. I scrubbed away Mathew's ghost with hot soapy water. By the evening I felt I was taking control of my life again. The house was starting to look more like my home than his. I took a hot bath and fell asleep quickly for the first time since the murder.

Tuesday morning, I found my old student paintings in the garage and put them up. Even if the house was soon to be taken from me, I felt a deep satisfaction at being able to do all the things I had given up on whilst Mathew was alive.

I received a call from Inspector Pride. She arranged to come round during the afternoon, with more information.

After lunch, James Harris phoned and asked if he could visit. He was ten minutes away.

"I'll be passing The Coffee Shop. Can I get you something?"

He came round holding a cardboard tray with two takeaway cappuccinos and almond croissants. James' long bushy hair looked slightly greyer than the last time we met. The waistband of his beige trousers looked a little strained. I took the tray from him.

"I am so sorry, Amanda. What a shock. I thought I should give you some time."

I had to stand on my toes to reach up and give him a kiss. He put his arms around me and gave me a strong bear hug. I could feel his paunch pressed against me. I was conscious of the coffees in my hand. He released me and stood looking at me with his hands on my shoulders. James' breath smelt rancid. I tried to hold my breath. Then as I turned and ushered him to the kitchen, I let the air rush from my mouth. We sat on Mathew's beloved shaker style chairs, sipping our coffees. James leant back, putting his hands behind his head.

I described finding Mathew. He slowly shook his head bunching up his eyebrows into a concerned frown. When I told him about the cash withdrawals, James lost some of his colour. He ran his hand through his hair several times.

"So what do the police think? I mean, what are they working on?"

"The inspector thinks someone must have been blackmailing Mathew and when he ran out of money, killed him."

"My God. I suppose this will mean a big investigation."

"Yes, it will."

"Who is leading the investigation?"

"Inspector Pride."

"Joan Pride?"

"Yes. You know her?"

James ran his hand through his hair again.

"From a long time ago."

"She'll be here soon."

James gulped down his coffee. I noticed him fidget with his belt. Perhaps the buckle was biting into the flesh of his abdomen.

"Oh dear. It sounds complicated. I suppose they will want to interview me as well."

"James, is something wrong?"

"No, no, nothing. Look, Amanda, I think I should go. I have a few errands to run. I just wanted to see how you are. I'll see you at the funeral and then later we can talk more. Now you are a shareholder, we need to decide what to do with the business."

James fumbled through the pockets of his leather jacket until he found his keys. He stopped and looked at me.

"Are you sure you will be alright?"

I shrugged my shoulders.

"Hey ho, life's a box—"

I managed to stop myself from completing my mother's signature line. James looked confused for a moment. Then he leant forwards and gave me a kiss. I caught his breath and thankfully it smelt of coffee now. After a sideways glance and half wave, he left.

I prepared coffee and biscuits for Pride. It was raining and Pride's brown hair was wet from the short walk from her car. It made her head look too small for her large body. The green puffy jacket added to the effect. A man she introduced as Sergeant Alfred Smiley accompanied her. He wasn't very smiley when I shook his hand. As I drew close, I smelt stale cigarettes and mint.

After we sat down, Pride reached into her bag and placed a folder on the table. Her demeanour was formal and cold. I felt myself withdrawing.

"Just to be clear, you are saying you had no knowledge of the loans taken out against this house or the cash withdrawals."

"No, of course not." I felt annoyed that I immediately started to feel guilty.

"Then how do you explain your signature on these forms?"

Pride place three documents on the table in front of me. She turned the pages to reveal my signature on each document. She rhythmically tapped one of the signatures.

"Is this your signature?"

"Yes, but I can assure you I did not sign these papers. There must be a mistake."

"Well, on the first loan your signature was witnessed by a Dr William Barnet. Do you know this man?"

"Yes, he is our doctor, but I can assure you he never witnessed me signing this." I swallowed several times. I noticed my eyes blinking.

"I see. A Mr Graham Parker witnessed your second signature. Do you know this man?"

"Yes, he is the solicitor who drew up our will." I swallowed again and felt drops of perspiration forming on my forehead.

"And the third witness, Mr James Harris, is the man your husband ran the shop with?"

"Yes, it is. He just left."

"Let me ask you again. Do you maintain you did not sign any of these documents despite these witnesses?"

Sergeant Smiley leant forwards a little as though to study my face more closely. I felt flushed. I knew I had not signed these papers and yet here I was, feeling as though I had. The terrible possibility crystallised inside me that I had just signed them quickly for Mathew, without paying any attention to what it was. Would I have noticed if he just said they were documents for the shop? Pride pushed the papers closer to me impatiently.

"Yes, I am sure I did not sign them," I pronounced unconvincingly.

Pride looked at me intently for an uncomfortably long time. I wanted to look away but felt I had to face her out. My left eye started to twitch and I had to put my hand over it. I fought back an impulse to cry.

"Mrs Blake, can you please tell us where you were at 1 p.m. on the day of Mr Blake's murder."

I felt nauseous. My voice cracked slightly.

"I finished teaching at 12:30 and then, as the weather was dry, I drove to the park to eat my lunch."

"Were you alone?"

"Yes, I like to sit on a bench by the ponds and read my book."

"What time did you return?"

"About 1:30 p.m."

Smiley asked the next question.

"Can anyone confirm that you were at the park?"

"No. I mean there were people there. I don't know if they would remember me."

"So, you would have had time to drive home, shoot your husband and get back to school."

I had to press my fingers against my eye again. I could feel the lower lid contract spasmodically.

"I suppose so. What are you saying? You think I shot Mathew?"

Pride coldly thanked me for my help and got up to leave.

I sat in shock. I felt myself draw my body in, as though I was sucking my skin and flesh inwards. I held my hands protectively across my chest and pressed my legs together. Reality and delusion swirled around. In my memory I was sure I had not signed those documents, and yet there was my signature on the papers and witnessed by people I knew. I was sure I went to the park for lunch.

Was there any chance, however remote, that I had come home, murdered Mathew, erased the incident from my memory and returned to school as though nothing had happened? I thought back to the day of the murder, were any clues to me being home with Mathew when I found him dead on the floor? Could I have made him lunch? I would typically make him a salmon, ham or salami sandwich with a salad. Isn't that what the inspector said he had eaten? I would be more likely to leave crumbs on the table than Mathew. My eye started to twitch slightly. I wanted to curl up on the sofa and let it all fester inside me but forced myself to stand up.

On impulse I decided to talk to Edward about the signatures and loan agreements. I needed another perspective. I walked across to his home to see if he was in. As I walked up the path, there was a tap at the window and I turned to see Edward's face. He indicated to go to the front door.

"It's just me, I'm afraid. Edwina has gone shopping."

"It's you I want to talk to."

I explained the signatures, whilst Edward listened intently. I felt relieved he accepted I had not signed them without any questioning. I still doubted the security and predictability of my world. A tiny seed of a thought was hiding in the darker recesses of my mind. It whispered, *You found out what Mathew was doing, shot him in a violent rage, calmly went back to school and blanked it all out.*

"Well that explains why Mathew got the loans. I think you need to face the reality that he was defrauding you. He effectively stole the value of your house from you."

"But why? Why on earth would he do such a thing? How did he get the signatures witnessed?"

"I don't know. Why would someone blackmail him?"

Edward stood up, stretched and effected a martial arts stance as though it helped him think.

"Did he want to leave you?"

I looked down at my hands. Did he? Was I so blind not to know?

"Um, does Edwina know you want to leave her?"

"No."

"So if you left now it would be a complete shock to her."

"Yes, I think it would."

"I never imagined Mathew wanted to leave me."

"Perhaps he didn't. Maybe it was blackmail after all."

"But how could he ruin me like this."

Edward shrugged his broad shoulders.

"I am even wondering if I could have somehow done it and blanked it all out."

"What?" Edward exclaimed with a curious expression.

I told him of Pride's assertion that I had not been to the park for lunch.

Edward sat next to me and put his arm round me.

"Amanda, that simply is not you. Be logical, you would have had to find a gun that could not be traced to you, arrange for Mathew to be home, get from school to your home without anyone seeing you, and then back to school. Could you do all that after finding out Mathew's treachery and not remember a single thing? Anyway, surely you would want Mathew alive to get the money back."

We were interrupted by the sound of the key in the front door lock. Edward jumped up and returned to his pose. Edwina came in laden with bags of shopping.

My desire to arrange Mathew's funeral had waned. My plans to entertain everyone at home after the cremation, to celebrate his life, had withered with each piece of evidence that Mathew had been cheating on me financially. With the realisation that he must have forged my signature on those documents, I began to question my relationship with the witnesses. No wonder James was so nervous. Could I even trust Graham Parker?

This was a terrible way to contemplate saying goodbye to Mathew. So many happy memories had become polluted by events. Did Mathew and I ever have the marriage I felt we had? My mind explored the times he seemed less interested in me, the times he would become irritated with my comments or the way he would get annoyed if I had to ask him to explain the plot of a film. I remembered the look of embarrassment on his face when I drank too much and let myself go at Pam's party last month.

As I got to know Mathew, I had been surprised at how hungry he was to be everything English. I once had to stop him buying a flat cap and tweed jacket. He read Shakespeare, Charles Dickens and Jane Austen as though he was at school. He had become an avid English history student and many Sundays were spent at historic buildings or sites. It was his unexpected academic side that most attracted me to him, when we first talked after our tango class.

Did the charms he found in me wear off? He used to call me his "English Rose." He liked to lie on the sofa with his head on my lap as I read to him with a pronounced BBC English accent. He would sometimes practice the words. Many of our early conversations centred on what it was like to grow up in England. Had he eventually become more English than me? Did he overcome his obsession with everything anglophile?

What did we have in common? We used to laugh a lot together. During the first few years we made a point of giving each other a candle lit massage with scented oils. I felt we had an intimate relationship. Mathew was not the most passionate or adventurous lover but I felt fulfilled. Then two or three years ago the massages faded away and we had a less physical relationship. At the time I felt it was a natural transition into a more mature relationship.

Thinking back, I changed too. At the beginning I was quite submissive and used to agree with whatever Mathew wanted. He chose the restaurants, set the itinerary for our holidays, decided what went into our home. I slowly emerged from my passive shell and started to have my own opinions. It culminated last year in an impasse over whether my painting could be put up in our home.

I remembered one incident that pained me. We went out for dinner at a new Vietnamese restaurant in London and sat at a table that was close to a couple from Spain who owned an art gallery in Madrid. Mathew spent most of the evening talking to them in Spanish. He kept translating bits to me, but it felt like just enough not to be rude whilst not enough to include me in any of the conversation. Had he tired of me? Perhaps he found my inability to follow an academic conversation embarrassing? Did he find a couple of Spanish strangers more interesting than me?

I set the funeral for Friday and chose the simplest, basic option. Edwina came round and helped me with the announcements in the local papers. I took the opportunity to voice some of my fears.

"I am beginning to wonder what kind of relationship I really had with Mathew. The first few years were so wonderful, but looking back I wonder if it was just a temporary phase for him."

Edwina looked at me curiously.

"How did you feel at the time?"

"Generally life was pretty good. We did not argue or anything like that."

"Well, why are you having doubts now?"

"I suppose finding out about the loans has unsettled me. He wasn't so passionate about me after the honeymoon period. I can't help feeling I was a disappointment to him."

Edwina smiled and put her hand on my arm.

"Lots of relationships go through ups and downs. Eddy and I have had our fair share of challenges. I can't tell you how much I want to strangle him when he jumps around with those ridiculous karate poses, but we've always come back stronger. Deep down, I know Eddy and I will always face our problems together and that our marriage will endure."

For a moment I thought Edwina was directing her last comment directly at me. She looked at me sweetly and continued.

"Even if Mathew was feeling a bit flat, how do you know he would not have grown more fond of you in a much deeper way later?"

I nodded. Part of me wanted to say, "Oh Edwina, you poor deluded fool. Edward wants to leave you." But then they were still together and perhaps, regardless of Edward's loss of love, would be for a long time.

Wednesday saw the return of Inspector Pride. She came alone this time. Her dry hair was back to its waves and curls. I did not make the effort to offer tea or coffee.

"I have interviewed all three of the witnesses and none have any knowledge of seeing these forms before. I therefore assume that all the signatures, yours and the witnesses, are forgeries."

I waited for an apology for her accusatory tone yesterday, but nothing was offered. Instead she produced a lemon and vanilla sponge cake. I relented and made some tea and sliced the cake.

"Were you aware of any skills your husband had for forging signatures?"

"No, not at all."

"I presume he would have had prescriptions from his doctor and could copy the signature from that."

"Yes, he did suffer from gout occasionally and had to take prescription medication. Also, we had various letters from our solicitor, so he could have practiced with those. And he must have lots of papers signed by James that he could use."

"So it seems he defrauded you by either forging your signature himself or getting someone else to. His engagement in criminal activity lends weight to the idea that he might have been blackmailed. If he was prepared to act against you in this way, I wonder what else he has been up to."

"In all the time I knew Mathew, he appeared completely normal. This seems so out of character."

Pride washed a mouthful of cake down with a swig of hot tea. She swallowed and distractedly asked me another question as she teed up another mouthful of cake.

"What do you know of his past?"

Pride loaded her mouth and an image of a washing machine with flour, eggs, sugar, tea, milk and saliva churning around her tongue flashed through my mind.

"Only what he told me. He grew up in Barcelona, studied European History and worked in a clothing store as a buyer. Then he moved to Potters Bar when he was thirty-six. He worked for John Lewis as a manager."

"That's all?" Pride mumbled through the yellow sponge. She held her hand by her mouth in case any crumbs spilled out.

"He was quite secretive. He just said the past was behind him, when I asked him."

I swallowed and bit my lower lips as I thought that perhaps he had previously been a criminal.

"Mathew Blake is not a typical name for a Spanish man."

"He said he changed his name by deed poll to fit in."

"Quite the man of mystery. Can you get me his passport, marriage certificate, deed poll papers, citizenship documents, national insurance, photographs, laptop, phone bills and anything else about him. I think I will do a little research of my own," Pride stated, brushing the crumbs off her fingers.

Being so neat and predictable, I found Mathew's documents in a maroon box file in his cupboard. Below, there was an envelope full of photographs. One, taken five years ago, was of him dressed in a blue suit and wearing black-framed sunglasses. He went through a phase of slicking his dark hair back. We laughed about his Italian look only last month.

I found a photograph of both of us from about two years ago. It was taken in Green Park in London. A Japanese tourist had enthusiastically taken several photographs of us standing under a large tree. In this one, Mathew stood behind me with his arms around my waist with his hands locked together over my navel. He was leaning forward so that his cheek touched my fair, wavy hair. I was about half a head shorter. I had my hands over his and my head tipped back slightly as though I was about to turn and kiss him. It was taken in the late summer and my cheeks looked a little flushed with freckles dotted across them.

I remember feeling particularly happy that day. I felt very much in love and our relationship felt secure. I had just started my new job teaching art at Sir Fredrick Osborn's comprehensive school and we had come up to London to celebrate. Mathew was in his light fawn trousers with a beige jacket and I had dressed up in a brown skirt and cream blouse. We looked stylish together, colour coordinated with a kind of 1950s fashion identity.

Oh Mathew, I just don't get it. I held my head in my hands, gripping my hair between my tense fingers. *We were fine, weren't we? How could we go from this to you forging my signature? I just don't understand.*

I felt a longing for the feeling I experienced in Green Park. I wanted Mathew to walk through the door and hold me again. I wanted to feel his face against mine, I wanted to smell him, I wanted him to hold me tight.

I collapsed on the bed holding the photograph to my heart and wept. I had lost the man I loved and now I did not even know if he really loved me.

Pride came in and sat on the bed. I felt myself roll down the dip towards her. I tried to compose myself. She gently rubbed my shoulder.

"It's just that it is bad enough that Mathew was murdered, but now it seems he was ruining me. I wonder if he ever loved me."

Pride smiled sympathetically.

"It is also possible that he was in some kind of mess and wanted to protect you from it. Maybe he was involved in some kind of illegal activity. It does not mean he wasn't in love with you."

I dried my eyes, gave Pride the documents and followed her downstairs. As she stood by the front door she turned to me, looking concerned.

"I'll organise some counselling for you with a friend of mine, if you like, and I'll let you know when I find out more about Mathew. Meanwhile we are trying to find someone who saw you in the park."

Pride walked down the path and then, as I started to close the door, she turned.

"I nearly forgot. When did you first become aware of the mortgages and cash withdrawals?"

"When I went to the bank to transfer the money from Mathew's accounts."

"It just occurred to me that if you found out earlier, it would give you a motive. I imagine I would feel enraged if someone forged my signature and stole the value of my house."

"I did not kill Mathew," I stated resolutely. Yes, I was sure that was the truth.

CHAPTER 4

Monday was the day of the inquest. I hardly listened to the sombre, monotonous tones of the pathologist, inspector and judge. The verdict, not surprisingly, was that Mathew was unlawfully killed by a person or persons unknown. I left feeling flat.

After some deliberation I willed myself to phone the school and request more leave. I felt too vulnerable to expose myself to thirty teenagers. I was not in the mood to have my boundaries pulled, stretched and tested.

On Tuesday I went to visit Pride's friend Steven Holmes at his clinic in Hertford. He started by asking me about my childhood. I wanted to say that I was here because the man I loved had been brutally murdered, borrowed so much against the house I would probably lose it and that he had deceived me.

Instead I explained how I was an only child. My mother had a miscarriage two years before I was born. Just after my third birthday she became pregnant, but my younger brother died during birth. Yes, I did feel a sense of loss. My mother had taken me out to choose his clothes and I persuaded her to buy him a mobile with bright profiles of cars, trains and aeroplanes. After his death, my mother became withdrawn and I spent more time with my father. Yes, I think I must have felt a sense of rejection. I don't know if they were similar to my current feelings. I found the mobile after my mother died.

We discussed my first day at school. I remember not being able to fasten my new yellow sandals and another girl, Anna, did them up for me. She became my best friend for the next six years. Yes, I do tend to have a few close friends rather than lots of acquaintances.

At secondary school I was one of the quieter children. I did all my homework but would typically be in the lower half of the class when our test results were handed out.

My first serious romantic relationship was with Paul when I was seventeen. We met in art class. He wore glasses and read books on Greek philosophy. We worked together on a sculpture. I liked his gentle touch. After a few weeks he took me out to a pub on his moped. When he took me home there was an awkward moment when I felt he wanted to kiss me but could not find the courage. I wanted to tell him I would welcome him, but in the end he left with a stiff wave of his hand.

On our second date we went to the Victoria and Albert museum. We stood in front of the sculpture of Neptune and Titon. I let my hand touch his. He turned and returned my gaze. As if in slow motion we moved towards each other and kissed. I was glad we waited; the setting felt perfect for my first romantic embrace. We became boyfriend and girlfriend. It was very innocent for the first few months. Then Paul became more insistent about making love and I gave in. No, I did not enjoy it. It was only my love for him that resolved me to try again a few weeks later. Yes, after a while I enjoyed our lovemaking.

It ended when I went to art school and he went to read history at university. We promised to continue but after the Christmas holidays, he made less effort to return my messages. Yes, I did feel abandoned. For many nights I put my head under my pillow and cried myself to sleep. I lost a lot of weight and took tranquilisers. No, I blamed myself. I felt as though I was not intelligent enough to keep his attention.

Yes, I did have similar feelings about my husband. Yes, my father was an academic. He taught art history at University College London. No, my mother was not academic and went back to working as a PA when I was about nine. I was not aware of my father finding either of us boring. Yes, I did try to impress him with things I learnt at school. Sometimes he would discuss them with me and sometimes he would just laugh and give me a hug. Yes, it is possible that my main motivation for my studies was to please him. I think I did choose art because he taught art history but it was also because of all the school subjects, it was the one I was best at.

By the summer I replaced tranquilisers with recreational drugs. During this phase I had a number a casual relationships. Yes, I became promiscuous. With the help of alcohol and drugs, I bloomed in full colour, centre stage.

No, I was not aware of feeling I had let my father down but I may have felt that, deeper inside. Yes, part of me does feel guilty about some of my sexual experiences at college. No, I never told Mathew about them. No, I am not in contact with any of my friends from college.

Steven brought our first session to a close.

He had hardly said anything, which didn't help with my current situation but I liked being able to talk uninterrupted. He listened, made notes and, when he did not understand something, asked for clarification. He was interested in how I felt and I appreciated that. I noticed a pattern emerging of not feeling clever enough, when around academic people, whilst at the same time being fatally attracted to them.

When I got home, I started making a salad for lunch. My phone interrupted me. It was Edward. He offered to take me out for lunch and I accepted. A few minutes later Edward was at my front door.

"I'm working from home today. So, I thought I would pop out for lunch and it occurred to me that you might like to get out."

I grabbed my coat and bag and climbed into his car. Edward was set on eating at an expensive French restaurant. He insisted we share a bottle of wine and displayed great insights into the various choices. I felt he was putting on a bit of a show, but it was nice to be entertained and taken care of. After a while Edward steered the conversation to Edwina.

"I'm still struggling to tell Edwina it's over. Do you have any suggestions? I've never done this before."

"How does she feel about your relationship?"

"Business as usual. Edwina has the rest of our lives mapped out. A long boring road to nowhere, devoid of romance and adventure."

"You sound resolved."

Edward nodded and looked glum for a moment. He took off his glasses and cleaned the lenses. I let him wrestle with whatever thoughts he had about his marriage. Then he looked up.

"So, what shall I do?"

"I suppose if it was me, I would like you to be honest, explain your feelings and give me a chance to change."

"My heart just isn't in it anymore."

"Well, you need to talk about it."

"Yes, it really is time to grasp the nettle."

Our conversation moved onto the food and wine. When we came to our coffees Edward looked into my eyes.

"Amanda, there is something important I want to tell you."

My hands were lying on the cream tablecloth, and Edward reached across to hold them. I felt awkward.

"I know this is a difficult time for you, but I wanted to say it now. You know, strike whilst the iron's hot, I thought rather than wait, I would see if you felt the same."

Edward looked into my eyes.

"I have developed strong feelings for you over the last year. It started at the New Year's Eve party and kept growing ever since. I kept persuading Edwina to invite you guys for dinner or to include you in social events, just to be close to you. Now I want to be with you. I have even fantasised about living with you."

He smiled and shrugged his shoulders.

"Well, there, I have said it. I've outed myself."

Edward looked proud of himself. I was stunned. Why on earth would he think I would want to talk about a new relationship when I had not even buried my husband? Mathew may have done a terrible thing, but I still had many, many happy memories with him. I did love him for all those years. Edward took off his glasses. He breathed onto them, misting the lenses before wiping them on his napkin. As he looked up, he smiled at me expectantly.

"Edward, how could you imagine I would even be thinking of a new relationship? And do you really think I would even consider it whilst you are still married to Edwina? I could never treat a friend like that. I am sorry, but I really am astonished."

I shook my head and looked away. The silence became unbearable.

"Even if you were single, I would want to get to know you properly and let my feelings emerge naturally. I can't believe you would be so selfish at a time like this."

Edward sighed. He became terse and abrupt.

"Fine, you've made yourself clear. I'm sorry I troubled you."

He stretched his arm out and looked at his watch.

"Well, it is time I went back to work. Do you want a lift home?"

I couldn't bear the thought of being in the car with Edward.

"No, I think I will do some shopping now I am here, and get a taxi home later. Thank you for lunch."

Edward stood and summoned the waiter for the bill. He turned and curtly shook my hand.

"I'll say goodbye, and let you go."

The fresh air felt good on my flushed cheeks. I felt angry as I walked down the high street. How could he expect me to be complicit in hurting Edwina? After all I was going through, I was looking for sympathy and support, not to be hit on. Did he imagine we would go back for a romp in Mathew and my bed?

I distracted myself by browsing through the new books table in the local bookshop. Then I wandered over to the self-help section and bought a book about dealing with grief.

CHAPTER 5

Wednesday, I woke to find my front doormat covered in letters. I had already received a few condolence cards but today there was a torrent. I scooped up the envelopes and took them through to the living room. I sat on the sofa and started cutting the envelopes open. Once I had read the card I put them on the living room table with the others. I could see I would soon run out of room.

Most of the cards included standard preprinted notes of sympathy with a signature below. Some of the signatures were indecipherable. One envelope stood out as being different. It was brown, long and my address was hand written in a scribbled style. I opened it and pulled out a tightly folded piece of plain A4 paper. I opened it out and just stared. To the right of the paper was a black and white photocopied picture of me. It had been cut out and stuck onto the sheet of paper. To the left was a picture of a man in a mask. He looked like a terrorist and must have been cut out of a newspaper. The sender had drawn a speech bubble from the mouth of the man with the words *u turn to die hore* scratched into the bubble with a thin biro. The picture of me had a bubble from my lips with *plees dont hurt me I give you good time* written inside. I groaned inwardly and said, "Oh no," to myself.

I recognised the picture from a trip Mathew and I took to Bath. It was part of one of Mathew's discover Roman Britain, historical excursions. We stayed in a room with a four-poster bed. For fun I made a sexy, flirtatious pose against one of the posts whilst Mathew took pictures of me. I was wearing a thin cotton cream dress with a pattern of pink flowers. On this shot I had pulled the left side of the dress up my leg slightly whilst cupping my right breast with my other hand. My head was tilted to one side and I pouted seductively. As part of our photograph album it looked amusing and the sort of composition you might smile at, but when cut out from a black and white photocopy and stuck onto the letter, I looked grotesque.

I felt cold and shivered. I looked up at the windows and door. I froze. It took some time before I could get up and phone Inspector Pride. Sergeant Smiley answered. Pride was not there. I tried to explain what had happened, but had to make several attempt to express myself clearly before he understood. He told me not to touch the letter or envelope. Almost as an afterthought, he instructed me to lock all the doors and windows just to be safe. He would come round within an hour.

Smiley rang the bell and for dramatic effect pressed his police ID against the glass. I opened the door and took him through to the living room. He smelt of stale cigarettes. Smiley did not attempt to make conversation. He took some cream plastic gloves and clear plastic bag from his case. Smiley put on the gloves and gingerly held up the letter by its edges.

"Do you know where this picture of you came from?"

The yellowing on his front teeth was darker today.

"Yes, from the photograph album that was stolen when Mathew was murdered."

"And did you make any copies?"

"No."

"Has this photograph been published anywhere?"

"No."

Smiley edged the letter into the bag with the envelope.

"Under the circumstances, I am going to request a PC stays with you."

Smiley left leaving me to a few hours of anxiety before the doorbell rang and I let in a uniformed PC, Jennie Peters.

PC Peters looked as though she was in her late twenties. She was slim and athletic looking but I could not imagine what she could do if we were attacked by an armed killer. She made a risk assessment of our home. Later a man came round and fitted locks on the windows.

Living with Jennie felt awkward. Although she insisted I carry on as though she was not there, I felt obliged to offer her food and drinks. I felt obliged to make conversation. Jennie became my quiet shadow. We went shopping together, took walks together and once went out to a Thai restaurant.

I found the photographs that made up my anniversary present in a folder marked *Love* in my computer. I wanted to test out Pride's blackmail theory. Was there something in the pictures? I made a careful study of each looking for anything in the background that could include something incriminating. Some outdoor photographs had other people in the background. I zoomed in to see if there was anything illuminating. I felt like the David Hemmings character in my favourite sixties film *Blow Up*. Having something to focus on distracted me from my inner turmoil. I turned it into a project, filing the photographs with anyone else in them into a new album and then making a description of the people caught in the background.

Friday came quickly. The funeral was at 2 p.m. I wore my black dress and a black hat I bought for the occasion. Jennie and I drove down to the crematorium. The crunching of the gravel, sounded jarring. I wanted to hide behind a mask, and insulate myself from the crowd in the hall.

James strode over and gave me a hug that squeezed the air from my lungs.

"We'll miss him," he said gravely.

"Yes," I responded weakly.

"Oh God, what's she doing here?"

I followed James' gaze and saw Inspector Pride at the back, talking to Jennie.

Edwina came over and gave me a big hug.

"Stay strong, I'm here if you need me."

Edward scowled, pointedly standing beyond Edwina. Then the awkward moment was broken, as a large, longhaired, bearded man came over and told me used to play guitar with Mathew at the blues club. He rambled on describing Mathew in terms of scales, chords and rhythm. My mind wandered and I looked past the man to see Miranda and Jessica from the shop talking to James.

Two profusely sympathetic teachers from the art department rescued me. I stood bathed in their condolences until Jeff, who looked after Mathew's old Alfa Romeo, shook my hand.

Thankfully, we were ushered to our pews. I could be on my own again. I started to shake a little as the coffin slid into the dark tunnel. Tears welled up and rolled down my cheeks. Somehow all the mystery about the missing money had smeared my final feelings for the man with whom I had shared so much with a thin veneer of betrayal. I felt I had been cheated of the real grief I should be feeling. Being part of this tarnished ending felt so very sad and incomplete.

Goodbye, Mathew. Thank you for the memories.

After I shook more hands. I noticed that I began to view James and Edward suspiciously. Was one of them the murderer? I looked around at the people slowly walking to the church doors. It could be any of them.

I was aware that neither Mathew nor I had any family at the funeral. I had never met any of Mathew's relations and he had not met any of mine. I had told Mathew that I would like to create a new family with him. I think I used the well-worn phrase – "Darling, I want to have your baby. I think it would be wonderful to have some little Blakes running around our home." He reasoned that it was not the best time. It never was – too soon, too busy, too expensive. Excuses included wanting to move house, the recession, travel. He felt the future was too uncertain. We might depend on my salary for a few years as the shop was in difficulties. Besides, he kept reassuring me, I was young and could wait a couple of years.

I regretted my decision not to invite people home. I experienced pangs of guilt as I said goodbye to everyone at the crematorium. When Jennie and I got home, I went upstairs, took my dress off and crawled into bed. Images of the coffin, people's faces and the crematorium, circled past my eyes. I turned onto my side forced myself to look out of the window at the billowing white clouds blowing past.

Later Jennie brought me some soup, bread and a salad.

I submerged myself into a dark black cloud all weekend. I lay in bed, slumped on the sofa or sat at the kitchen table with my head in my hands. Jennie eventually gave up asking if there was anything she could do. She read and listened to her iPod. My favourite thoughts were: why me? What had I done to deserve this?

CHAPTER 6

Monday morning, three weeks after the killing, PC Fiona Mills replaced Jennie. Fiona was more outgoing and chatty, with a jolly manner. My responses were minimal, having lost my need to keep up with social convention. Fiona persisted with snatches of conversation each time we met in the kitchen or living room. She would be an excellent nurse.

We drove back to the crematorium to collect Mathew's ashes. I wondered what to do with them. I thought of burying them in our garden, but if I was to lose my home what was the point of leaving them there. I forced myself to search through my memories for a time and place Mathew might like for his final resting place.

I remembered a time early in our relationship when we enjoyed a picnic in a meadow, near the River Mimram. Wild flowers swayed in the warm breeze, as butterflies fluttered over colourful petals. We lay on a brown and red tartan blanket under a large oak tree. I had packed sandwiches, juices and fruit into a large wicker hamper. It was here that Mathew proposed to me. He was so gallant, as he held my hand and knelt next to me. Mathew gazed into my eyes as he spoke eloquently of his love and desire to be beside me forever. When he asked me to marry him, I became overwhelmed with emotion and cried. He embraced me and I kept whispering, "Yes," into his ear. I wanted him to be part of me as we lay in each other's arms. I felt so close, so open to him.

Now, I was struggling to hold onto the validity of those memories. It was so easy to question his intentions, and dismiss any expression of his love as being the cynical seeds of eventual betrayal. Somehow I had to keep a part of Mathew sacred, untainted by his duplicity. I had to believe that what he said at the time was true.

I collected the ashes and we drove to the meadow. I walked along the same path as all those years ago, towards the oak tree. Instead of holding Mathew's hand I was holding a pot of his ashes. It was cold and bleak. I reassured myself that the flowers would grow back in the spring and that Mathew's ashes would feed them.

I knelt down close to the spot where Mathew and I were consumed with love and started to pull the soil away with my hands. I tipped the ashes into the hole and pushed the soil over with my palms. Fiona stood behind me in silence. I prayed that Mathew would find peace.

By Tuesday I noticed I was looking forward to seeing Steven again. I drove to Hertford with Fiona.

When I was seated, Steven looked up at me from his notes.

"So we left off with you at art college. Would you like to proceed?"

"I think you should know that since last week I have received a death threat. I buried my husband on Friday and I have been feeling very depressed."

Steven made notes.

"I see. Do you want to skip forwards?"

I nodded.

I told my therapist how my father died suddenly, about my mother's unexpected death, meeting Mathew and our relationship. I described finding Mathew dead on the floor, the bank details and the threatening letter. I went on to tell him about my depression.

"I think it would be unusual if you did not feel depressed under the circumstances. Giving yourself some time to grieve might be very healthy."

When I was ready, we went on talking about adjustments, change and challenges. Once my hour was up, I felt a bit more open.

On the way home, I engaged in conversation with Fiona for the first time. I found myself interested in her new relationship. I wanted to know where they met, what he was like, how they spent their time together.

When I pushed open the front door, I could see three letters on the floor. A long brown envelope caught my eye. I turned it over and saw the same scribbled handwriting. I looked at Fiona.

"Oh no, it's the same style as before."

"Put it down and I'll call in Inspector Pride."

Pride arrived nearly half an hour later.

She put on gloves and carefully unsealed the envelope. She pulled out the white paper and unfolded it. A picture of me was positioned to the right and to the left was a photograph of a masked man holding a gun. Both were black and white photocopied images, cut out and stuck onto a plain sheet of paper.

This time the bubble coming from my mouth said *me big prostitute. me turn man on and get him do wat I want.* The words in his bubble were *Now u pay big time bitch. I get closer.*

We sat looking at the paper for what seemed like a long time. Pride was the first to speak.

"Where did this picture of you come from?"

"The same album. It is a picture of me with Mathew taken on the beach near Nice. In the original, Mathew and I are leaning against a rock holding hands. He must have copied it and cut around my profile."

I was topless. Again in the original setting it looked completely natural but here, weird and creepy. I had my purple and black bikini bottoms on. My picture had been cut just along the top of my bikini line so that it looked as though I could be posing naked. I had a slightly seductive look. Whilst our friend Janis was getting ready to take the photograph, Mathew had pinched my bottom. I had cuffed him across the back of his head playfully, so when the camera clicked I still had a half smile.

Pride turned and fixed me with a stare.

"And you cannot think of anyone who could be sending you these?"

I shook my head. Pride sighed. I watched as Pride carefully placed the envelope and message in an evidence bag. She took off her gloves and continued.

"It's just that I find it strange that someone would go to all this trouble for no apparent reason."

"What do you mean?"

"It strikes me that the logical conclusion was that you have upset someone who is trying to get back at you by sending these notes. Did you take Mathew away from another woman? Did you lead someone on and then reject him? Was someone else in love with you leading up to the time you started a relationship with Mr Blake?"

I started to say no, but remembered Edward.

"My neighbour Edward did recently tell me he had strong feelings for me for a year, and that he wanted to leave his wife."

Pride made notes.

"Good, so now we are getting somewhere. How did you react?

"I told him I did not share his feelings and, of course would not hurt Edwina even if I did."

"And was this before the first letter appeared?"

"Yes."

"So Mr Edwards claims he has secretly been in love with you for a year, your husband is murdered and then you reject him and you start receiving these letters. Does Mr Edwards work in London?"

"Yes, in Holborn."

"The first letter was postmarked as being sent from King's Cross, London. Unfortunately the stamp and envelope were of the self-seal variety so we have no DNA or prints. I think I will talk to Mr Edwards next."

Pride looked triumphant. I felt a slight pang of guilt, as though I had betrayed Edward. Would he be visited by the curse of telling Amanda his feelings?

"Can you think of anyone else?"

"No."

"Come on, it took my probing to get you to tell me about Mr Edwards. I've known weaker motives drive people to violence. Was anyone interested in you when you started your relationship with Mr Blake?"

"I was seeing someone called Patrick Larkin. We were just friends, nothing serious."

"Where did he live?"

"London. Notting Hill."

"How did it end?"

"I just stopped calling him and he did not call me. As I remember, it was me who initiated the friendship and did most to keep it going."

"Was Mr Blake in a relationship when you met?"

Pride leant forward and stared into my eyes. I felt intimidated and blinked.

"He did mention that he was just coming out of a relationship."

Pride looked a little flushed.

"Who with?"

"I don't know. I think he said she was a distraction for him and did not mean anything to him."

Pride looked down at her notebook and wrote, with an intense stare. Two deep vertical lines ran up between her eyebrows. Her cheeks were quite red. Her lips appeared to be slightly purple and pressed tight against each other. Pride got up to leave.

"So far, no one remembers seeing you in that park."

After she left, I felt disturbed. There was a gnawing in the pit of my stomach, my heart was beating faster, my mind was spinning and I felt disorientated. The inspector had become something of a bully. It was almost as though she thought I had brought it on myself.

CHAPTER 7

My next visit from Pride was two days later. I did not feel moved to welcome her. She strode in and slumped onto the sofa.

"Have you thought anymore about possible suspects?"

"Yes, but I cannot think of anyone else. Do you really think Edward is a suspect?"

"He has not provided a reliable alibi for the time Mr Blake was murdered."

"And Mathew's past? Have you found any details?"

"He is recorded as being Ramon Vilanova before he married a Veronica Blake. Veronica Blake is currently residing in Venice. She had a stroke last year and is slowly recovering from damage to the left side of her brain. I don't think she warrants a visit to Venice, unfortunately, nor do I think she is a suspect in her current condition."

I was shocked to hear Mathew was married. He had never mentioned Veronica. Why would he be so secretive? I felt slightly out of breath as I absorbed this new chapter in his history.

"Did they have any children?"

"None recorded."

"How long were they married?"

"Just over three years."

I wondered what had happened. Was the break up so painful he could not talk about it? Perhaps she had run off with his best friend. I felt a twinge of sadness that he could not tell me about it. I considered myself to be a sympathetic, understanding woman. I could have comforted him, if the memory was so painful.

"I cannot find any record of a Ramon Vilanova living in Spain. I am working on the assumption that he either changed his name or illegally entered the country and took on a false identity. So far I have not turned up any missing person's reports for a Ramon Vilanova.

It may be that we will never find out more about his life prior to his marriage to Veronica Blake."

Pride then tried to sit up. The sofa was too low for her and instead of her body moving forwards, her knees lifted. For a moment I felt too embarrassed to do anything. I hoped with the next surge forwards she would be able to lever herself up onto the armrest. She didn't and I forced myself to stand up and offer her a hand. We grabbed each other's wrists and I leant back so Pride could get her weight over her feet.

"I would like you to look at your husband's phone bill and let me know if there is anyone unusual on the list."

She found her bag and got out Mathew's phone bills. Someone had called the numbers and noted the names of the people. There were several calls home, calls to my mobile, to the shop, to James' mobile, to several friends I knew of, the bank and the tax office. No telephone numbers that would reveal a potential blackmailer appeared on the bills. On the morning of his murder, Mathew's last call was to James. I told Pride there was nothing suspicious and she left.

I thought about Veronica. I assumed Mathew would have had other relationships, although he had not even indicated he had ever been married. I supposed he would have had to marry a UK citizen to have a British passport. I felt disorientated thinking of Mathew with a previous wife. I had a desire to see a photograph of her, or even Mathew and her together. I didn't want to leave it to my imagination.

My next task was to visit the building society. I sat in a black office chair looking across a dark wood desk at large drooping cheeks and jowls. In a low, gravelly voice, devoid of emotion, the man told me Mathew set up the loans. The society had agreed three loans that added up to eighty per cent of the value of our home at the time. Our home had since lost value, whilst unpaid interest on the loans had increased to the point that the manager mechanically suggested I was now in negative equity. The current repayment charges would consume my full salary after tax. I stared at the prospect of my home being repossessed with a numb daze. I could not summon the will to get out of my chair. An assistant came and helped me up, leading me to the reception area.

Halfway through my life I had lost my husband, house and lifestyle. I would have to start all over again from nothing. I felt as though I was staring into a black abyss. I was slipping from my warm, safe, predictable world into the cold, lonely, unknown. I cannot remember feeling so sad.

That night I woke from a dream about Mathew. He was looking at me pleadingly, as though he was begging for mercy. I felt remote and disconnected from him. I could not hear him. He reached out towards me with open hands but there was a gulf between us. I just stood there feeling cold, watching him.

I lay in the dark with my eyes open, curled into the foetal position, with images of Mathew spinning around my head. The awful question that I could not push away was, had I killed him? Was my dream a distant recollection of a traumatic event that I had buried deep in my subconscious? Did I really go to the park on the day of the murder? My heart was beating fast, as I tried to remember details. What was in the sandwich? What was I wearing?

I was distracted by the sound of creaking on the stairs. I thought it must be Fiona. The steps sounded heavy. I pulled the duvet tightly around my neck. As I stared at the round brass doorknob, I thought I saw it turning. I thought I heard the sound of someone breathing deeply. It was as though the breathing was already in the room. I felt paralysed. As the breathing became heavier, mine froze to tiny, quick shallow gasps. The sounds disappeared as quickly as they came. Had the ghost of Mathew visited me?

In the morning I asked Fiona if she had got up in the night. She said she had not. I wanted to believe she was lying, but I couldn't.

Fear was following me. I became suspicious of Fiona. I began to watch her. I checked my valuables, in case they were the object of her nightly prowls. They were still there.

I thought about Edward and his reaction to me at the end of our lunch. As Inspector Pride pointed out, I received the first threat after that incident. Oh my God, could he have murdered Mathew, to get him out of the way? Could he have coolly walked across and rang the front door? Of course, Mathew would let him in. Then he could have shot Mathew in cold blood and took any photographs of me he could find.

I remembered the way Edward would touch me when he brought me my morning teas, when I slept in his spare room. I wondered why he was so intense, but now it all made sense. I was his prey, and there I was in his lair. I remembered once watching a wasp attacking a caterpillar in my garden. The buzzing black and yellow, overwhelming the soft, pale, silent green. Edward had started preparing me by telling me it was over with Edwina and then, when he was ready, made his move.

Could rejection turn love to hatred so quickly? No, not love, it would have been lust, desire or a primal attraction. I considered that if Edward could kill Mathew so easily, then why not me? As I stood by the living room window I saw Edward leave his house. I ducked back behind the curtain quickly as he looked round. I opened a small crack between the curtain and window frame. As Edward walked past my home he stopped and turned so he looked straight at me. His eyes were piercing, cold and unblinking. He affected one of his martial arts postures. I squatted down on the carpet keeping my eyes just above the window ledge. He was wearing a yellow jacket and black trousers. I gulped as I looked down at my long, pastel green top. Sweat formed across my forehead.

"Fiona, Fiona, please come quickly!"

I heard the kitchen chair scrape across the floor, footsteps, and then saw Fiona enter the living room.

"He's outside."

Fiona looked alarmed.

"Who?"

"Edward. I think he killed Mathew and now he wants to kill me."

Fiona walked over to the window and looked out.

"There's no one there. Look, come and see."

I heaved myself up and peered up and down the road with my face pressed against the cold glass.

"See, no one's there," Fiona said comfortingly.

"He must have gone. He was there, I assure you."

I noted the look Fiona gave me. Suddenly I was playing the mad victim in a Hitchcock film. I told Fiona my theories about Edward. She sat passively. At the end she told me that her boss had interviewed Edward and that they had searched his home. They had nothing to link him to Mathew's murder or the threatening letters.

The next morning Inspector Pride came round unexpectedly. Fiona had left and was to be replaced by a new PC, so I assumed Pride was bringing my new companion, but she trudged up to my door alone. I showed her into the living room.

"Mrs Blake. I would like you to come down to the police station so I can ask you some more questions."

"Can't you ask them here?"

"I would prefer a more formal setting and to have one of my colleagues present. In particular I would like you to go through your version of the events that took place the day Mr Blake was murdered."

My heart missed a beat and I stood motionless. The inspector's eyes looked cold. She swayed slightly from one foot to another. She raised her eyebrows and glared at me. I snapped out of my trance. I picked up my large brown, floppy shoulder bag and loose black coat. Just before leaving, I went back for my laptop. If police stations were like hospitals, I would have plenty of time on my hands.

We got into Pride's green Ford Mondeo. There were boxes and paper bags full of files on the backseat so I sat next to her. The smell of cheap perfume was repulsive. I leant against the window and opened it slightly. I realised there was something I was not comfortable about with Pride. She veered from being sweet to sudden displays of aggression.

So now I was the suspect. Did she think I was sending myself those awful letters? Although, I was almost absolutely sure I was innocent, the seed of a thought that I killed Mathew had sprouted. Each time it only lived for a few seconds, before my rational mind recovered, but during those brief moments, the rogue thought induced a feeling of terror.

Pride felt too big for the car. The intensity of her mood was oppressive. I became nauseous with the violent swaying of the car. My fists tightened around the edges of the seat. I began to have a panic attack. My heartbeat doubled, I felt a pounding in my chest, my breathing became frantic and yet I could not get enough air. I was too scared to let my lungs open. My eye twitched strongly. I kept rubbing it but a nerve just below my eye kept contracting spasmodically.

Pride drove through the country lanes. The car radio played "Summertime" even though it was winter. We came to a small village with cottages arranged along one side of a village green. I felt a pain in my chest each time I breathed in. I felt starved of air. The November sun was low in the sky and shone onto the dirty corners of the windscreen the wipers could not reach. Pride lowered her sun visor. I thought I must be having a heart attack. I wanted to tell Pride but no sound came from my throat. Three children were riding bicycles on the grass, chasing each other. As we approached, a child in a red top nudged a boy in a black top causing him to lose balance. In an effort to regain stability, he swerved into the road in front of the car. The inspector slammed on the brakes, throwing me forward against my seat belt. The box and bags flew forwards off the rear seat. I could feel something hit the back of my seat.

The inspector flung the door open, heaved herself out of the car and slammed the door shut. The black-topped boy got up, pulling his bike off the road. He must have been about eleven. Pride started yelling at him. I opened my door for fresh air. The cold felt good, not sitting next to Pride felt good, being still felt good. I undid my safety belt and let myself expand.

I could hear Pride yelling at the children. She turned, kicking a stone as she returned to the car. Pride slumped back into her seat. Our eyes met. Hers looked fierce. I panicked. I could not be in the car with her. I could not go to the police station with her to be interrogated. I turned to scramble out of the car. Pride grabbed my sleeve. I wriggled out of my coat, grabbed my bag and ran across the green. I heard the inspector start her car and drive fast around the end of the green to cut me off. I ran across the road ahead of her but she sped up. I could hear the engine screaming. She swerved the car and aimed it at me. I jumped across the ditch at the side of the road as the car flashed past and crawled through the hedge. I felt pain in my left leg. I limped across a small grass verge and into the woods beyond. I heard Pride yelling to me.

"Amanda, come back! I know you did it!"

I did not turn back or stop. I ran with a wounded half-skip through the woods. I felt a mild pain in my left knee each time I put weight on it. I began to pant as I pushed myself deeper into the woods. The cold air started to rasp against my throat causing an increasing pain around my tonsils. I could feel my heart pounding inside my chest as my legs began to weaken. I had visions of Pride calling out the whole of Hertfordshire's police force and that I would be tracked down by police dogs. My right foot got caught on something and I tumbled forward. I put my hand out in front of my face as I fell to the ground.

"Fiddlesticks," I cried out.

I lay trying to get my breath back. The pain in my chest had gone. I scrambled upright and looked around to see if anyone had heard me. I started to trot more carefully. My right hand was bleeding. I slowed to a fast walk and hobbled down a narrow path avoiding a tangled mesh of brambles.

The path led to an old hut. It was covered in sheets of corrugated iron, moss, ivy and leaves. The dark entrance faced me like an open snarling mouth. It looked distorted and misshapen. I was struck by a childish fear. I felt like running back from it. For a moment I could not pass. I recoiled and tried to talk some sense into my distorted mind.

I forced myself forward, picking my way through the undergrowth around the hut. I crossed a muddy ditch and then walked down a steep hill. At the bottom was a deep, red-bricked lined pit. I looked over and saw black liquid mixed with leaves and branches at the bottom. There was an upturned shopping trolley in the corner. I baulked for a moment like a hypersensitive horse, afraid to pass. I moved on into a clearing. I joined a larger path and met a silver haired man in a green, waxed cotton jacket, taking his black Labrador for a walk. I smiled as he said, "Afternoon."

I panted, heavy footed, along the path. My mind tried to make sense of everything. What was Pride's intention? She said she wanted me to go through the events leading to Mathew's murder. She screamed out that she knew I did it. What did she know?

I could see a lane ahead of me. As I approached, a police car passed slowly. I instinctively crouched behind a tree. The greenery was thick here and although I could see a uniformed policeman peering out of the passenger seat, he seemed to look straight through me. The car drifted on. Once the car was out of sight, I edged up to the road. I needed to get my bearings. I listened carefully before walking out of the woods. I could see the lane led down to a main road. I could follow the woods on the right most of the way. I started walking along the edge of the road, ready to jump back into the woods as soon as I heard or saw anything. I paused to wrap my bleeding hand in my handkerchief.

About halfway, the sound of a car sent me diving back into the woods. I lay behind a fallen tree. I could smell the peaty, damp earth. A small maroon hatchback passed. The driver was an older lady. I continued along a small track, parallel to the lane. As I approached the field leading to the main road I saw a police van speed past with its blue lights flashing. Now I needed a plan. I sat on a raised earthy mound and thought. Oh Mum and Dad, what should I do? Please help me out of this mess. My father would want me to go back to the police. My mother would be more inventive and creative. An image of her sewing my fancy dress party clothes flashed through my racing mind.

Yes, I needed a disguise. I frantically searched through my bag. I had some long nail scissors, sunglasses, a pink scarf, mascara, lipsticks, a small mirror and black leather gloves.

I started cutting my hair as short as possible. My hands were shaking. Long strands of soft, fair, wavy hair fell among the leaves around me. It took longer than I thought but the end result was that

I now looked like a weird leftover from the punk era. Clumps and tufts of hair covered most of my skull but here and there I could see bare skin showing through. Perhaps kinder people would think I had alopecia or was undergoing chemotherapy and feel sorry for me. It kind of matched my emotions.

Next I found my old sunglasses. I painted on the brightest lipstick, a glossy pink. I used my mascara to darken my eyelashes and then smudged some across my eyebrows. I took off my brown sweater and put it in my bag. I tied the pink scarf around my neck. It clashed with my red stretchy top, but added to the image of a slightly mad woman who was stuck in her wild days. Finally I rolled my jeans up three times so they ended half way down my calves, exposing my brown and mauve striped socks.

I felt refreshed in my new identity. A new horizon opened up. I was not going back to my home. I could not face Pride after this. I wanted to run as far as I could from Edward. No more banks, building societies and bills I couldn't pay.

I needed somewhere to stay for a few days. I had some cash, plus my credit and bankcards. Local hotels would be risky and I assumed easy for the police to look for new guests. I needed to get some distance between myself, Edward and Pride. London was the obvious place. The only person I could think of was my mother's sister-in-law, who had a flat in London. I vaguely remember visiting her about ten years ago, after my Uncle Roger died. My uncle was, I think, eight years older than my mother. His wife must be in her late sixties now. As I remember, we took the train to London and a tube to Belsize Park. My mother kept calling her Dotty. I think she found it funny, as the woman was quite eccentric. I could not remember their last name. With no better plan, I decided to aim for Belsize Park and retrace my steps from all those years ago. If that did not work out, I would have to stay in a cheap hotel for a few nights until I could come up with a better alternative.

A hedge ran along the side of the lane and I walked close to the edge through the muddy field. Nobody would see me from the lane and if I crouched down, I would be hard to see from the main road.

I kept a close eye looking for anything that could resemble a police car. When I got to the main road, I picked my way through the hedge. Now I was highly vulnerable.

No taxis or busses were likely to pass so I had to wave someone down or hitch. I froze, wondering how I would know which vehicles would be safe. What if I jumped out straight into the path of Pride? The sound of dogs barking in the woods behind me gave me the extra incentive I needed. I walked along the road with my thumb out. Several cars passed without even slowing. I tried looking smiley but my appearance was probably putting people off. As I became more desperate, I became more assertive. I turned to look at the drivers and stood on the side of the road so they had to make a conscious effort to steer around me.

A white van slowed and stopped further up the road. I ran up to the Transit and pulled on the door handle.

"Hello, love. Where are you going?"

He looked like a builder. I quickly decided to trust him and climbed into the passenger seat. He turned the music down.

"I just need to get to London. Are you going anywhere near a train station?"

"I can drop you off at Stevenage. You're not this mad killer that everyone is looking for?"

I swallowed and felt my stomach tighten.

"No."

He laughed loudly. "Pretty Vacant" by The Sex Pistols radiated from the foot well speakers. The driver turned the volume up.

"Is this your scene or are you more of a Goth?"

"This is good."

So I looked more punk than chemotherapy patient. I tried to join in the small talk with a casual manner, but it was hard not to be consumed with thoughts about Pride. Had the police issued a warning?

When we arrived at the station, I thanked him and hopped out. I climbed the stairs and slowed as I saw a policeman by the ticket counter. He was watching passengers passing through to the platform.

I reminded myself that I looked different. They would be looking for a woman with long wavy, fair hair and a brown sweater. As I walked to the ticket machine, the policeman looked me up and down. I bought a single to King's Cross. I had to pass close to the police constable to get through the barrier. I resisted my impulse to look away and pushed my hands into my pockets trying to behave as though I was a punk with attitude. I gave the constable my impression of a *what are you looking at* face and he lowered his eyes.

The London train was due in sixteen minutes. I leant against the wall at the far end of the waiting room. It felt out of the way and secluded. Please give me strength, I am almost there, my mind cried out. I used the time to take the handkerchief off my hand. I could see a graze across the side of my hand and knuckles. The wound had dried. I finally saw the white lights of the oncoming train in the distance.

Seated in the carriage, I tried to remember my aunt and uncle's surname. It would have been the same as my mother's maiden name. My thoughts raced on to what to do when I got to London. I had seen all the footage of the London bombers being traced through their journeys into London using CCTV. I assumed I had already been filmed at Stevenage station. If Pride worked out my disguise, it would be easy to follow me through the system to Belsize Park. I needed a change of clothes. Besides, I was starting to feel cold.

The train slowed and pulled into King's Cross, interrupting my thoughts. As I passed the ticket barrier the name Hope popped into my head. Yes, that was it. Dorothy Hope. I walked out of the station and asked where I could find a clothes shop. A short walk took me to an outdoor clothing shop. I found a mid-length black jacket with a large hood. I tried pulling the hood as far forward as it would go and was pleased it obscured my face. I found some brown leather hiking boots and a green and grey backpack. I paid cash. I put my brown sweater back on and packed my shoulder bag, muddy shoes and pink scarf into the backpack. I unrolled my trousers. Standing in front of the mirror I looked gratifyingly unrecognisable.

By the time I arrived at Belsize Park tube station, it was getting dark. The air felt wintery. I looked around vaguely remembering the shops, cafes and cinema. I felt nervous using my mobile. Could they trace where my calls were made from and to whom? I found a public telephone box, phoned directory of enquiries and got the number for Dorothy Hope.

"Hello my name is Amanda Blake. I am Mary Birch's daughter. Mary was your sister-in-law."

There was a short pause.

"Yes, of course, I remember you. You came to Roger's funeral with your mother. How lovely to hear from you. I hope you are keeping well."

"Well, actually, I'm in some trouble. I am in the area. Could I come round?"

I put another coin into the slot.

"I have my little meeting this evening, but yes, please do. You might enjoy it."

I memorised the address and set off following Dorothy's directions.

CHAPTER 8

The house was about a ten-minute walk from the phone box. It had a white façade, with a column on either side of the front door porch. It was four floors high. I pressed the buzzer feeling a flutter of anxiety. My aunt invited me in and I pushed hard against the door. My aunt's flat was on the first floor.

Dorothy was standing by her open door and held her hands out in a gesture of welcome.

"Hello, dear, do come in."

Dorothy held my arms and looked in my eyes. She smiled warmly and gave me a hug. Then she turned and walked through the hall and into the living room. I followed.

"You are in some trouble, you say. How exciting. Please, do sit down."

My aunt waved me to the sofa. She looked at me more closely. The hyacinths next to me threw off a sweet fragrance.

"Has this trouble led you to take on some kind of disguise?"

"Oh, is it that obvious?"

My voice sounded a bit shaky. With my aunt's encouragement, I told her about the murder, the photographs, Edward, the letters, the loans, the cash withdrawals, Pride and my escape. My hands trembled slightly as I told her about the imminent loss of my home.

"My goodness, what an adventure. And how mysterious."

She went off to the kitchen to make some tea.

"I only have herb teas. Do you have a preference?"

I thought for a moment and said peppermint, but I realised she did not hear me as she spoke from the kitchen.

"No? Well, I will make my special blend for you."

She came back with a small wooden tray with cups, saucers and a teapot. To the side were two small plates, each with a slice of cake.

"I thought I would try my new apple and cinnamon cake on you. It is made with corn, rice and ground almond flour." I groaned inwardly. I was not sure I could eat anything. The knot in my stomach was still present. My mother used to make such scathing comments about my aunt's strange habits. She used to refer to her cooking as witches' brew and rolled her eyes at her sister-in-law's odd herbal remedies. Dotty was considered abnormal in our family and lived up to my parents' nickname for her. I used to enjoy hearing their stories of ghastly meals and weird behaviour and laughed at the antics of my crazy, dotty aunt.

"So, you think Edward is our murderer?"

"He has the motivation and the opportunity. He was quite aggressive with me. Who else could it be?"

"Yes, indeed. Although, all you have to go on is that he said he had feelings for you and seemed upset when you rejected his advances. To murder your husband and send you threatening letters seems a trifle extreme. Your theory does not explain the loans and cash withdrawals."

I felt irritated with the ease my aunt pointed out the flaws in my theory. I took a deep breath. I certainly did not want to start on the wrong foot with my aunt.

"Yes, I suppose you are right. I have no idea why Mathew withdrew the cash each week. It would be good to get it back."

"Good to get it back?" Dorothy repeated softly.

I looked at Dorothy blankly.

"I remember my English lecturer, Professor Prendergast, would say to me, 'Come on Miss Petal' – Petal was my maiden name – 'you can do better than that.' Then I would say something like, 'It would be a great relief to recover the money.'" Dorothy looked out of the window at the passing white clouds for a moment. "Yes, those would be the describing words."

Dorothy went back to the clouds and then as if giving voice to random thoughts muttered, "I suppose for the blackmail theory to hold true, Mathew would have to have done something he would pay everything to conceal. Is that likely?"

I shook my head as I tried the cake. Although it tasted a little bland it had a satisfying homemade taste. I realised we had not discussed the possibility of my staying.

"Dorothy, do you think I might stay with you for a few days? I would not impose, but I don't have anywhere else to go, unless I find a hotel."

"No, no, you must stay. I insist. Besides it would be fun to help you solve your little mystery. Now, do tell me how you feel after the tea. I used fresh mint from the garden, camomile, some verbena and grated lemon rind."

"I like it."

"But how do you feel, Amanda?"

I shut my eyes for a moment.

"Good, I feel good."

"Describe, my dear. No need to judge."

I shut my eyes again.

"Warm, more relaxed and a soothing feeling in my stomach."

"Excellent, excellent."

Dorothy suggested we play a card game.

"It is rare that I have the opportunity."

I did not feel like it, but she seemed so enthusiastic. I nodded. It gave me a chance to observe her. As we began the game, Dorothy put on her reading glasses. She carefully held the metal frame with two hands as she slipped them into place. Dorothy wore a long flowing maroon skirt with a blue blouse. The skirt looked to be made from silk whilst the top from a heavy cotton. She loosely tied a green and brown patterned scarf around her neck. On her feet were fawn sheepskin slippers over long grey socks.

To my sense nothing matched. Perhaps her sight was poor or she was colour blind. I heard my mother's voice proudly exclaiming Dotty had the dress sense of a medieval druid. I am not sure why she assumed druids had no dress sense but where that comment used to make me laugh, I now felt a twinge of guilt. Dorothy looked healthy, whilst being on the cuddly side. Her grey hair formed tight curls. There were wrinkles around her eyes that gave her a playful appearance. Her eyes twinkled invitingly.

"So how do you feel about life after all these dramas?"

"I'll never trust someone with my money again, that's for sure. I never want to be in love again. I am sure I'll always carry an emotional scar from all this."

I took a deep, shaky breath in and sighed.

"Never and ever," Dorothy mused putting down her cards. "Always, too. They are such absolute and final words. Is life ever like that? Tell me Amanda, would you feel different if you thought to yourself that I do not currently feel like trusting someone with my money, I do not want to fall in love for a while, or that I am aware of an emotional scar that needs healing. It might leave more room for other possibilities."

I became defensive, shrugging insolently. Dorothy smiled sweetly.

"If we think in words, our choice of words may become very important as they shape our thoughts and out of that, what we think is possible."

I reminded myself of my situation and nodded.

After we finished playing a second round she looked at the clock on the mantelpiece and got up to get ready for her meeting.

"What is this meeting?"

"It's a little hard to explain. They are always unpredictable. Why don't you think of it as a story that will unfold in its own way."

We set out cups, saucers and plates on the low living room table. With Dorothy's supervision, I arranged the sofa and three chairs so everyone could see each other. Dorothy brought out bowls of dried fruit, nuts, olives and fresh fruit. She placed an array of candles on the table and I lit them for her. Then I lit the incense in the corner of the room. Dorothy drew the full length, purple and gold curtains across the large bay windows at the end of the room.

For a while it felt like we were preparing for a séance. Were my parents right and she was the leading member of a witches' coven? Everything was done with a calming ease. Although she exhibited an eye for detail, her arrangements were made as though she had just thought of them. In that sense, her actions were quite childlike. It reminded me for a moment of when, as a child, I used to play house and arrange things in my bedroom. Nothing really mattered but everything was interesting and particular.

"What do you think, dear? Shall I move these candles over here? Sit down in that chair and tell me how it feels."

I sat on the soft, beige chair indicated.

"It looks good. I like the candles where they are."

"Feelings, Amanda, feelings, dear."

I shut my eyes again and tried to access my feelings.

"I feel quite relaxed, but a little excited at the same time. I suppose I am wondering what the meeting is about."

"Just describe, dear. No need to justify or analyse."

"I feel a sense of anticipation."

"Wonderful, wonderful. Now I am going to turn down the lights and you can tell me if you feel any difference."

This time I kept my eyes open.

"I still feel the anticipation, but I am also feeling a bit more secure."

"Well, I think that just about does it."

As if we were in a stage play, the doorbell rang.

CHRYSALIS

CHAPTER 9

The caterpillar finds a place on a stem or branch and attaches itself by spinning its own silk. About a day later it will wiggle frantically and shed its exoskeleton revealing the chrysalis beneath. Although still on the outside, tremendous activity is taking place inside the chrysalis. The caterpillar is deconstructing itself and recreating itself as a butterfly.

The first to enter was an elderly man. I guessed he was from India. He looked to be slightly older than my aunt. Dorothy introduced him as Nirmal Rajan. As he took off his long, black coat, I saw he wore a white shirt and grey Indian-style tunic. I smelled a hint of spice. When I looked down at his feet, I was surprised to see he was barefoot, wearing only sandals. He took off his sandals and lined them up neatly by the door. My aunt bent down and put a pair of wool slippers by his feet. Nirmal smiled and said, "How do you do, Mrs Blake." He then sat on the furthest chair and pulled his legs up so that he sat cross-legged.

The bell rang again and two people came in together. My aunt introduced the first as Sandy Vox and the second as Henrique Huber, whilst announcing me as her niece. They stood congested by the front door as they took off their coats and hung them up. Sandy slid off her red trainers, slipped on a pair of slippers and came over to me. She gently put her hands on my shoulders.

"So you're Dot's little niece."

She looked me in the eye as she gave me a smile and a little squeeze before removing her hands. Sandy wore a long fawn skirt and brown V-neck sweater. I could not see any makeup or jewellery. I watched her take a seat next to Nirmal and curl her legs under her. There was something feline about her movements. With her right hand she pulled her long blonde hair back behind her shoulder. Her blue eyes sparkled in the candlelight. I thought she must be about fifty years old. Henrique Huber interrupted my observations.

"Good evening, Frau Blake."

Herr Huber shook my hand firmly. His hand was very large and warm. He wore a black suit with a blue shirt and red patterned tie. Henrique had a large face with curly, dark hair that was greying at the sides. He let his facial hair grow in front of his ears so that it was level with the bottom of his ear lobes. I looked up at his long, bushy eyebrows. He was at least a head taller than me. Huber took off his polished black shoes, carefully slid his foot into each slipper and walked over to Sandy. He pinched his trouser creases just above the knee and pulled his trouser legs up slightly before sitting down. I imagined he was somewhere between Sandy and Nirmal in age.

Dorothy waved me to the seat next to her and began by introducing me. She suggested I tell the story that brought me here.

"It might be therapeutic and interesting to hear other possible perspectives."

I swallowed hard as I fought off my initial impulse to hide away. I finished with the line, "I have gone from being a happily married woman with a job and home to being on the run with nothing."

I had expected them to be shocked, to exclaim surprise and concern, to make suitably sympathetic remarks and offer condolences. I felt very self-conscious in the silence that followed and then to my horror I heard myself saying.

"Hey ho, life's a box of chocolates."

They remained still. Sandy looked at me.

"You know, nothing can be a lovely place to be."

Sandy paused for long time, searching into my eyes.

"From nothing, everything and anything is possible and your transformation can begin."

She paused and looked at me with sincerity.

"If I can be so presumptuous to offer you a tiny piece of advice…"

Another moment of silence.

"Try to make that transition with love. Feel the love inside you first and out of that create life. It would be a shame to colour this rebirth with fear."

I felt Sandy was sincere, but I did not feel in the mood for any kind of airy-fairy, new-age advice. I needed practical suggestions for sorting out my situation with Pride and for dealing with Edward or whoever was sending threatening letters. I felt quite irritable. I suppressed an urge to say something like, "If you had just been through what I have been through, you would not be sitting there dishing out platitudes." Henrique Huber lifted his large head. His hands rested on his lap and he opened them and turned the palms upward.

Herr Huber rubbed his face.

"I found your story absorbing and I suppose a part of me kept asking why you made the assumptions you stated? As is our nature, you have become entombed in illusions that limit your thinking."

I could feel my heckles rise. I was not sure I understood him but he seemed to be accusing me of making it up.

"I can assure you, everything I told you is fact."

Herr Huber looked at me for a moment.

"Possibly. May I deconstruct a little? It may help. If not, you can disregard it as the insane ramblings of an old German fool."

I nodded cautiously.

"We find ourselves," he waved his hand to the group, "questioning everything."

Huber looked at me again with a probing expression. I was beginning to feel angry. I anticipated his little talk was going to be annoying and I wanted him to get it over with.

"Go on."

"You claim your husband was being blackmailed. I wonder whether there are other choices. Was he a secret gambler? Could he have something like a love child, been part of a secret organisation, involved in a cause that is dear to him? I am fascinated by why you would choose to jump to the assumptions you have. Out of one event you have, as is the human habit, spun a web of illusions that you now believe are real. Do you even know if the police are, as you say, after you? You ran away, on your way to an interview, you were not arrested, and you only have a policeman at the station to support your assertion. I suspect we construct situations that put everything beyond our control and ultimately exonerate us from any responsibility."

I felt a storm rage inside me. The injustice welled up. I stood up. I wanted to shout but my voice wavered and instead of yelling abuse, I stammered. Tears ran down my cheeks. I looked around wildly, trying to find some way of venting my anger. I grabbed a glass of water next to me with the intention of throwing the liquid into Herr Huber's face, but the glass slipped from my hand landing halfway between us, before rolling under the living room table.

Four pairs of eyes looked back at me. I ran into the hall, slammed the living room door and stumbled into the doorway ahead. I fell onto a large bed and curled up sobbing. The mix of despair, rage and fury became uncontrollable. I pounded the pillow with my fists hysterically. I lifted myself up and flung myself back down onto the bed. I swore and yelled obscenities. *Oh Mathew, how could you? Why did you do this to me? Did you hate me so much to drop me into this hell? You've stripped me of everything, left me with nothing. Now, as a final evil twist, the police think I killed you.*

I felt as though I was six years old again and my father had just laughingly dismissed my desire to stay home from school. Was Herr Huber was another in a series of intelligent men that I wanted to respect me, but who treated me like a fool?

My mind returned to Mathew. After all the love, all the compromises, all the giving in to your needs, all the care, this is how you leave me. I put so much into you and you have left me with nothing, except debts, terror and humiliation. My anger turned to a deep sense of hopelessness. Why do men treat me like this? What was so horrible about me? I sunk into despair, feeling the cold grief pressing hard against me. I tried to breathe but my chest felt crushed. I closed my sore eyes tight, as a painful gnawing in my stomach gripped me.

I heard the door open softly. I heard slow footsteps on the carpet. I felt a hand between my shoulder blades. I slumped. I was aware of someone sitting close to me on the bed. Another hand rested on the back of my head, still at first, before making slow, gentle, stroking movements. I started to feel frozen and empty. I shivered. I turned onto my back and saw my aunt. There was a soothing smell of wild flowers. She leant across me and put one hand over my heart as she tenderly wiped the tears from my face with a handkerchief. Through the darkness of the room I could see her eyes looking back at me. My breathing was shaky, sending spasms and tremors through my body. I could feel my emotional eruption subside. I started to speak but my aunt put her finger across my lips.

"Shhhhhhh, Amanda, just rest."

My aunt pulled the bedspread across me from the other side of the bed and tucked me in like a child. She rearranged the pillow under my head. Then she lifted a blanket out of the chest at the bottom of my bed and slowly unfolded it before wrapping the wool around me.

"I'm so frightened."

"I'm here and I will stay with you."

She put her left hand over my aching stomach and held my hand with her right hand. I felt warmer, cocooned in my aunt's presence.

"Try starting each breath with your mind. You decide when to breathe in and when to breathe out."

I tried following my aunt's instructions. I was still gulping the air in.

"Feel each breath, Amanda. Feel the cool air with each inhalation and the warmth of your breath as you exhale. Focus your mind on just feeling each breath."

As I focussed on starting each breath and feeling it, I became drowsy. Exhaustion slowly crept over me.

"Try to breathe in whatever way feels loving to you."

My eyes became heavy. I must have fallen asleep, as when I next opened my eyes, my aunt was sitting in a rocking chair next to the bed. I could hear the rhythmic clicking of her knitting needles. I reached out and she gave my hand a squeeze.

Next time I woke, light streamed into the room through gaps in the curtains. The room had a sweet scent. I saw that my aunt had put pots with hyacinths in full flower by my bed. There was a note next to me. I pulled the curtain a little to read it.

Dear Amanda,

I have gone to my bedroom for a snooze. Wake me up if you need anything.

Love D x

She had drawn a heart below. Tears welled up in my eyes. I showered and dressed again. I began to think of Huber's speech. He did bring up lots of interesting possibilities. I realised I had relied on Pride's theory and become too narrow in my thinking. My mind raced around different options, including gambling and even giving our money to Scientology. I resolved to be more open to other ideas. In that respect, Herr Huber had been a great help. I still felt it was completely ridiculous to imply it was all an illusion of my own making. A hot flash of anger rose through my body and I quickly moved onto other thoughts.

Over breakfast, my aunt helped me think through practical steps. I found it hard to get used to her. Sometimes she would make remarks that impressed me. She seemed wise, clever and insightful. At other times she appeared forgetful, confused and unsure. Conversations would break down when she could not remember someone's name. Sometimes she would seem to lose interest and drift off altogether.

We decided that if I remained anonymous and continued my disguise, I would be safe from Edward and the person sending the threats. I would need a wig and new clothes. My aunt suggested I write to Pride explaining why I ran away. Dorothy offered to go out and get the wig first. She measured my skull.

Dorothy returned later with a wig of long straight black hair. She bought matching dye for my eyebrows and dark purple lipstick. I could now go out and buy new clothes. Dorothy gave me two hundred and fifty pounds.

I left the home mid-afternoon for central London. I felt safe walking under the heavy, dark clouds and light rain with an umbrella. My first stop was to get a new phone. I picked up a cheap pay-as-you-go mobile and twenty pounds credit, confident that my new phone would be untraceable.

Walking along Oxford Street, I consciously played out new images for myself in my head. I settled on the opposite of my previous dress sense. I decided smart, neat, black, conservative. I was aware that I envisioned the look that would have most pleased Mathew. Wondering why I did not dress this way for him whilst he was alive, I entered a clothes shop.

I felt weird standing in front of the mirror modelling my new outfit. With the wig and clothing I looked taller, more elegant and slightly mysterious. I felt different as though I had taken on aspects of the character of the woman I imagined would create such an image. I judged a woman dressed like this to be intelligent, uptight and fixated on looks. It was miles away from my earthy, art teacher robes.

Something that had been playing on my mind was the inspector's accusation that I might have created an enemy by taking Mathew from someone. She seemed so intense when questioning me.

Whilst I was out I decided to call James. He had known Mathew longer than I had and I wanted to find out more about that last call Mathew made to him. I used a phone box. I did not want him to have my new mobile number. He was still at the shop.

"Hello, James."

"Where the hell have you been? I've had the police round looking for you."

"I've been receiving threatening letters. Pride seemed to accuse me of bringing it on myself by taking Mathew away from someone. She took me in for questioning and I panicked and ran."

"Wow, good for you. Pride can be a bully."

"James, do you know who Mathew was in a relationship with before me?"

"There was someone, but I never met her. Wait, I do remember Mathew saying she was a police constable. He claimed she could get me off a speeding ticket at the time, but she couldn't."

"Could she have been Pride?"

James laughed heartily.

"I hardly think our Inspector would be Mathew's type."

"Maybe six or seven years ago she was slimmer."

"So you think she was in love with Mathew, you stole him from her, and then she lost it emotionally, became a chocoholic, put on loads of weight, rose up to the rank of inspector, and all this time was plotting to kill Mathew and get her revenge on you?"

"Well, no, not like that."

"I had a run in with Pride before and she was large then."

"What was that for?"

"Oh, it's not important. My girlfriend at the time accused me of attacking her, but it was all made up and didn't come to anything.

I didn't form a favourable impression of Pride at the time. She crossed a few boundaries that my solicitor took up with her superior."

"That kind of backs up my experience."

"Where are you, Amanda? Do you need help?"

"I'm in hiding. You know you were the last person Mathew spoke to on his phone."

"No, I had not considered that."

"What did you talk about?"

There was a slight pause.

"Oh, um, just shop talk."

I let it go for now.

"James, do you know anyone in the North Herts police force?"

"I know where you're heading and I'll make some enquiries. How do I get hold of you?"

"I'll call you. Bye."

Dorothy was impressed with my new look.

"I am just about to take a short walk. Would you like to join me whilst you are all dressed up in your new disguise?"

We strolled through residential streets to Hampstead Heath. Dorothy kept pointing out interesting architectural features on the houses. When we arrived at the heath she touched the branch of a tree and then held it between her hands as though she was warming it.

"I do so love being in contact with nature," she exclaimed.

We walked along the path, past the ponds. The air was cold and the ground wet. Every now and then the sun shone through a gap in the clouds warming my back. We came to a wooded area and Dorothy knelt to push the soil down around what looked to be a very young tree. She put her hand into some nearby soil and a worm slithered across her fingers. She lifted her hand to the light and observed the worm crawling around her thumb before gently returning it to the earth.

Dorothy looked up at the sky and then around her as if she had just been dropped there.

"Goodness, we are here already. Well, I think I am ready for tea."

We took a new path to Hampstead and found a table in a café. I was aware that people treated me slightly differently in my new clothes. I watched as two men looked me up and down. I felt other women were more conscious of me.

Over tea Dorothy asked me to describe everything I saw on the day I returned home and found Mathew laid out on our carpet. She was particularly interested in the photographs.

"Would the album have been easy to find?"

"I suppose so. It was in the living room on a shelf. It has a thick, blue cover with a spiral for the pages so I think anyone would recognise it as a photo album."

"Pictures, money and a watch."

"The watch wasn't really valuable."

"No, I would think it would be for sentimental value. Watches are given for retirement and inheritance. Photographs form a record of someone's life. I wonder whether the attacker expected the pictures to all be of you and Mathew."

"What do you mean?"

"Well, if I was in a friend's house and took out a photograph album, I think I would expect lots of different family pictures. Children, grandchildren, parents, holidays. You know the sort of selection. Perhaps a set of images of just you and your husband were not appreciated."

I thought of Edward. Did he assume that my marriage was on the rocks and then steal an album that would have projected images of a couple very much in love?

My aunt had arranged another of her meetings for the following evening; same people, same time, same procedure. Whilst Dorothy's friends intrigued me, another part of me felt I had some unfinished business with Herr Huber. I also felt awkward about meeting them again after my outburst at the last meeting.

"Oh goodness, Amanda, don't be silly. No one will even think about that. They are far more interested in the present, dear."

CHAPTER 10

Dorothy did not have broadband and I had not even touched my computer since arriving. I felt an urge to get my emails. I went out in disguise to a café in England's Lane where there was a Wi-Fi connection. I found a seat at the far end of the restaurant and ordered. I read through my emails. A woman sat opposite me and ordered a triple espresso and a pastry. I moved my computer to make room when her order arrived. I noticed the woman impatiently pour sugar into her cup, gulp her coffee and bite into her pastry. She attacked her order with the hunger of an addict. Then she looked up and stared at me.

"Oh my God, oh my God, it's you, isn't it?"

I jumped slightly as the woman burst into life waving her arms. Her round red face beamed at me.

"Amanda Birch. Anarchist Amanda."

I had not heard my art school nickname for over ten years. Then I recognised her. Ruby Ellis. Ruby brushed flakes of sticky pastry from around her mouth.

"Ruby?"

The woman started beating her chest. I shut my laptop.

"Yes, it's me, Ruby."

Ruby grabbed both my hands and squeezed them.

"How amazing is this? Here we are sitting opposite each other. You've changed, Amanda. What have you done to your hair? Well I guess we all have developed." Ruby ran her hands up and down her torso to emphasise the sparkly low cut top, tightly embracing her curvy body. "I still have so many great memories of those arty-farty days. So what are you up to, who are you with, where do you live, what do you do?"

I remembered Ruby's capacity for nonstop talking. Sitting opposite her, I felt she was going to take off. I imagined her floating up above the tables waving her legs and arms around, talking loudly, riding a wave of excitement and drama. I spoke flatly and quietly. I think I wanted to shock her into actually listening to me and show her how serious real life dramas can be.

"A few weeks ago I came home from teaching art to thirty out-of-control fifteen year olds and found my husband murdered on the living room floor. I then received gruesome death threats and found that my husband had forged my signature to borrow against our home, leaving me homeless. Now I am on the run."

"You're kidding!? No, you really are serious. You are, aren't you? Oh my God, Amanda. Oh Amanda, murdered?"

I instantly regretted my need to shock. Ruby became animated. Her voice rose, becoming piercing as she worked herself up into a frenzy. People were starting to look round. She knocked my empty coffee cup over with a frantic gesture.

"You're on the run! Someone's trying to kill you! Why, Amanda, why? What are you going to—"

Ruby seemed to be on the verge of becoming hysterical. My legs felt weak. I wanted to run out but I could not send the message to my legs. Ruby kept on, trumping one exclamation with another more sensational. I threw my glass of water into Ruby's rosy face. Cold water cascaded down her cheeks, chin and neck, soaking her purple shimmering sweater. Ruby gasped as she took in a sharp intake of breath. I thought she was going to scream. In a panic I grabbed her arms and pulled her close to me. I started to talk slowly and quietly.

"Listen, do you want to get us both killed? Why don't you announce to the whole of London who I am and why I am on the run? Why do you think I am wearing this wig? Be quiet and calm yourself, quickly."

I held onto Ruby's arms whilst she took deep breaths and counted to ten. I remembered this ritual from art school.

After a minute she stretched out her fingers as a sign of regaining control. I let go of her arms. We both remained silent. Ruby picked up a napkin and dabbed her face. I did not know how to begin a conversation without risking another outburst.

"Let's talk about something else. Tell me about your life. Please keep yourself calm."

"Okay, I'm better now. It was just the shock of seeing you again after all these years and then finding that, you know. Um, well where to begin? I'm in a lousy marriage with a pig of a man, Bill, who is only interested in himself. I would like to say we've been to hell and back, but we are still there. I have two children, Robin and Sam. Both girls. We chose androgynous names, so their gender would not matter when they arrived, bless them. They are five and seven. My life is full of taking Sam to ballet classes, piano lessons, parties, art school, theatre club and school. We live round the corner. Bill works, I spend his money. Do you have children?"

"No, Mathew never seemed ready."

Ruby lowered her voice.

"Mathew is the one who was—"

"Yes," I answered cautiously.

Ruby looked up at the clock.

"I'm late. Give me your mobile number and I'll call you."

I hesitated. So far only Dorothy had my number. Ruby was not a threat, but unless she had changed, she was a liability. Ruby must have sensed my caution.

"Look, here's my number and email. Call me and we'll do caffeine soon."

She wrote on a napkin with a gushing, flamboyant flourish and surged through the crowd of people waiting for a table. I had forgotten how tiring she could be. For a while after I felt distracted and disorientated.

Late afternoon Dorothy and I repeated the same procedure of setting out the room. It was as though last time never happened. Although Dorothy put the candles in more or less the same places, it was as if it had just occurred to her.

"I like to live out of my beginner's mind, when I can, my dear."

This time Henrique Huber arrived first. It must have been raining. His black umbrella was dripping, forming a pool on the mat. I took it into the bathroom. Dorothy took Henrique's heavy wool coat and hung it up in the hall. Dorothy and I took our assigned seats. Again I noticed Henrique pinch the creases of his pressed trousers and lift them a little before sitting. This small action was his signature, his icon in my head. I saw him relax, look up at me, tilt his head slightly and smile.

"Well now, Mrs Blake, how are you today?"

"Much better than the last time we met, thank you."

The doorbell rang and I jumped up to let Sandy Vox in.

"My goodness, what weather. Quite invigorating."

Sandy handed me a wide brimmed, green, waxed cotton hat and slipped out of a long brown cape. Sandy curled up on the sofa next to Henrique. They made quite a contrast. Henrique upright, straight lines and composed. Sandy was all curves and flowing folds as she stretched out.

Nirmal Rajan arrived wearing the same outfit as to the previous meeting. He had protected himself from the rain by wearing a mackintosh and a small folding umbrella. As soon as Nirmal was seated, Sandy spoke.

"I would like to explore love if that is acceptable to everyone."

No one objected.

"I am seeking to live out of a feeling of love," Sandy said, looking at me.

"How do you do that?" I asked cautiously.

"You simply unwrap your soul."

This was the first time I had heard Nirmal speak in one of the meetings. Having looked into my eyes to say five words he smiled. His eyes twinkled and then he went back to looking into the far distance. Herr Huber raised his hand.

"When I was young I found it fascinating that we could describe our universe through observation, analysis and formulae. Then I went through my philosophical phase, as my mother described it. Following in the steps of Descartes, I began to wonder what is real. I realised that my reality is my experience of life, lived through my senses."

Herr Huber turned up the palms of his hands in a gesture of openness. He continued.

"Later, I realised that we all think differently. So a theory takes on as many forms as the number of minds it is thought through."

I thought about the children at school and how frustrated I got when they heard what I said differently. Henrique continued.

"I realised science was humans' clumsy attempts to explain our universe. Later I found that philosophy was tying my mind up in knots and I was spending too much time thinking about life rather than living it. It was then that I moved into my deconstructionist period. I examined every belief residing in my head and realised they were not real but what I had chosen to think was real. Most of them were just a distraction cluttering up my head. Something very surprising and wonderful happened. I unwrapped my soul of some of those layers I built up over my lifetime. The image I so carefully constructed to help me impress my friends collapsed. The successful strategies, coping mechanisms, learnt behaviour, dissolved, letting my soul shine through."

I nodded and smiled. I had the feeling that they felt I needed to be helped or even converted.

My aunt cleared her throat and then paused. For a terrible moment I thought she had forgotten what it was she wanted to say. Then she began again.

"Do you remember when you were a child how you loved to play games?"

I nodded.

"The big question is, do we ever stop? Do the games just change? Does hide and seek or chase me change to winning friends and passing exams? Do boyfriends, art school, teaching, marriage and socialising become other games?"

I felt myself react.

"No, not at all."

"What do you need for a game? Rules and regulations, competition and some way of knowing whether you are winning or losing. Isn't that what happens with money, status, prestige, husbands, children, looks?"

I remember feeling incredibly proud of Mathew and wanting to introduce him to as many friends as possible. I liked the way Mathew played up to them and turned on the charm. I did feel like I had won something. Not having children felt like losing. Little comments from my friends would hurt and leave me feeling sad and upset. Herr Huber interrupted my thoughts.

"Is it possible that even now we are all playing a game? Could it in any way be that going on the run is part of another game you are engaged in?"

Now I could feel my anger rise. I felt my face redden and I started to protest. As I struggled to find the words, Sandy spoke quietly and slowly.

"Amanda, we are not here to judge you. It really makes no difference whether you have unwrapped your soul or not, whether you feel love or whether you are immersed in a game that has taken hold of you."

Nirmal started to speak softly.

"We can only engage in the process of transformation when we are ready. Perhaps this moment is not your time. Sometimes we protect ourselves from pain, hurt and fear so deeply that we are afraid to let go. If you feel a resistance, don't force it. There will be other times and it may be that at each of our meetings you will feel a little closer. One day you will want to take off the bandages to see what is underneath. I like to think of it as learning to swim. It takes a while to get used to the water and after some time of watching other people swimming, one day the trust and self-belief reach a point where it feels time to launch off and swim on our own."

There was a long silence. Nirmal appeared to meditate for some time. Then he started to speak again. His tone was slightly warmer.

"We all like to dig. We wander through life along our chosen path and when we come to a place we feel comfortable, we start digging. Sometimes we become completely absorbed with our hole – the soil, the roots, interesting stones, different creatures. We become identified by our particular hole and what is in it. We want to deepen our sense of self so we keep on digging. Digging deeper into our beliefs, assumptions, values and judgements. As we get deeper into our hole we see less of the land around us. After a while we see only the sky above. At these times we need a friend to come along and offer a hand to pull us out so we can see the beautiful expanse beyond."

Nirmal looked into my eyes for a long time before smiling. Sandy continued.

"We all dig our holes. The four of us here dig holes with our discussions. We all benefit from a friend offering us a hand to climb out again. Once we are back out in the open, the temptation is to find another Eden and dig in again. So Amanda, please do not think of any of this as personal. We are here for each other as much as for you. You may want to stay in your hole for a while and that is wonderful. We will still be ready to help you out when you feel the impulse to leave, and I hope you will help me out of mine."

After another pause Henrique finally spoke.

"Trusting other people to help keep me moving, exploring and discovering is an amazing gift I have given myself."

Then Sandy led a meditation. I tried to breathe in with the intention that I was loving myself.

After we described how we felt. I felt strangely calm, content and peaceful. The anger had passed easily, like mud washed away by the rain. After some time Nirmal, Henrique and Sandy got up. We hugged each other before our guests dressed for the cold, wet night outside.

When we were settled on the sofa, Dorothy put her hand on my arm and spoke softly.

"Do you think my home could be your chrysalis for a while?"

"What do you mean?"

"I wonder whether this could be a place for you to experience some kind of transformation?"

"I think that may be happening already."

Dorothy smiled.

"Well, we will see."

CHAPTER 11

I woke thinking about Veronica Blake. It was strange that I had taken her last name. Mathew became a Blake, left Veronica and met me, giving me the name Blake. I had assumed Blake was Mathew's name. He insisted that his past was behind him. He didn't want old relationships invading ours. I was happy with that at the time. I did not want to imagine my Mathew kissing other women. I liked his fresh clean start approach to our life together. Now his previous wife had walked into my life. Mathew was developing a past and I could not shut it out. Dorothy thought learning more about Veronica would help answer the mystery of why Mathew was shot.

Breakfast with Dorothy was a curious affair. First we sat feeling what we wanted. She wanted me to escape habits and any idea of what I should eat. I always felt like tea, toast, butter and marmalade.

I put on my disguise, packed my bag and went out to Oxford Street to pick up some new clothes with the money Dorothy leant me. On the way I sent Ruby an email telling her of my plans and asking if we could meet up. Whilst I was in Oxford Street, I phoned James to find out if he had heard more.

"I spoke to someone who has been in the force for over twenty years. Look Amanda, I really think we should meet up. I can explain it all properly."

"No. It's not that I don't trust you, James, but I feel safer being anonymous for now."

"Well, at least tell me where you are."

Why was James so keen to find me?

"That would hardly help. Tell me what you have discovered and hopefully it will bring all this to an end and I can go back to normal."

"Okay, he remembers Joan Pride but cannot recall her having any relationship with Mathew. He thinks during the period before you and Mathew met, she was in a relationship with Inspector Lenga. They were notorious when it finally became public. Not only was the relationship interracial, and therefore the source of jokes, but there were suspicions that Pride was made a sergeant because of Lenga's influence."

"One last question: Have you remembered what your last conversation with Mathew was? It would help me to know a little more of what was happening to him in his last hours."

There was a slight pause.

"Sorry, nothing coming back to me yet."

As I left the phone box, I saw Edward walking along Oxford Street towards me. He was wearing a long fawn coat with brown leather gloves. His movements appeared hurried. I pretended to look into a shop window. I could see him in the glass reflection. He strode quickly right up to me and then stopped. My heart missed a beat. Surely he could not recognise me in my disguise. He was looking straight at me. I looked down at a pair of expensive red sandals. I noticed Edward look at his watch out of the corner of my eye. He seemed distracted by something and then crossed the road. I turned to watch him walk, until he was lost in the crowd. I felt shaky and unsettled. Had he recognised me? Would he follow me home?

I went home, making an effort to place myself within crowds of people. I hopped onto the tube train at the last minute. When I reached my station I waited to see if Edward left the train too. Satisfied I was alone, I made my way home.

Dorothy was out. I removed my wig and makeup. I was getting a headache and lay down on my bed with a wet cloth over my eyes. My mind was frantically analysing, going round in circles. Speculation, assumptions and opinions ran wild. Edward, James, Pride? My headache got worse. I got up and looked through the bathroom cabinet for painkillers. Dorothy would probably make a special herbal tea. She did not have any medication.

Finally I could not stand it any longer and went out to the chemist in Belsize Village. As I collected the painkillers, I saw myself in the mirror. I had no disguise. No jacket, hood, wig or hat. I immediately felt exposed and naked. My eye started to twitch immediately. I rushed home with my head down. I felt someone following me, but when I turned round there was just a young woman with a pushchair. I looked up and down the tree-lined road before darting up the steps to the front door. My nerves overcame me and I could not get the key to fit the lock. My hands started to tremble. I looked round. There was a young man waiting at the bus stop, two women talking in front of the church and an older man in a long fawn mackintosh walking past.

I took several calming breaths and tried again. When I looked down I realised I had the inner flat key between my fingers. Once I swapped it for the outdoor key, I was quickly inside and safe. When I got into the flat I heard footsteps coming from the kitchen. My heart leapt.

"Is that you dear? I just got some lovely plums for you to try."

I told my aunt of the headache and my trip to the pharmacy. She put one hand on my forehead and the other across the back of my neck.

"I think I have just the thing for you."

Dorothy made me a strange drink of hot water, apple cider vinegar, lemon and mint leaves. She then suggested I try some pieces of a very sour, salty, Japanese pickled plum called umeboshi. I went to my room to lie down.

When I woke my head was pain free. I suddenly felt very sad that my parents couldn't see beyond their prejudices and realise what a wonderful person Dorothy was. They seemed trapped in a kind of tribal self-righteousness that meant they wanted to prove outsiders like Dorothy as being wrong. For a moment I felt ashamed of them. Then I thought that perhaps they had just dug themselves so deep into their holes, as Nirmal said, that they just couldn't hear Dorothy's different ideas.

I got up and sat in the living room with Dorothy. She wanted to know, in as much detail as possible, what the threatening letters said. I drew out the images on plain paper and wrote out the messages for her, with all the misspellings, as best as I could remember.

"Let me get my reading glasses."

When she returned, she sat close to me.

"Well, this is interesting. The wording looks like it has been written by a child or someone who has very little education."

"Lots of people use the text style of writing. Couldn't it be someone wanting to remain anonymous?"

"Yes, it could but I think the person who wrote this was emotional. The words are chosen to hurt, offend and frighten."

Dorothy lay back against the back of the sofa and closed her eyes. Then she asked me how the photographs were attached to the paper. She was intrigued by my description.

"Photocopying the photographs, cutting them out and sticking them onto paper suggests someone with no access to a computer. I am no expert, but I am told you can scan pictures into a computer and then easily put them on a page and write the captions so that it all prints onto one piece of paper."

"Yes, all my pupils would be able to do that easily."

"Even the idea of a cartoon style suggests someone quite young to me."

We sat in silence for some time.

"Something else that is bothering me is that James had a telephone conversation shortly before Mathew was murdered and he claims he cannot remember anything about it."

"That does sound suspicious. The human mind works in mysterious ways, and I imagine it is very good at remembering someone's last conversation, however mundane. The question we need to ask ourselves is how we can open James up to revealing the contents of that call?"

"I think it would help me, even if it has nothing to do with Mathew's killing."

"Sometimes I find the best thing is to meditate on something else and see if an answer pops into my head. Why don't you help me repot these plants? They have outgrown their homes."

Dorothy encouraged me to get absorbed in the feeling of the soil, roots and pots. She suggested I get lost in observing the plants.

Then she wanted me to feel the plants emotionally and try to connect to them.

"You are so full of life. Are you thirsty?"

I started to answer before realising she was talking to the plants. When we finished, Dorothy sat in her chair and shut her eyes. I cleared up the loose soil and put the new pots back by the window.

"You know dear, I think is time you visited Mathew's ex-wife. What is her name?"

"Veronica."

Dorothy shut her eyes for a few minutes.

"Well I think it is a splendid idea, my dear. Venice is such a beautiful city. Roger and I went there. We stayed in a lovely hotel. What was the name?" Dorothy held up her hand as though to stop me answering. "It was close to St Mark's Square. I remember the host very well." I let her talk on until she trailed off.

"I can't. My passport is in my home and even if I did have it with me I would feel nervous going through passport control. Pride could have put out an alert. I would hate to be arrested trying to leave the country."

My aunt must have been tired. She fell asleep on the armchair. I put a green and brown, tartan wool blanket over her and tucked her in gently. I felt blessed to be staying with Dorothy. As I got up she mumbled.

"A solution will present itself."

As my aunt drifted off again I sat down. My mind was consumed with questions about Edward. Then I thought about my aunt's comments about the notes being written by a young man. That did not fit at all. It made no sense. I could not imagine Edward would have hired some youth who could hardly speak English to send me notes.

As thoughts of suspects, murderers, revenge, hate, span around my head I became increasingly fearful. My body contracted and tensed. My heart raced. I gripped my cold clammy hands together. I could feel myself perspire as my headache returned. I cursed my situation. I sat forward in the chair and rocked back and forth. Then I jumped right out of the chair as the door buzzer sounded in alarm. I walked cautiously to the entry phone and pressed the video button. There was a stocky, bald man standing in front of the camera. He buzzed again. I looked over at my aunt. She looked peaceful and calm. I lifted the receiver.

"Hello."

"I'm looking for a Mrs Amanda Blake, is she there?"

I dropped the receiver. It clattered against the wall before dropping to the table below knocking over a glass vase with red carnations. I felt I was having another panic attack.

"What is it dear?"

My aunt sat up.

I glanced at the video screen. The man was still there. I hardly dared look at him. I could feel the nerve below my eye tighten intermittently.

"There is someone at the front door asking for me."

My voice was high pitched and shaky.

"Do you recognise him?"

"No. He looks short, heavy, about fifty and is wearing a suit."

I picked up the receiver and dropped it again as the buzzer sounded close to my ear.

"Tell him I will come down."

I took a moment to steady myself.

"Hello, I will come down. Give me a few minutes."

My aunt got up and straightened her clothes in front of the hall mirror.

"Well, this is all most exciting. I wonder who it could be. You stay here Amanda, and lock the door whilst I am downstairs."

My aunt turned and winked at me as she left, closing the door gently. Two things stood out in my mind. Firstly, that all this appeared to be a game to my aunt. She seemed to be genuinely interested to find out more.

Secondly, that even with the drama of a potential murderer at our front door she closed the door gently. So far nothing had shaken her from the gentle calm she lived in. It must have been infectious. I was beginning to regain my self-control.

I locked and bolted the door and tidied up the carnations. With the answer phone receiver pressed against my ear I could hear everything at the front door whilst watching through the screen.

I could hear the man introduce himself as Mr Ron Peterson from Investigative Services Ltd. He reached into his jacket and took out a clear plastic wallet with an ID label inside. He then handed my aunt his card. He went on to explain that he had been hired by the North Herts Building Society to trace Mrs Blake so she could agree to the building societies proposal and remove her possessions.

Dorothy went on to explain that Mathew had been murdered and that I had received several death threats and was in hiding.

Mr Peterson laughed and said it only took him two days to track me down. My aunt asked him what made him think I was here.

"I watched a woman of about the correct age with a wig leave this address in the morning at 9.23. She returned at 14.09. Then she left again at 15.04 without her wig and returned at 15.31. In the meantime you came home at 15.17. I took photographs from my car and they match the photographs I have on my computer. I know Mrs Blake is in your home right now."

I felt weak and started to shake slightly. He continued.

"I think it is in Mrs Blake's best interest to discuss this and reach a formal agreement regarding her home and make arrangements to remove her things to a safe place."

"How do we know we can trust you? For all I know you could be the man sending threats and using this as a guise for gaining entry."

"I have here a letter from the building society and copies of the mortgage agreements. I suggest you call Mr Davies at the credit department. You are welcome to have your solicitor present, or any other person that would reassure you of Mrs Blake's safety. We can meet in a public place. I noticed there is a café close by."

My aunt said something and turned to come inside. I saw Mr Peterson walk away. I ran over to the window and watched him cross the road and get into a dark blue saloon car. I noticed he had a slight limp. I walked back to the hall and let my aunt in.

We discussed the options. I realised I would have to confront the situation regarding my home. I phoned the building society and Mr Davies confirmed that Mr Peterson was engaged to find me. Dorothy offered to call a neighbour, Henry, to see if he could escort us to the café. I agreed. I heard her talk. She made it sound like a very exciting proposition. Next, Dorothy phoned Mr Peterson and said we would meet at the café at 5 p.m. She turned to me and looked into my eyes.

"Amanda, how do you feel?"

I groaned inwardly. I did not want to discuss my feelings whilst in the middle of a crisis. I persevered to try and humour my aunt. She had been so helpful and I knew she was well meaning.

"Frightened, scared, nervous, a little cold."

"Do you feel love?"

I shook my head. Dorothy reached out and put her hand on mine.

"Listen Amanda, you are coming to an important point in your life. Things are happening and this is not the time to get lost in illusions, this would not be the ideal time to get lost in the layers around your soul. Now is a time to be connected, centred, clear and present."

I went to put on my disguise.

My aunt's phone rang, she answered and she told me Henry was waiting downstairs. Dorothy suggested I stay in a mindful state by consciously feeling every step as we walked to the main door. We met Henry outside.

"Hello, Henry. How kind of you to help us on our little adventure."

My aunt then introduced us. Henry was over six foot with long, curly, blond hair. He wore a tight grey polo top under his open jacket. Henry looked slim in an athletic way. His mouth broke into a big smile as he made a joke about bringing his penknife for the occasion.

As we walked towards the café, Dorothy and Henry made small talk about a new delicatessen that had opened nearby. Then she turned to me.

"Feel every step, dear. There is no rush. Just walk at your own pace. We will be beside you. Breathe, Amanda, breathe."

She then turned back to Henry as if nothing had happened. I saw Henry give me a quizzical look and then went back to his conversation with Dorothy. I heard their conversation move onto Henry's practice. He was an acupuncturist working in a clinic in England's Lane.

I was aware of a change inside. I did feel more connected and in this state, some of the swirling emotions evaporated. I cycled between listening to Dorothy and Henry, to feeling each step, to focussing on each breath.

As we approached the café, Dorothy suggested Henry sat at a nearby table where he could observe us. We entered the café with Henry waiting outside for a minute. Mr Peterson was already seated at a table to the rear. He got up stiffly to greet us. His handshake was quick, tight and strong. I noticed his hand was wet.

Once all the introductions were made and we had ordered, Mr Peterson leaned forward onto his elbows and outlined the situation.

"As I am sure you can understand, my clients are keen to conclude this matter. Every day the interest on your mortgage means your debt is rising and the building society is keen to gain possession and sell its asset. You can imagine that the society was worried when unable to contact you and hired me to find you. My job is simply to deliver these documents to you."

He patted the large brown envelope on the table. I nodded. I could feel a tightening in my abdomen at the thought that I was now actually losing my home. A feeling of being overwhelmed washed over me. What would I do with all my things? I saw Henry walk dreamily into the café and take a table close to ours.

"I suggest you take these documents to a solicitor for impartial advice and then arrange to meet Mr Davies. I would also like you to sign that you have received these documents. My clients are keen to work with you through this difficult time. However, failure to engage in any form of dialogue may result in legal action that will include the loss of your home, all the contents and ultimately personal bankruptcy."

Our teas arrived and my aunt fussed around Mr Peterson, making sure he had everything he needed. She then spoke.

"I must commend you on finding Amanda. I am intrigued on how you found her so quickly."

Peterson rubbed his knee before turning to my aunt.

"It was fairly simple. I found that Mrs Blake's mother was originally Mary Hope and her father Alfred Birch, both deceased. I then looked for the next tier of relatives. Mary Hope had a brother, Roger Hope, who had died, but his wife, Dorothy Hope, was still alive."

"And after that I suppose it was easy to find me."

"Well, not that easy. There are thirty seven Dorothy Hopes residing in the UK. I had to get access to your date of birth and then find matches. You married in St Mark's church in Primrose Hill so I made the initial assumption that you stayed in the London area. I was surprised that you lived so close."

Dorothy pulled her mauve cardigan around her more tightly as though she suddenly felt a chill.

"So in your opinion, it would not be difficult for anyone to find Amanda."

"If someone knew how to use the resources, no, it would not. But not many people would know where to begin, or how to access all the records."

"Certainly not a young person who is new to this country," Dorothy mused.

"He could simply hire someone like myself."

Dorothy looked up surprised.

"Yes, how stupid of me. I had not considered that. It must be my age. One last thing Mr Peterson. How easy would it be for a detective inspector to find Amanda?"

"In theory, very easy. In practice, there is rarely enough time for this kind of research. Mrs Blake would have to be of great concern to warrant the resources."

Dorothy turned to me and put her hand on my arm.

"How do you feel about signing Mr Peterson's receipt for these documents, dear?"

I shrugged, not really knowing how I felt.

"Well, it is simply a statement of fact, Mrs Blake. It does not obligate you to anything."

I looked at my aunt.

"I would sign it and take the documents to Martin Ledbetter to look at." After a short pause she added, "Martin has been our family solicitor for, let me see, he first helped us with the purchase of our home in Hampstead. When would that have been?"

I looked up and saw Ruby push her way into the café. I could feel myself tense. I did not want Ruby to impose herself on Dorothy or Mr Peterson. She stood at the counter surveying the cakes. I resolved to sign. After some small talk Mr Peterson excused himself and left. Henry came over and sat at our table. Compared to Peterson, Henry looked as though he was sitting at a school desk. His spidery legs and arms enveloped the table.

"That all seemed very civil. No daggers, poison or raised voices. There I was ready to spring into my Bruce Lee stance," he made a feeble, mock karate pose with his hands, accidently knocking a jug against the teapot. "And my big moment never arrived."

I laughed and caught his eye.

"It is, 'big moment did not arrive,' Henry."

Henry laughed and slapped his hand.

"I stand corrected, Mrs H."

Ruby had sat at a table near the door. I let Dorothy and Henry walk ahead of me and as I passed Ruby I waved and made the hand sign to indicate I would call her.

When we got home, Dorothy phoned Martin Ledbetter and made an appointment for me to see him the next day. My aunt asked Henry if he could escort me to the solicitor's office.

Dorothy invited Henry to stay for dinner. We ate a large salad with stir-fried vegetables. After Henry left, my aunt went to bed. I stayed up for a while thinking about the events of the day. Seeing Edward was unnerving, I still found him intimidating. In contrast spending time with Henry was fun. He was easy-going, relaxing and comfortable to be around. A feeling of anxiety gnawed at my stomach as I thought about Mr Peterson and the impending loss of my home. I was scared of the unknown and my life was bereft of certainties. There was so little to hold onto.

Henry arrived punctually. He pressed the buzzer keeping his finger on the button so that our quiet apartment was filled with a jarring noise until I could pick up the receiver. I put on a quick disguise and left the flat. Henry walked with me to Rosalyn Hill where Ledbetter, Rose and Crankshaw had their offices. I had to trot along beside him every now and again to keep up with his long legs. Henry made a big play of looking around for potential hit men. We saw a pair of elderly women in the church garden, a small heard of mothers and pushchairs near the school, a young man in a grey hoodie at the bus stop, a large woman with shopping and a group of builders. None looked suspicious.

Once Henry had escorted me to the solicitor's offices he arranged to meet me in half an hour. I sat in reception for what seemed like a long time until a little, old man with white hair and a stoop came out of his office and beckoned me to enter. My first thought was that he must be past retirement. He wore a dark pinstriped suit with a waistcoat. He looked like a city gent from an old black and white film. His shiny, squirrel like eyes darted between his papers and me.

His hand shook slightly as he held the documents. In his initial opinion I would be obligated to pay back the loans to the building society, even though they were made with a false signature and with false witnesses, as it would be difficult to prove that the society had been negligent. However, there was an element of doubt and this put the society in a difficult position. He suggested writing a letter requesting that no interest be added to the debts from the date that the fraud became known. That in the meantime they make me an appropriate offer, given that I was the victim of fraud. Mr Ledbetter said he would look into whether I needed to arrange for probate.

We then moved on to the issue of Inspector Pride. He recommended writing to the police informing them of my new address and stating that Mr Ledbetter would represent me and that it was my wish that he be present at any further interviews. He suggested writing that I wanted to make a complaint about Pride's behaviour. I agreed. Martin Ledbetter informed me of his fees and I signed a letter authorising him to represent me.

Henry arrived a few minutes late. He tripped on the reception mat and lost his balance momentarily causing his long arms to flap. I smiled at the thought of him being my bodyguard.

"All sorted?"

"Yes, thanks."

"Good. I have a client in twenty minutes, so do you mind if I take you straight home?"

It had not occurred to me that he would do anything else.

"Henry, do you have a car?"

"Yes, I have an old MG. You know the one with the chrome bumpers. It limps from one MOT to the next, but it is currently working."

"I was wondering if you could take me to my home one day so I can pick up a few things. I would pay you, of course."

"Sure. I usually keep Thursday afternoons free for my tai chi, but I can give it a miss."

In the morning I walked to the café and sent Henry an email. I was feeling playful.

Brave Knight, Please collect your princess from 56 Belsize Park and take her to Tewin in your strapping charger. A

I pressed send and immediately regretted it. Reading it back, I felt immature and silly. Oh fiddlesticks.

A little later the reply came.

Pick you up Thursday at 1 p.m.

CHAPTER 12

I woke feeling some trepidation about visiting my house. I had found a kind of warmth at my aunt's home and part of me wanted to stay cocooned in the feeling of love and contentment that I enjoyed there. The world of murders, banks, mortgages, police and teaching was something that happened outside. Henry arrived and took me to his small, white car. I felt like I was being led to an unknown fate. I hoped Pride would not be waiting to ambush me and that Edward would be in London.

I was initially ill at ease sitting so close to the road. As Henry accelerated I felt a buzz of vibration through my feet on the floor. The car had a damp smell. Once I became used to the slightly claustrophobic interior it felt quite cosy. The heater took a while to warm up, eventually sending a warming draft of air to my legs.

Henry insisted on giving me a guided tour of the dashboard, explaining every switch and dial. I drifted in and out of his story about finding the car and organising its renovation.

We drove to Tewin under heavy grey clouds. I thought they would burst but somehow the pregnant forms held onto their waters. When we arrived at the house I felt nervous. On the short walk from the car to my front door I looked round several times. I half expected Edward or Pride to ambush us.

I pushed the key into the lock. The idea of a cup of tea flashed through my mind. I heard the draft strip brush across the mat as I leant on the door. Inside my home was cold, damp and uninviting.

"Do you want to come in, Henry?"

"Sure."

"Do you mind putting on the kettle, whilst I collect my things? There should be some herb teas in the far kitchen cupboard."

Henry loped along the corridor whilst I climbed the stairs. I found a couple of suitcases and put some of my warmest clothes into them. Then I remembered the idea of flying to Venice and found some dresses and lighter tops. I grabbed my passport, chequebook and file with all our legal documents. I went into the bathroom and scooped up various toiletries into a large wash bag. I noticed black mould growing around the upper lip of the bath and on the shower curtain. There was condensation on the window, mirror and tiles. The bottom of the bath had a yellow stain. The plants on the windowsill had died.

I stood still and felt a tear come to my eye and run down my cheek. This had been the scene of candlelit baths, with Mathew reading poetry to me. We had washed each other in the shower; it used to be full of beautiful smells, warm and clean. Now it was cold, empty and musty. A happy part of my life had died.

"Do you mind if I put some music on?" Henry shouted from downstairs.

"Sure, help yourself."

I left the bathroom and slid my cases down the stairs. I looked through the living room for any personal items to pack. Henry had unwittingly put on one of Mathew's favourite tracks, "Unit Seven" by Wes Montgomery. It was a jazz recording that Mathew claimed had some of the most fluid guitar playing he had heard. I started crying again.

"Tea's ready."

I walked into the kitchen and almost fell into Henry's arms. My body collapsed as my emotion deflated. He remained standing awkwardly next to the table, holding me upright. I let my face rest against his chest and put my hands round his back. I felt soft lamb's wool on my cheek and could detect the faint smell of orange and lemon. He moved his arms to my back and held me. We stayed in our embrace for a while. Then I looked up. I put my hand softly on the back of his head and felt the waves of his long hair. Henry leant down and we kissed. First our lips touched gently and then I pressed a little harder and I let my lips part. I felt his tongue. A feeling of excitement warmed and revitalised me.

"Hello, Amanda. I thought I saw you on the drive."

I jumped and took a sharp intake of breath. I turned and saw Edward standing in the kitchen doorway. His broad frame filled the opening. With his thick white wool sweater and baggy blue jeans, Edward looked unusually large. His face looked slightly contorted and intense.

"Oh fiddlesticks," I whispered to myself.

"Is this a bad time? I just wanted to see if you were okay. We have been worried after you disappeared. The door was ajar, I hope I have not blundered in on anything. Bull in a china shop. No point standing on ceremony." Edward's voice collapsed to a mumble so I could hardly hear the last few words.

I broke away from Henry and put my hand over my heart as I took a couple of breaths to calm myself.

"No, its fine. I'm sorry, you startled me. This is Henry. He kindly drove me here so I can get some things. Henry this is Edward, our… I mean, my neighbour."

Henry offered Edward a mug of tea and poured another for himself.

We sat down and Edward tried to make a conversation, asking me questions about where I was living and what I was doing. I could not think of how to answer. I certainly did not want to reveal where I was staying. After an awkward silence, to my horror, Henry answered for me.

"Amanda's living near me in Belsize Park. She's staying with her aunt."

I wanted to scream out, "No!" Instead I sat frozen to the chair.

After a while Edward asked if he could talk to me alone.

"Sure," Henry replied.

I assumed he meant it was okay with him but he seemed to have answered for me. Henry got up and walked through to the living room, taking his mug with him. I could hear the muffled sounds of Mathew's Django Reinhardt LP.

"I'm sorry about bursting in on you like that. Is he your new boyfriend?"

I shook my head.

"Amanda, have you thought any more about what I told you? I still feel a longing for you, if anything more so. I know you need help and I want to be there for you. Let me be your knight in shining armour."

There was a pause whilst neither of us spoke. That last comment shook me. It was too close to the message I sent Henry. I looked at the carpet not knowing how to respond.

"Amanda, please let me look after you. Let me take you away from all this. I know you think it is just some crazy impulse coming from falling out of love with Edwina, but I have been wanting to be your other half for over a year."

Edward stroked my forearm.

"Edward, I want to ask you something. Can you answer honestly?"

"Yes, of course."

"Have you been following me?"

"What do you mean?"

"Did you follow me in Oxford Street?"

"No, of course not."

"Did you murder Mathew?"

Edward sat up, looking indignant.

"My God, Amanda, who do you think I am? Are you crazy? No, of course I didn't kill Mathew."

"Have you sent me any letters?"

"How could I? I don't know where you live."

"No, I mean, did you send notes to me here, before I left?"

"If I wanted to tell you something, I would come in person, like now. Can we get back to my question?"

"Edward, I just don't share your feelings right now. Sorry, but I am certainly not thinking of romance. What you saw in the kitchen was just a moment of weakness. Coming here was more difficult than I imagined. I hardly know Henry and do not have any romantic feelings for anyone right now."

"Well, we could meet up in London. At least let's keep our options open."

"After you took me out for lunch, I received two threatening letters. Since then I have been suspicious of everyone. I have been very frightened.You must be able to see that after the way you behave in the restaurant, and then receiving those letters, I would be scared of you."

Edward looked genuinely concerned.

"I am very sorry I was ungracious. I felt sad and reacted badly. Amanda, look at me, can't you see that I want to be in a loving relationship with you, not hurt you?"

"I'm sorry, I just can't see anything clearly for now."

"Why don't we at least keep in touch by email?"

"Yes, we could do that. I would like to get ready to go now."

We said goodbye. On the way out I scooped the pile of mail that had been sandwiched behind the open front door into a plastic bag.

We drove off, making a slight detour so I could withdraw money from my bank account. We did not talk much on the drive home. I felt uncomfortable about the kiss.

I thought about Edward. He was slightly older than me, he had a well-paid job as a management consultant, he was quite attractive in a rugged way and apparently in love with me. However, there was no way I would entertain getting involved with him whilst he was still married.

I wondered whether Edward had said anything to Edwina. Then a thought occurred to me that made my stomach tighten and heart race. Perhaps he had and that Edwina was sending me those letters. Could she be disguising them as the work of a child? If so it had worked. She had got me out of my home and away from Edward.

I was becoming paranoid, jumping at every shadow. Next it would be Henry, my aunt or her friends. I started to meditate. Slowly the fear and anxiety washed away with a feeling of contentment. The realisation that I had the means inside me to create such a change of my emotional state felt inspiring. I noticed a fiery glow slowly spread up from my heart to my cheeks.

When Henry parked outside my aunt's flat, I felt warm and more self-assured. Henry helped me in with the cases. I felt relieved to find

Dorothy in the living room and impulsively gave her a big hug. She returned my affection.

"Oh, something has changed about you, my dear. You feel warmer, more radiant and loving." Then she looked over to Henry and said in mock admonishment, "What have you done to my niece?"

Henry looked embarrassed for a moment and then tried to make a joke by alluding to the prince kissing the frog. I tried to laugh and Dorothy did not seem to understand what he was saying.

"Where did you find the frog?"

"Let's step back a couple of minutes. I tried to make a joke but it failed miserably. Time to move on. I've got to go."

"'Got,' Henry?"

"I would like to leave now. Does that pass, Mrs H?"

"Perfectly."

I gave Henry a hug and thanked him for all his help.

I tipped the bag of letters on my bed. I sat down and started to separate the junk from personal mail. My eyes homed in on a familiar brown envelope. I held it in my hands feeling a wave of despair wash over me. I called out to my aunt. She came through.

"Oh goodness, let me get my glasses and a paper knife."

Dorothy put on a pair of white gloves and carefully parted the flap of the envelope with her paper knife. She gently pulled out the white paper. There was a picture of a man and another picture of me, photocopied from the same album. I was standing on the world's first iron bridge in Ironbridge Gorge. A noose was drawn around my neck and the rope leading to the figure stuck on the left of the page. A bubble from the man's mouth contained the words *u have lost me i find u and then u die.* The bubble from my mouth said *i give you good time.*

"Goodness, it is the same style as you described the previous two. No grammar whatsoever. Last time I went for tea with Mary Pitchford, she was most pessimistic about modern education. Reading this, I tend to agree."

A shot of anger infused my veins. My aunt's obsession with grammar was distracting us from the horrific message.

"Anything else?" I asked impatiently.

Dorothy held the paper in front of her and closed her eyes.

"You know dear, it feels to me that there is a lot of pain here. Something has happened that has caused a great trauma. Then you die. Death and dying. Has our friend been upset over a death recently? He or she seems to keep implying you are a prostitute. What kind of relationship has this soul had with women? Where does the sex come in, I wonder? Now, how can we heal all this?"

My aunt did not seem to expect an answer and I did not feel like giving one. I felt irritated that she referred to Mathew's killer as our friend.

"At least this confirms you have lost him. Do you want to call the police?"

"I don't think it adds anything to the previous letters."

Dorothy put the letter and envelope into a clear plastic bag.

My sleep was disturbed with nightmares, sweats and the need to get up to go to the bathroom. After breakfast I went to the café to read my emails. On impulse I phoned Ruby and suggested she meet me. Ruby was a reassuring thread back to different times. I craved those art school days as an escape.

I received an email from Edward urging me to meet him. After some deliberation, I gulped down my fears and wrote back agreeing to meet him in a pub after his work. I thought a quick drink and then back home with all the office workers would be safe. I wanted to find out how much he had told Edwina about his loss of love for her and feelings for me.

Afterwards I read an email from Martin Ledbetter's office with an attachment from the Hertfordshire Constabulary confirming receipt my new address and stating that they would contact me if I was needed for further interviews.

Ruby arrived slightly breathless. She sat across from me and ordered a double espresso and cheesecake. I was no expert but their seemed something compulsive about Ruby and food.

"Oh Amanda, I've had such a lousy day. We are decorating our bedroom and the colour I chose looks absolutely ghastly. Somehow it looks more rancid urine than summer corn. Now I'll have to put up with a grilling from Sergeant bloody Major Bill. Just the thought of him sticking his fat stubby nose into the bedroom and making one of his caustic comments sends me into a rage."

I reached out and gently lay my hand on her forearm.

"You could choose a different perception."

Ruby's cheeks reddened and her eyes flared wider. I thought she was going to erupt. I squeezed her arm a little and tried to look calmly into her eyes.

"Look Amanda, I just say it how it is. Bill is ruining my life, fact."

"Doesn't thinking like that mean you lose control of your life? You are giving all the power to Bill, putting yourself in a hopeless situation."

I moved my hand away and smiled at Ruby.

"I see through where you're going with this. Bill's an obnoxious jerk, end of story."

She slapped the table for emphasis. I just smiled and looked at her.

"Okay, let's talk about something else."

We drifted through a compilation of the highlights of our time together at art school and then we said our goodbyes. Walking home I felt uplifted. By trying to help Ruby I had somehow helped myself. Perhaps Ruby was so entrenched in her battle with Bill that it would take something special to pull her out of her trench and into the open. I wanted to be there for her if she ever felt ready.

Walking up the stairs to Dorothy's flat, I was aware of my thighs straining to lift me up each step. I used the slight pain to help me feel each step.

I shouted out a cheery hello to my aunt as I took my coat off. As I hung it up something sharp brushed against my hand. I looked down and saw the edge of a brown envelop pointing out of the pocket. I pulled it out and let out a short cry.

"What is it dear?"

"Another letter. He must have put it in my pocket. He's been so close he reached into my coat."

Dorothy came into the hall.

"Shall we take it through to the living room?"

Dorothy got her white gloves, paper knife and another clear plastic bag.

i find u again

i very close

soon time come hore

when i ready u will know me an taste dead.

"Oh dear, the English is even worse. Why does he call you a whore? He reveals his shadow. It feels like a lot of pain. Do you think he is asking for help? If he could slip the letter into your pocket he must have the opportunity to physically harm you. Why tell you first?"

Dorothy closed her eyes and sat still for several minutes. Then she seemed to lose interest. She put the letter into the clear plastic bag and went into the kitchen to make some tea. I sat fixed to the spot. I was totally numb. I couldn't think, feel or move. Now I really had been found out. Dorothy came back with two cups of tea and took her knitting out.

"You know, the more I think about Venice, the better I feel about it. I think it would do you the world of good to get away from all this. Time can be a great healer. Francis has a small flat in Venice she rents out to friends. Why don't I see when it is available?"

Dorothy carried on knitting whilst I collapsed in my chair. She went back to the time she went to Venice with Roger but trailed off when she could not remember the name of a seafood restaurant she wanted to recommend. I felt I was going to explode. My life was hanging by a thread and Dorothy had become distracted by clams.

"What am I going to do? I can't go on like this," I yelled. I jumped up and paced the room. Dorothy sat in meditation.

"Oh, God!" I screamed in exasperation and threw myself onto the sofa.

"What would you like to do?" Dorothy asked quietly.

"I don't know, what can I do?"

"Well, you are already doing. You have done a lot. And you are going on. Even since you said you could not go on, time has passed and you are still here, taking another breath."

I grunted with frustration. Dorothy continued.

"When I was a little girl I would start a novel, and as soon as I got to the exciting part, I just had to turn to the end to see what happened. I spoilt so many stories."

I thought Dorothy was going to go on and explain how my own story would unfold naturally and there was no need to jump to the end, but she remained quiet, leaving her memories alive in the room.

Later Dorothy came back to the letter.

"Shall we inform the police? I could ask Martin to come if you like."

"Sure, whatever," I responded rudely.

Dorothy made the phone call and reported that a PC would come and collect the evidence this afternoon. I was relieved it was not Pride.

In the afternoon I felt calmer and told Dorothy about my meeting with Ruby. I explained how dismissive she was about my attempt to offer a different view, how attached she was to her version of events even though it clearly upset her.

"When I sit down with someone, I like to remind myself that I am with the most incredible creature. This is another human who represents millions of years of evolution or has been created in the image of God. Someone whose every cell is a piece on wondrous magic. I find their eyes, skin, hair, mouth, hands utterly fascinating. More than that the person before me has his or her own amazing life history. And here it all is, wrapped up into an extraordinary life form, right in front of me. I just want to explore, ask questions, listen, discover and most of all understand. There is no need for me to impose my ideas, dear. Better to wait until asked, I think."

"Okay, I'll try it next time and perhaps I'll get a better response."

"Oh no, Amanda, it is not to get a response. Only ask questions if you really are interested. Be interested in Ruby because you genuinely are fascinated. Try to understand her and out of that let a natural connection develop. Please do not create expectations. Let Ruby respond in whatever way she feels at the time and accept it, dear."

Later PC Fiona Mills came round to take a statement and collect the letters. I felt anxious, wondering if I was still a suspect for Mathew's murder.

"How is Inspector Pride?"

"Detective Inspector Pride is on indefinite leave. I'm reporting to Sergeant Smiley."

I asked her what happened, but she would not say anymore. So now the police knew where I lived and Pride was on the loose. What had happened? Did she blame me? My anxieties started to resurface. I was only a hair's width from returning to paranoia.

CHAPTER 13

I left to meet Edward mid-afternoon. Since receiving the last threat I gave up on my disguise. I felt exposed and vulnerable. I walked quickly, looking around constantly for my hunter. Would I recognise him if I saw him?

Edward suggested meeting at the Nags Head in Covent Garden. I carefully picked my way through Soho and then across Charing Cross Road to Covent Garden. I found the Nags Head, but I was early. There was an old style red phone box across the road and I went over to phone James.

I felt safer with my back to the wall, peering out of the glass. We discussed the shop. James suggested he take my shares. He said the shop was practically worthless, as the debts had risen to the value of the stock. There was the customer base and some goodwill that had been built up over the years. James had tried selling out but no one wanted to pay money for a liability in the current financial climate.

I asked him again if he could remember more about his conversation with Mathew before he died. He said he couldn't.

After I put the phone down I felt flat. I was still ten minutes early and I did not feel like going into a crowded, noisy pub. I walked along a side road. Vans and trucks were parked on the pedestrian walkway unloading boxes of products.

I had little interest in Mathew's share of the shop. There was some sentimental value in that I had helped Mathew through the early stages and been a part of all his challenges. I had joined in the excitement and the successes. I had also been with him when staff left unexpectedly, when a floor manager was found to have been systematically stealing from the till, when an assistant took them to a tribunal for unfair dismissal.

I stumbled forwards as someone barged into me from behind. I started to look round but a firm hand clenched my neck and jaw, pushing my head forward. I tried to shout out but I couldn't make a sound. A hand pressed against my lips. My body felt limp. After all this time, after all the fear, my attacker was finally upon me, I lost the ability to fight.

I was led up a ramp, fast, into the back of a fruit and vegetable truck. My left arm brushed against crates of tomatoes as I was forced to run along the narrow passage between the boxes. As we neared the end, I was thrown forwards violently. I lost my footing and fell against the end wall. I felt a strong pull on my neck again throwing me off balance. I landed heavily on the plywood floor.

A spasm of panic flew up through my chest. I was frozen with fear. My attacker threw himself on top of me. I could smell alcohol. He clamped my neck to the floor with his forearm. I tried to beg him to stop but no sound could pass my throat. I could see the tip of what looked like a gun in my peripheral vision.

We were at the end of the truck behind a tower of crated cabbages. I was lying on my side with one arm pinned underneath me. I felt his free hand reach round and pull my coat open. He started to rip my top apart. His breath was close to my ear. He grabbed the exposed cup of my bra and pulled it down hard. He was breathing heavily. I started to sob. I felt weak, hopeless and resigned. I had been totally overpowered. Suddenly a terrible wave of failure consumed me.

He leant on my neck as he reached for my bag. I felt faint. I concentrated on the pain to keep myself conscious. He released the pressure slightly as he shook the contents out of my bag with his free hand. I tried to say "Please spare me," but could only make a whimpering sound. I felt a swift blow to my mouth. My lips stung. I saw him grab a handful of banknotes.

The man shifted his position and I felt the cold steel of his gun against my temple. He pulled my top out from the waistband of my trousers and I felt his cold hand move across my bare abdomen. He squeezed my breast hard. I tensed with pain and let out a gasp. "Please give me another chance," I cried out to myself.

I tried to move. I wanted to get away from his whiskey-sodden breath. My ear was folded against a sharp edge on the floor and was hurting. It was hard to breathe with the pressure against my neck. He let out a sigh. It sounded like a groan of great emotional pain. Drops of liquid splashed against my ear and cheek. I felt my head being lifted, I sensed relief, and then he smashed it down. Immediately there was a flash and loud noise. Out of the blackness my head was filled with a vision of the inside of the truck. It was a weird lighting. I could see the vivid pattern of the plywood floor and walls. On the floor were scraps of leaves, Brussels sprouts and a squashed tomato. The image faded quickly. There was a loud rushing sound in my ear. Then blackness. Time stopped for a moment. I thought I had been shot.

I realised my arm was free. I held it to my eye. Suddenly there was an eerie stillness. I turned slightly so I was cowering in the foetal position. I expected the final shot. Instead I felt a hand on my back. Then someone gently held my hand. I moved my hand from my eye a little. I could see blurred shapes. I started to focus on the face of a young man. I could see his mouth moving, but not hear anything. He helped me up into a half-seated position. I could just make out the words "Are you hurt? Are you okay?" with my better ear, over the rushing sound in my head. I burst into tears.

I could see the man more clearly. He wore a maroon hoodie and his cheeks were covered with red acne. I felt a new rush of fear. An older man in a heavy, black coat came in holding a mobile phone to his ear.

"Don't worry, love, you'll be okay. The man with the gun ran off towards the tube station. You're safe now," the youth reassured me. I wanted to believe him. He gave me a tissue and I held it to my face.

I wondered where I had been shot. My senses were returning. I could feel a sharp pain from my ear and side of my head. I could taste blood in my mouth. My knee hurt. I felt sick. My head started to throb.

The youth pulled some crates of cabbages round to support my back. I pulled my coat across my chest. My heart was still pounding and spasms of distress convulsed my abdomen. I could now see down the truck and out into the street. A crowd peered in.

"Looks like you've been mugged."

The older man started to put my possessions back into my bag.

I heard a siren. The truck lit up with a blue flashing haze. A policeman approached talking into the radio on his shoulder.

"What's happened here?"

The older man spoke.

"I heard a loud bang from inside this truck. Then a man ran out with a gun in his hand. This lad jumped in and I followed. We found this woman curled up on the floor."

"I thought she was dead," the youth added.

A second policeman spoke.

"Can you give us a description of the attacker?"

The older man replied.

"About six foot, white, long black coat, black hat pulled low and sunglasses."

"Which way did he go?"

"Ran up James Street, towards the tube."

The policeman turned and shouted an order to someone outside and started talking into his radio.

"Suspect, about six foot, white, wearing a black coat and hat, last seen running up James Street. The suspect is armed and has recently discharged his weapon."

The policemen moved to allow the ambulance men through. A man in fluorescent green knelt next to me.

"Are you in pain?"

"My head hurts."

He examined my head and looked into my eyes. Then he felt my pulse.

"You received a nasty bump on your head and cut your lip. Can you move your fingers and toes?"

I tried and nodded.

"I don't think you have been wounded by the bullet. Do you feel ready to be taken to the wheelchair?"

I nodded again. The two men helped me up and carried me to a wheelchair at the bottom of the ramp. I sat down and one of the men started to wrap me in a blanket. I felt a surge of self-loathing. I hated myself for being so weak. I should have grabbed his balls and wrenched them from him, I should have kicked out, bitten his arm—

"Amanda, Amanda!"

I looked round and saw Edward trying to push through the crowd. A policeman restrained him.

"Do you know this man, madam?"

"Yes."

Edward was let through and walked to me.

"My God, what happened? What a bloody mess."

Edward leant over and put his hand on my shoulder. His face was close to mine. He was sweating. His glasses were starting to mist.

"I am so sorry, Amanda. I should have been here earlier."

I smelt alcohol on his breath. In panic, I recoiled and turned my head.

"Get away from me. Leave me alone."

Edward stood up looking startled.

"Would you please come with me, sir?"

A policeman led him away.

A small army of armed policemen converged next to me. They were dressed in black, with white writing on their uniforms, holding matt machine guns. There was a constant chatter from their headset, whilst shiny black helmets shrouded their heads. I could see more uniformed men closing the road with tape. I was lifted into the ambulance and a paramedic made me comfortable for the journey.

In the ambulance, the thought that it was Edward kept travelling my mind. Sometimes it was quiet. Sometimes it receded. But it was always there creeping back into my thinking. Why Edward? Why would he do such a thing? One minute he is telling me he wants to be with me, and the next he attacks me. I began to consider the possibility that he was schizophrenic, a real life Jekyll and Hyde.

My emotions subsided into an anesthetised numbness, similar to my state after finding Mathew dead on the floor.

After an examination in the hospital I was diagnosed with trauma to my ear, bruises, cuts and grazes. The doctor decided to keep me under observation overnight. I still could not hear in my right ear.

"Is there anyone we can contact?"

I gave them Dorothy's telephone number.

Dorothy came to visit me with a basket of herb tea bags, fruit, nuts, vegetables and hummus. She took out a wide-mouthed thermos and poured me some hot soup. She forgot my nightclothes and toiletries.

"Here you are, dear. You will soon be feeling better. What a calamity. And in the middle of Covent Garden. How extraordinary. What did the police say?"

"They will come round tomorrow and talk to me."

Painkillers helped me fall into a deep sleep.

Dorothy arrived early with a change of clothes, my toothbrush and toothpaste.

The rushing sound had subsided and my aches were manageable. My lip felt swollen. I had to drink my teas through a straw. When I returned from the bathroom, Dorothy had made herself comfortable next to my bed and started knitting.

Detective Inspector David Williams and Sergeant Janet Gough arrived at 10 a.m. The inspector was short, broad, shaven headed and I imagine about forty, whilst the sergeant was very tall and slim with long black hair. I guessed she was thirty. They made an interesting visual mix. They showed me their IDs and I introduced my aunt. Williams pulled over two chairs.

They wanted me to talk them through the whole incident. Sergeant Gough took notes. After I described the events they wanted a description of the assailant.

"I did not see his face. I think he was taller than me. I saw his hand, which was white. His cuff was dark. He smelt strongly of alcohol."

"We have a limited description from witnesses. His age has been placed between twenty and forty."

Then my aunt put down her knitting and spoke.

"You do know my niece's husband was murdered nearly three months ago and that she has been receiving threatening letters since."

I saw the inspector's eyes widen. I explained about the murder, the photographs, the loans and missing money, escaping to London and being followed.

"You understand I will need to talk to Sergeant Smiley?"

"Yes."

"So far, we have been through the local CCTV and we know your attacker ran into Covent Garden underground station. He then ran down the stairs. He took off his black coat and left it on the stairs. I presume he also removed his sunglasses and hat. He then could have got on a train unrecognised."

Dorothy cleared her throat. I thought she was going to correct Williams for saying "got." My mind even ran through more descriptive options; jumped, ran, leapt, stepped?

"Excuse me, Inspector, but is it not possible that he could also have come back up in a lift and made his way back to Amanda?"

"Yes, that is possible."

"It's just that my niece considers Mr Edwards to be a suspect in both her husband's murder and the threatening letters she has received. He arrived as she was being taken to the ambulance, also smelling of alcohol."

The inspector looked confused for a moment. He glanced at Dorothy and then at his sergeant. Sergeant Gough looked through her papers.

"Isn't he the man who was at the crime scene? Edward Edwards. I thought that was a strange name. He was detained and gave his address. I have it here," Gough said.

"Yes, that's him."

My aunt continued.

"My own feeling is that you should be looking for a much younger man. I feel sure the stolen photographs, the missing money, Mathew's murder, the threatening letters and this attack are all connected. The letters seem to me to be the work of someone quite young and illiterate. If only we could find out more about Mathew's past."

Dorothy's voice trailed off as she stared across the ward. Sergeant Gough's phone rang and she stepped into the corridor to take the call. Inspector Williams tried to regain control.

"Was anything taken from your bag?"

"Yes, I had nearly two hundred and fifty pounds. He took it all. Nothing else. Oh, wait; there was one strange thing. Just before he fired his gun, I thought he started crying."

Dorothy looked at me wide eyed.

Janet Gough returned.

"Excuse me, Inspector, the coat was reported stolen from a bar in Leicester Square. The owner just came into the station and identified it. A Mr Patrick Legsworth."

Williams looked at me enquiringly.

"No, I don't know anyone of that name."

The inspector turned to his colleague.

"We'll need to keep it as evidence. Check it in with forensics. I think we need to do a little research and then we will have another talk. Meanwhile I'll arrange for a constable to watch over you."

The inspector and sergeant rose to leave. Dorothy looked up from her knitting.

"I presume you will check to see if the bullets from Mathew's murder match the bullet from the truck."

I cringed at my aunt trying to tell the inspector how to do his job. The inspector smiled and waved goodbye. I sighed as I slid down the bed to relax my head against the pillow.

My mother's chocolate phrase reverberated around my head for a moment. Perhaps it brought me some obscure, motherly comfort.

"It's the winter solstice in a few days. I thought I would invite my friends round for tea. Do you think you would feel up to it, dear?"

"I'm sure I can manage a cup of tea. It is just that I feel so angry when Herr Huber keeps talking about illusions."

"Do you get angry because you feel attached to the illusions? They can be so sticky sometimes. It is one of those dilemmas." Dorothy became lost in thought for a moment and I let her think. "How long do you leave a child believing in Father Christmas, if you start such a story?" Then she sat up straight. "Oh, my dear, it will be Christmas in a few days. How would you like to spend it?"

"With so much happening, I have not thought about it."

"Why don't I take you out for a long relaxing lunch, just the two of us?"

"That would be nice."

"I always think 'nice' is such an insipid word."

I smiled and felt a pain in my lip.

"That would be really lovely, Aunty."

Dorothy smiled at me and pressed her hand on mine. Neither of us spoke for some time. Dorothy went back to her knitting and I lay back feeling drowsy.

"I still can't come to terms with how ferocious the man was. I felt he really hated me. As though years of pent up rage were being released."

"I know. I don't think shooting Mathew gave him the resolution he was looking for. I think all these letters are his way of trying to make it more of a healing for him. He is building up slowly to a longer, drawn out ending. I am sure he did not want to kill you this time. A drunken, impulsive act, perhaps."

I felt a wave of dread at the thought that my torture would be someone else's healing. My fears returned, ferociously gripping me in an ice cold vice. Dorothy reached out and held my hand.

"Don't worry, dear, there are many ways to bring about a healing and we will find another way for him. We just need to understand him first, get to know more about him. Oh, by the way, Francis' Venice flat is free in the new year."

My eyes felt heavy and I drifted in and out of my aunt's musings before falling asleep. I remember thinking Venice would be good. Next time I woke, I listened to Radio Four and remembered my mother.

CHAPTER 14

My second interview was at my aunt's home. Detective Inspector David Williams and Sergeant Janet Gough arrived in the morning. This time Williams was dressed in black and Gough in white. It seemed too much to be an accident.

My aunt fussed around getting tea for us all.

"You two look most interesting. Did you plan to dress as a yin-yang combination?" she enquired.

Sergeant Gough laughed.

Williams ignored the comment and spoke.

"Amanda, would you mind if we are joined by Sergeant Smiley? We need to connect the two incidences."

"That's fine with me."

Smiley arrived after a few minutes and greeted me as though we were meeting for the first time. Something seemed wrong and then I realised the sergeant had whitened his teeth. His seasoned smoker smell felt out of place with his shiny, snow-white dentistry.

"Mrs Blake, I must inform you that Inspector Pride has been removed from this case. I understand from your solicitor that you had some concerns about her behaviour and I would be happy to report any official complaint you would like to make."

We agreed I would make my complaint after Williams and Gough left. Williams started to update us. My aunt leant forward turning her left ear to hear the inspector better.

"We now know that the gun fired in the truck was the same that killed your husband. We are therefore working on the assumption that the same man killed Mr Blake and later attacked you. We think it reasonable, given the history of when you received the letters and their content, not to mention the use of photographs taken from the murder scene, that the same man who shot your husband and attacked you wrote the letters. I understand you have since found three more letters; one at your home in Tewin and two since moving here. Could I have those please?"

Dorothy got up and retrieved the folder with the letters. Now Janet spoke.

"We have looked through CCTV and it shows your attacker running up to Covent Garden tube station and then seven minutes later Mr Edwards exits the station and walks down to find you. We have checked and this provides sufficient time to run down the stairs and return up in a lift."

The sergeant glanced at Dorothy and quickly moved on.

"We have analysed the coat found on the stairs and there is nothing incriminating on it. We were hoping to find hairs on the collar but having tucked his hair into his hat and worn a scarf, no evidence remained on the coat. We noted that your assailant and Mr Edwards are of a similar size and build."

"Have you checked his Clam?"

Everyone stared at Dorothy.

"I thought you could check a person's Clam to see where they have travelled and when."

"Oh, you mean Oyster card," the inspector said with a smile. He turned to Janet. "Have we?"

"It's on my list," said Gough whilst writing.

The inspector took over.

"In the meantime we have questioned Mr Edwards and searched his home, office and car." At this point Dorothy leant so far forward I thought she would fall from her chair. "Nothing incriminating has been found, although he has yet to produce a convincing alibi for the time prior to him exiting the tube station. Sergeant Smiley, I believe he did not produce an alibi for the time Mr Blake was shot either."

"Correct, that morning he was working from home alone. His wife returned just before 2 p.m. but that puts him alone at the time Mr Blake was shot. He did show us numerous emails he had written, but Inspector Pride was convinced he would have enough time to run across the drive, shoot Mr Blake and return."

"Yes, but why take the photographs, money and watch? Surely that would only waste time and risk incriminating himself if he were searched?"

Everyone turned to Dorothy.

"We did search the Edwards' home and they were not in his house," Smiley said whilst looking at the floor in front of him.

"It's all so confusing. Part of me felt sure it was Edward attacking me. His smell and the way he acted just before I was put in the ambulance," I said.

"No, I don't think he is in enough pain to want to kill and attack you like this," my aunt added.

Sergeant Smiley cleared his throat.

"I understand that you were calling a Mr Harris from a phone box shortly before the attack." Smiley turned to Williams. "Mr Harris ran a clothing shop with Mr Blake."

"Yes, there was a phone box on the corner."

"Did you call Mr Harris's mobile number or landline?"

"His mobile."

"It's just that Inspector Pride had considered Mr Harris to be a suspect. There had been previous prosecutions and convictions."

Dorothy became interested.

"So you think he could have been waiting for Amanda, taken her call and then attacked her."

"It's possible. What has your contact with Mr Harris been, Mrs Blake?"

"We have had several phone conversations. He does not know my mobile number and, as far as I know, does not know where I am. We have been trying to sort out what will happen to the shop."

Smiley leant forward to rest his elbows on his legs.

"May I ask how that is proceeding?"

"He claims my shares are worthless."

Williams said he would arrange to have an officer outside and that he would send a crime prevention unit round to ensure the flat was safe. Gough then went through the writing of a statement with me. As Williams and Gough rose to leave, Smiley hung back and turned to me.

"Do you mind if I hear your complaint?"

"What do you want to know?"

"First, I would like your account of what happened the day Inspector Pride collected you for questioning."

I told him about the interviews, her aggressively restraining me in the car and running me off the road. Smiley made notes. Then he wrote out a statement on my behalf. I read through and signed it.

"I thought you should know Detective Inspector Pride is on leave and unlikely to resume working on your case. I cannot divulge any more for now."

I felt slightly guilty. Pride had been very kind to me at times.

CHAPTER 15

December twenty-first came quickly. The winter solstice began with breakfast meditation and then fulfilling my feeling for green tea, apricot juice and whole oat porridge with nuts and raisins. I had got to the point where I enjoyed my new foods so much and felt so much better, I could not understand why I ever consumed my sugary, commercial cereals, toast and breakfast tea.

Dorothy sat opposite me and spoke softly.

"I am really enjoying watching you return to your true self, my dear. Rather than wandering through life in some kind of virtual reality on autopilot, acting out of habits, you are engaging with your world."

Henrique, Sandy and Nirmal arrived midmorning. It was a cold but sunny day. There had been snow overnight. Sandy needed to stamp her feet and rub her hands to bring the warmth back. She crouched by the living room radiator warming her back.

This time Henrique was dressed in casual brown trousers and a maroon cashmere sweater. It took me a while to get used to his softer, cuddly form. Nirmal silently took his usual chair and sat in stillness.

We drank the various teas that Dorothy had made for each of us. The talk was of how London looked so different with its white coating. Then Dorothy turned to me.

"Amanda, after your ordeal we would like to offer you a treatment. We want to put ourselves in service to you and make this your special moment."

I looked back quizzically, unsure what my aunt meant. Sandy explained.

"Think of it as an hour at the spa. We will give you a healing session and gently lead you to a place where you may feel like generating your own healing from within."

"Well..."

I hesitated not sure what it would be like, but then I looked at my aunt and stumbled forward into agreeing. A massage table was unfolded and set up in the living room.

I climbed onto the table and lay on my front. Someone went to great trouble to arrange a horseshoe shaped sock so that my head felt comfortable.

I felt a blanket being laid over me. Warm hands then tucked me in. My memory flashed back to being tucked in as a child by my mother. We had the same routine every night. I would run to my bed in anticipation of a story. My mother would tuck me in and cuddle me whilst my father read me the next chapter in his deep, growling voice. After they would each kiss me and quietly leave the room making sure to leave the door open, so I could hear them downstairs. A nightlight flickered on the chest of drawers.

These beautiful memories led me to an emotional brink. I felt a great longing well up in my stomach and overflow into my heart. Tears flowed freely, running to the bridge of my nose before falling to the floor below. I felt steady, reassuring hands on my back, head, legs and feet. The touch was gentle and the hands remained still. Sometimes it almost felt as though the boundary between us had melted and their hands were inside me, gently massaging my inner organs.

It intrigued me that all this had been done in silence. It felt that my four healers were somehow connected and harmoniously working with perfect, seamless synchronicity. I used their hands as a form of meditation by focussing on the feeling of each hand.

When lying on my back I encountered an amazing free-falling sensation. I had an unusual dream where I learnt how to fly. I just needed to trust myself and I could launch myself forward and fly across the garden. My mother and father watched as I flew around a tree and back to the kitchen patio.

When I woke my thoughts were unobtrusive, soft and calming. I still had memories of flying. I felt open, as though some kind of restraint had been released. My cheeks felt very hot.

I slowly opened my eyes. The curtains were drawn leaving the room dusky. As my eyes slowly surveyed the room from my position on the massage couch, I saw long flickering candles. I smelt the essence of a burning incense stick. Then I turned my head and saw the four sitting on their chairs in meditation. I watched them for a while. There was incredible stillness in their faces.

I lay for some time in a contented bliss. I didn't want to move, I didn't want to break the spell. Finally Dorothy came over slowly and placed her hand on my arm.

"Just relax and I will help you up."

I was left curled up on the sofa whilst my friends went into the kitchen to prepare lunch.

When their cooking was complete they carried in large dishes of vegetables, a salad and bean soup. The table was laid with an effortless grace. We ate a hot stir-fry, some roasted sweet potatoes and very crunchy steamed broccoli. I savoured each mouthful. Sandy caught my eye.

"Can you feel love, Amanda?"

"I do feel kind of loving inside."

"How would you describe it?"

"It's just a feeling."

After lunch and after the table had been cleared, Henrique moved to the sofa, lay back and appeared to fall asleep with his hands over his abdomen. Nirmal sat on the floor and made some very slow, long stretches. Sandy took out a leather bound notebook and began writing. Dorothy sat looking at me.

"I am enjoying your transformation, Amanda. You are a caterpillar turning into a butterfly."

I smiled back. It was one of those easy smiles that spread across my face and would have been very hard to stop. I felt very young and strangely innocent. I think for the first time I appreciated the meaning of the word serene.

After some time Sandy put her book away, Henrique opened his eyes and Nirmal returned to his chair. Henrique spoke softly.

"I suppose we are engaged in ontology, the study of being. To use that well-worn cliché, we are students of life, but students who only want to explore, discover and question through our natural curiosity rather than answer, construct or conclude. If along the way we stumble upon our own insights or revelations, then that can be a beautiful experience."

After a silence Nirmal began to speak.

"Questions guide our exploration and whilst we were born with so much curiosity, we often replace it with what we like to think of as knowledge. Memorising what passes as fact may be great exercise for our minds, but how does it develop us as a person? Does each assumed fact simply stop the process of exploration and lead us to live within a self that has been defined by our beliefs, rather than a self that has an unlimited capacity for further evolution. I hope I never, find myself, as we used to say. I want to enjoy the process of discovery for a lifetime."

I was intrigued by the way they communicated. Someone spoke and then it was almost as though they digested their words for a while before another person spoke. In all the time I had been with them, no one interrupted, spoke over another or dismissed another's thought. I could not always tell if they were agreeing but they had a patient, calm, considerate way of interacting that felt that each was really able to express him or herself and be heard. This was very different to my conversations with my fellow teachers or with my friends. After a while Sandy took up the conversation.

As they spoke I wondered how this group of people came together. What was my aunt's role? She hosted the meetings. I noticed that my aunt did not say as much as the others. Sometimes she just seemed content to listen without contributing.

"Do you mind if I ask a question?"

All eyes turned to me.

"How did you all meet? How did you find you had this common interest?"

Sandy laughed.

"You really don't know?"

I shook my head. Sandy looked over at Dorothy and smiled affectionately.

"We were all introduced by your aunt. She brought us together and initiated these discussions. It was your aunt that helped us experience our different ways to encourage someone to heal. She spoke about love, divinity, our soul and launched us off on our own journeys of discovery."

Henrique nodded.

"I was a banker, married, a father and product of my past, but now I am myself. I attribute the little stumble and helping hand that brought about such a metamorphosis to your aunt."

Then it was Nirmal's turn.

"I thought I had found enlightenment through my yoga and meditation rituals, but realised I was wearing the packaging of what I learnt enlightenment should be rather than what it was. It was your aunt who very gently helped release me from the web I was entangled in and set me free."

I looked over at Dorothy and noticed she had fallen asleep. Henrique put his finger to his lips and got up quietly. The others followed and silently made their way to the door. We hugged and kissed, and they prepared for the cold. I held the door open as they quietly descended the stairs and I gave one last wave as they turned the corner.

My head was spinning with ideas of who my aunt was. In my mind she had been elevated from someone with lots of quirky, but sometimes quite profound, ideas to a kind of guru. It amused me that I had assumed that the others were leading my aunt and that she revelled in their wisdom. It never occurred to me that she was their teacher.

CHAPTER 16

On Christmas Eve, Sergeant Gough came round to update me on developments and finalise my statement. My aunt prepared a tea made from dried bay leaves and lemon rind. The taste was so engaging I could not concentrate on anything else for a moment.

"Mr Edwards claims he got on a tube at Holland Park after a business meeting and missed his stop at Holborn. He says he woke up at Liverpool Street and got a tube back to Holborn and then changed to Piccadilly for Covent Garden."

"Did you check his Clam?"

"Oyster, Aunty."

"Oh, how silly of me. Did I say Clam again? Now I have that word stuck in my mind."

"Yes, we did check his Oyster card and that part is correct. However, it would be possible for Mr Edwards to buy a one-day Travelcard at any newsagents and use that to exit at Covent Garden, and enter again before finally leaving again using his Oyster card."

"That would imply that he had planned it out. Bought the pass, stolen the coat, carried the hat and dark spectacles before finding Amanda. How do you feel, dear? From your description it seemed more opportunist. Was the alcohol for courage or is that his normal habit?" my aunt mused.

I thought back. It happened very quickly. There was no way of knowing. Dorothy spoke again.

"And why fire his gun? If he wanted to kill you, surely he could have done so. By firing the gun we now know that this man has the same gun that killed Mathew. To me that makes me doubt he was either Edward or James."

"Unless it was an accident. He was trying to grope me and just before the gun was fired he lifted my head and smashed it back onto the floor."

Gough wrote notes.

"Have you interviewed Mr Harris?" Dorothy asked.

"Yes, we have. He could not provide an alibi but we have not identified him on any CCTV footage from the area either. So he was either in his disguise or not there at all."

The policewoman then went through my statement again and when I was satisfied I signed it.

Christmas Day arrived. There was still enough snow on the ground to make it a white Christmas. Dorothy and I exchanged greetings and sat down to breakfast.

"I hope you do not mind, my dear, but I put together a little gift for you."

Dorothy left the room and returned with a green package. There was a card taped to the ribbon.

> *To Amanda,*
>
> *I just want to express the joy and pleasure I have experienced with you being part of my life. Although the circumstances that brought us together may have been difficult for you I hope in later years you will look back on our time together affectionately.*
>
> *All my love,*
>
> *Dorothy*

I hugged and kissed my aunt.

"I know something special is happening to me, although I cannot really describe what it is. I also know it is because of you that I feel these changes."

"Not me, Amanda. Only you can initiate and sustain the transformation that is happening. Please do not give any of your power to me. I have enough of my own."

I unwrapped the present and found several balls of wool, knitting needles and a pattern for a sweater. The colours were mauve, green, pink, purple and brown.

"The colours reminded me of the hills to the south of Edinburgh. I hope you enjoy the process of knitting; feeling the wool, listening to the clicking of the needles and seeing the colours come together.

If it is not for you, I will not be offended, as you must know by now."

"I tried to knit once as a child and I think it is time to have another go. Thank you so much. I feel embarrassed, with all that has happened I have not got you anything."

"Would 'bought' or 'chosen' be a little more descriptive? For me, you being here is more than enough."

We enjoyed a relaxing morning in which Dorothy guided me through the process of knitting. She somehow turned it into a Zen art where knitting became another means to meditate and stay connected to my senses.

Later we took a taxi into the centre of London for our lunch. A grey car followed us. I presumed it was my police protection. Dorothy had booked us a table at a grand hotel and we sat down in an oak panelled lavish dining room. I slowly observed the chandelier, ornate furniture and glowing fireplace.

Once we ordered, Dorothy wanted to know how I felt in this atmosphere. I felt excited, stimulated and alert but also slightly guarded. The formality of the place reminded me of my father and his anxiety over my manners in public. I looked at the array of silver cutlery and made a mental note to start from the outside. I asked Dorothy how she felt.

"I feel my energy is a little faster, moving up and to the surface. Like you I notice my mind is stimulated. I feel engaged with my environment and enjoy looking at the different colours and textures. The open fire calls out for my attention and is warming."

"How did you get started with this way of life?"

"It was 1961 when I turned twenty. I knew I wanted to be different. My first experience of an alternative world was yoga. In those days the church complained it was anti-Christian, my parents thought I would be brainwashed and for the angry *Times* reader it was the beginning of the end. I enjoyed sitting in the lotus position in public, affecting a dazed trance, just to annoy passers-by. For added effect I became vegetarian. That was the last straw for my parents. Probably hard to imagine in this age."

"Do you have any pictures from then?"

"Yes, I still have a few. From yoga I became absorbed in Zen Macrobiotics, and after I consumed macrobiotics I became a Buddhist for a couple of years. When the seventies arrived, I studied philosophy, became a communist, joined CND and finally devoted myself to love. I met your uncle and we were like chalk and cheese. He was so straight and conventional. I introduced him to wild love making, free thinking, herb teas, lying in bed all day talking about the meaning of life and holidays in the south of France."

No wonder my mother was so critical of Dorothy.

"What attracted you to him?"

"He gave me my rhythm, routine, stability and consistency. If it were not for Roger, I would not have created the impulse to be of service to others. Roger was a man of great integrity, honesty and ethics. I learnt how to harness what I had, and began giving meditation classes. Once I started to connect to other people everything else evolved naturally. By the end of the seventies I had cleaned myself up and was starting to live out of my own intuition, insights and revelations. I became more myself. Then I learnt to trust myself, be loving and accept a divine connection."

"Do you talk to God?"

"I allow impulses to come through me and act on them. God does not speak to me. He is not a language."

"And what did Roger think of it all? My parents seemed so straight. They were horrified at the things you did."

Dorothy laughed.

"Yes, I think I was a little challenging for them. I think Roger generally liked it as long as I did not talk about my interests with his friends. He was quite self-conscious in public and I tried to be very understanding of that. In the end I think he really enjoyed my healing, natural foods and herb teas. He said it helped his arthritis and meant he could enjoy the last ten years of his life."

"How did he die?"

"In his sleep. Peacefully. We knew the time had come. He was much older than me and quite weak. He caught a cold that developed into a chest infection and he passed on one night."

I remained silent for a while, as Dorothy seemed to be in a state of remembrance. I had spent so long eating Dorothy's simple, clean-tasting foods; the rich hotel dishes quickly filled me up.

"Seeing as it is Christmas, what do you know of Jesus, Amanda?"

"I liked learning about him at school. The Old Testament seemed to me dark, fearful and threatening. When Jesus appeared, love, forgiveness and healing shone through. I liked the way he stuck up for the un-clean, the prostitutes and the lepers."

Dorothy nodded and gave my hand a squeeze. I looked up.

"I would not have imagined you were religious."

"Oh no, darling, I am not particularly anything. I would rather give myself the freedom to be everything, as and when I feel like it. So I am very happy to be religious today. I sometimes wonder how we would be if we could try out all the religions, ideologies and practices. Would humans reach a greater understanding? Could we let go of some of our prejudices, righteousness and judgements?"

"Oh, you mean be a Christian for a year, then study Judaism for a year, become a Muslim for a while, try being a Hindu, experience Buddhism and so on."

"Yes, something like that. It would be interesting to deconstruct all those barriers people have erected."

We finished with dessert and herbal teas.

That night it took me a while to sleep and then I woke to wild colourful dreams.

After Christmas I decided it was time to book myself a cheap flight to Venice. As I left home for the café, my laptop tucked under my arm, a man eased himself out of the car opposite.

"Miss Blake?"

"Yes."

"I'm Constable Pilkington. I'm part of your protection team."

He held up his identity card.

"I'm just going to a café. Do you want to come?"

We set off together, joining the families, lovers and friends, carefully stepping over the ice and snow.

We chose a seat at the end of the café, where I could survey everything before me, including the entrance. I booked my flights and then we chatted. Ruby walked in wearing a huge wide brimmed pink hat. When she saw me, she stormed over.

"That pig of a husband ruined Christmas Day. He ate too much at lunch, drank until he could not get out his chair and fell asleep on the sofa. We had planned a lovely walk in the snow. The children were so looking forward to it."

I introduced her to the constable. Ruby suddenly switched from outrage to being slightly flirty. The constable offered to take his latte to another table so Ruby and I could talk. I thought she must have intimidated him with her dramatic personality.

"He's quite dishy. Does he stay with you?"

I shook my head. The waitress saved me having to explain about the attack. Ruby ordered a feast of cream, sugar, flour and caffeine.

"You were telling me about Christmas."

Ruby continued her rant. This time I remembered Dorothy's suggestion to just ask questions, be interested and try to understand.

"How did you feel?"

Ruby flashed a suspicious look at me but answered.

"I was devastated. It was all I could do to keep the tears back when I saw Sam and Robin all dressed up in their coats and wellingtons. All their father could do was to roll off the sofa and mutter something about his favourite Borolo."

"Did you go out anyway?"

"Yes, of course. I wasn't going let fat Bill ruin the day."

"Did you have a good time?"

I kept just asking questions and trying to listen to each answer with my full attention. I bit my lower lips to stop myself offering my own opinions or making suggestions. I did notice being more open to Ruby and better able to understand her. It was interesting not needing to make her "wrong" and provide the "right" answer.

After Ruby left, I opened my computer and booked cheap tickets to Venice. Excitement and apprehension blended into mixed emotions as I instigated a new step into the unknown.

That night when I undressed for bed I noticed how much slimmer I had become. I was close to my art school figure. My skin felt smooth. The dry patches around my elbows and knees had gone. My nose and chin no longer felt greasy. I ran my hands through my hair and enjoyed the soft lustre. I felt healthier inside. My digestion worked well and I was regular. Somehow my new lifestyle and eating had rejuvenated me. Perhaps I was slowly transforming myself physically, mentally and emotionally.

A few days later I packed for Venice. The Internet predicted cold, wet weather, so my case was bulging with sweaters. I was ready to investigate Mathew's past. I wanted to discover how he was with Veronica. I wondered what his ex-wife knew of Mathew's early years. I travelled by bus from Finchley Road very early in the morning. The streets were empty, just me and three other people trundling our suitcases along the pavement. I became caught up in the rhythmic clunk as the wheels of my case hit the cracks in the pavement; a sound of the times.

CHAPTER 17

I arrived at Marco Polo airport and boarded the Alilaguna airport boat. We glided across the calm water towards the San Zaccaria vaporetto stop. I watched Venice come into view and marvelled. I slowly made out the details as we approached. This was my first visit to Venice and my excitement rocketed as I saw the façades of the buildings. It was a bright, sunny day and the water across to San Giorgio Maggiore sparkled in the sunlight. A cold wind blew across my cheeks. I climbed onto dry land and felt the ground of Venice beneath my feet.

With a map in one hand and pulling my case with the other I walked through the maze of narrow streets leading to my temporary home in Calle della Madoneta, to the west of St Mark's Square.

I found the large, black iron gates leading to a small courtyard. A moment's panic as the key did not seem to work and then the latch slid open. The second key opened a bare wood door that led to my flat. My first instinct was to get out and look around. I unpacked, showered and changed into warm clothes. I set off for a day's sightseeing with my camera, map and guide.

Within an hour I was lost. Some of the streets were so narrow it was hard to get my bearings. I mostly walked looking at the buildings, water and bridges. I ate dinner in St Mark's Square listening to Vivaldi's "Gloria Magnificat" as Dorothy had instructed me and paid with the money she had kindly given me for the trip. The rising and falling choral harmonies over what seemed to me to be his trademark violin phrases leant a kind of spiritual or even religious atmosphere to the evening. I returned home with aching feet. It was a relief to pull off my long, black boots and let my toes spread out on the stone floor.

My last information regarding Veronica was that, according to Inspector Pride, she was in hospital in Venice. I had located

Ospedale Civile di Venezia as the main hospital. It was close to Francis' apartment and I walked round in the morning. I was told that Veronica Blake had been discharged two months ago. Naturally they would not give me her address. Back at home I searched for Veronica Blake, Venice, Italy on my computer. Using an Internet phone directory, I managed to get her phone number and called.

"Hello, my name's Amanda. Can I speak to Veronica?"

I heard a woman's voice with a strong Italian accent.

"Veronica is not well and will not speak to anyone."

"I am sorry, and I know she had a stroke, but I have some important information about her ex-husband, Mathew, and would like to tell her in person."

"Wait."

I heard the phone being put down and footsteps.

"You may visit Mrs Blake at five this afternoon. Give me your email and I will send you directions."

I spelt out my address. Just as I started to say how I was looking forward to seeing Veronica, the phone disconnected.

I realised I could walk to Veronica's house taking in the Ponte di Rialto and on towards the train station. The weather had clouded over and the air was now quite cold. I wore my wool coat, hat and gloves.

I found the address I was sent. I was just over an hour early and walked back to an interesting restaurant I had passed earlier for a very late lunch. I had no particular plan. Dorothy advised me to just ask questions and listen. Allow my intuition to guide me. Nevertheless, I could sense some anxiety as I sat eating my pasta and salad. The woman who answered the phone sounded unfriendly. I suspected Veronica still harboured ill feelings towards me.

I rang the bell for apartment C at exactly 5 p.m. The buzzing of the electronic lock instigated some frantic pushing of the heavy, green door that scraped across the warped stone floor. I walked up the dark stairway aware of the uneven wooden steps creaking under my weight. When I reached the second floor, I met a tall woman with long, greying hair, who I placed in her early fifties. She held herself as though she was a dancer. Introducing herself as Claudia, she turned to lead me into a beige hallway. Claudia knocked sharply on an old wood door, opened it and ushered me in without speaking. I saw a slim woman dressed in a white wool sweater and blue jeans sitting in a large maroon chair by the window. The natural daylight lit her face. She looked beautiful with pale skin, wavy brown hair, dark eyes and long, thick eyebrows.

"Hello, I am Amanda."

Veronica lifted her left arm. I shook her hand gently.

Claudia carried a small chair and placed it opposite Veronica. She waved for me to sit in it.

"I am Amanda and I married your ex-husband Mathew."

I paused, looking for a reaction. The right side of her face moved slightly.

"I have some bad news. Last September Mathew was shot dead. As yet the police have not found his killer."

Veronica looked straight ahead to my right. There was no movement in her face. Claudia stood behind Veronica and put her hands on her shoulders. Veronica raised her left arm and placed her hand over Claudia's. Claudia turned to me.

"Veronica had a stroke about the same time that Mathew died. She is making progress, but as the stroke was on the left side of her brain she finds talking difficult."

I looked at Veronica who remained passive.

"I am very sorry to hear about your stroke."

Claudia spoke again.

"It is very kind of you to come and tell Veronica in person, but I am sure a letter would have been sufficient."

I waited and felt my breath before I spoke.

"I want to tell you some more. Since Mathew was shot I have received several threatening letters and was later attacked in London. As part of the investigation, the police tried to learn more of Mathew's past. They could only trace him back to your marriage in Barcelona. I realised that I knew little of the man I married and shared my life with. I am hoping that you could fill in some of the gaps."

Claudia stiffened.

"Where are the police with their investigations?"

"They have one suspect, my neighbour."

"How did you find us?"

"The police located Veronica in the hospital."

Claudia looked pale.

"Are they coming here?"

"No, I am sure they would not."

"Veronica finds talking difficult, so maybe you have wasted your trip."

Veronica reached out and touched Claudia's arm. Very slowly and with great effort from the right side of her face she managed to speak.

"I will try."

"I really want to know anything you can tell me about Mathew's past, particularly up until you met."

Veronica took a couple of long breaths. Claudia sat down.

"Met in Barcelona. He came from Argentina. Did not have an EU passport. Worked in a bar."

Veronica leant back and rested her head against the back of her chair.

"Do you know anything about his family or past relationships?"

"Did not say. Friends in bar knew him from Argentina. Wanted to move on. To go to London."

Claudia scowled.

"And then he dumped you once he got his UK passport. Took half your home in the process."

Claudia got up and gave Veronica a kiss on the forehead. Veronica looked up and smiled crookedly.

"How did it end?"

"Became critical and angry. Nothing good enough. Ashamed of me."

I felt a slight shudder remembering similar experiences.

"He met a policewoman."

My heart jumped.

"Was her name Joan Pride?"

Veronica shrugged her shoulders.

"Perhaps you are tired," Claudia said and looked at me.

"I can come back tomorrow. I can give you some healing if you like."

I did not know why I said that. I had never given any healing before. Perhaps it was one of those intuitive moments. Veronica looked ahead blankly. Claudia stared at me. I felt embarrassed and nervously tried to explain myself.

"Sorry, that might have been weird. It's just that you look to be in pain and I instinctively wanted to help. I would just place my hands on your back and help your body heal. It's like a very gentle massage. My aunt has been teaching me. After I was attacked, it really helped me, so I thought—"

"Same time,"Veronica whispered interrupting me.

Claudia got up, making it clear it was time to leave. I gathered up my coat, hat and gloves. I waved, but Veronica just stared ahead.

"She is tired now," Claudia offered as way of explanation.

As I walked out of the door Claudia spoke.

"Do the police know you are here?"

"No."

I walked home beside green water, over arched bridges, along stone walkways. It was dark. I stopped by a shop window to look at my map. I thought I saw a person dressed in black step back around the far corner in the reflection of the curved glass. My route took me from the busy street into a quiet residential area. As I walked the sound of my boots echoed slightly off the walls. There was an eerie stillness. I was surprised to find myself alone.

I walked on with a slight feeling of anxiety. After I rounded into a new street I felt a creeping sensation in my back as if someone was close behind. I turned quickly to see a figure in black dart into a doorway. I set off again quickly and found myself in another popular street. I walked past a party of colourful people. Some were wearing ornate masks. I presumed they were going to a carnival. I crossed a bridge and found myself walking alongside a church. My boots made a rhythmic cracking sound. I sped up increasing the tempo. When I reached the end of the church I felt something behind me again. I turned and saw the black figure walking fast towards me. The streetlight behind turned him or her into a silhouette. I walked on searching out people and sanctuary. I tried to focus and stop the fear welling up inside me, spilling over and flooding me with a paralysing terror. I crossed a small bridge and turned to see if I was still being followed.

I could see more clearly now. A black hat similar to the one worn by my assailant in Covent Garden, black costume face mask, thick black sweater, trousers and trainers. The person started to run towards me.

I turned and ran. Every part of me was consumed with a sickening, cold horror. I was ill equipped. The boots made running precarious and my trousers were so tight I could not stretch my legs out. In my panic I careered into a new street. My exertions created a frantic staccato beat that reverberated off the stone walls. I careered over another bridge. I was now panting hard. The cold air rasped across my tonsils. Rather than running in a straight line, I was unbalanced, crashing into the walls for support. The street appeared to be a dead end. My attacker was closing in quickly. I screamed for help in desperation. At the end of the road there was a small alley to the right and I turned the corner as I sensed my pursuer was almost in reach.

Ahead of me a thickset man wearing a brown leather coat strode into the walkway blocking my path.

I saw the entrance to a tiny bar to my right and put every last drop of energy into reaching the entrance first. I fell in through the door and into the arms of a large man in a suit. I turned to see a black form run on down the alley. It might have looked like the person was out for a casual run. Moments later the man in the leather coat walked past glancing towards the bar.

I couldn't catch my breath or calm down. I started crying. When I tried to answer questions, all I could do was pant. Then panicked thoughts shook my mind. Who could know I was in Venice? Claudia had seemed hostile. Why did she ask if the police knew I was here? Each question was pushed out by another so quickly that I resolved nothing.

I sat down on a stool. Another man brought me a glass of water. After I calmed down I explained, with a shaky voice, that I had been chased. A bald man in a maroon jacket looked around outside and said no one was in the street. He suggested I get a water taxi home. Two of the customers walked with me to a stop. I was trembling as the men helped me onto the narrow boat. I sat down gripping the seat. The motor revved and we launched out into the cool breeze, past floodlit decaying walls.

"Hey ho, life's a box of chocolates," I reminded myself on autopilot.

I was taken through the canals to a stop almost outside Francis' apartment. I got my keys ready and walked quickly to the main gate, escorted by the kind man from the water taxi. Once I was in, I began to relax. My mind went into analysis mode. Was this a new predator? Could it be the same person who had sent me those threats in England? Was it Edward? I did not get a good look in the dark but it could have been Edward. He must have started following me after I left Veronica's home. Was someone watching Veronica? Did Claudia phone someone? Should I call the police? What could I say? That someone followed me for a while? Hardly a crime. I considered calling Dorothy, but it was late, and what could she do? It took a long time to fall asleep.

I awoke to hear a creaking on the stairs. My heartbeat increased as I sat up. My ears were highly attuned to any slight sound. I heard steps and movement outside the apartment door. I leapt out of my bed and into the kitchen. I picked up a knife in one hand and a wine bottle in the other. I stood frozen, watching the door. I heard the sound of a key being pushed in a lock. I looked around starting to feel frantic. I thought of locking myself in the bathroom but I had noticed that the lock consisted of a thin hook and loop. Even I could force the door open. Then I heard a girl giggle and a man say something in Italian. I heard a door shut and then further footsteps followed by the floorboards creaking above my head. I sighed as I realised it was my neighbours returning from a late night.

In the morning I made a conscious effort to wear a very different outfit. I wore a hat and found a pair of sunglasses to wear. The winter sun was still bright enough. No boots this time, but a pair of blue canvas trainers. I pulled my reversible coat inside out, so that was now blue.

Once I was out I realised that worrying about yesterday's incident would not help. I needed to get back to the moment and trust in myself to deal with whatever happens. Despite everything, I was still alive. I had not eaten since yesterday afternoon and my appetite returned. I found a café close to the hospital with a beautiful view across a square and canal. I looked at my map and plotted a new route to Veronica's past a museum.

I started to enjoy my new route winding through to St Mark's Square and on towards Veronica's home. I located her home from another direction and then retraced my steps back to a new restaurant that had attracted my attention. I had plenty of time to explore. I walked into one of the many tourist shops selling masks, and tried one on. It would help me to be less recognisable. I bought a plain looking emerald green mask that covered my forehead and cheeks. At precisely five, I rang the doorbell and climbed the stairs to Veronica's apartment.

Claudia was dressed in black. She felt slightly imposing and gave me a cold stare as I walked up to her. I followed her into the living room. Veronica was sitting in the same chair.

"Hello, how are you today? I am really enjoying—"

"Where do I lie?" Veronica said with effort, cutting me off.

I looked around the room and suggested she lay down on the chaise longue. Claudia helped Veronica across the room and had to roll her onto her front. I could see she found it difficult to move her right leg. Once her neck was comfortable I asked Claudia for a blanket and gently placed it over her. I remember the care with which I was 'tucked in' and tried to ensure my movements had a loving, motherly feel. I then sat next to her and placed my hands on Veronica's upper back. I remembered Dorothy's instructions that I just meditate and let Veronica guide me.

After a few minutes my hands began to feel hot. I focussed my mind on my hands and the feeling of Veronica's back. It was bony.

I could feel her ribs. Her lower back felt cold and I instinctively wanted to keep my hands there. Claudia sat staring at me. Then she must have got bored, as she sighed and left the room.

When I finished I slowly walked over to a comfortable looking chair and sat quietly. I still felt some kind of connection to Veronica and it felt natural to continue my meditation, as though it would continue her healing. About fifteen minutes later Veronica slowly opened her eyes and looked at the ceiling.

"How are you feeling?"

"Sleepy."

"Perhaps I should go and let you rest."

"Ask me."

I was unprepared.

"What was Mathew like when he was with you?"

"First passionate, gallant, funny."

Veronica rolled her head on the pillow so she faced away from me.

"Later critical, aloof, distant."

Was Mathew checking out on me too? After a silence Veronica spoke again. Each word felt painful and bitter.

"When I heard he married you, I hated you both."

"I am very sorry. I did not know much of his past then."

"Now I have Claudia."

"I am sure she does a much better job looking after you than Mathew."

There was no reply and we sat in silence for a while. Claudia came in and sat on the chaise longue and held Veronica's hand. I stood up to leave. Claudia accompanied me to the door.

"When I left last night, someone followed me and then chased me."

I thought I saw Claudia's cheeks flush.

"You should be careful. Perhaps it is time to go back to London."

Claudia shut the door before I could reply.

I walked back out into the cold air and darkness. I had a small hand mirror in my bag and I placed it in the palm of my hand. I had also packed a vegetable knife from the kitchen, although I could not imagine using it.

As I walked through the streets I checked in the mirror to see behind me. I saw people in colourful masks. They were laughing, holding hands, and apparently on their way to a party. I noticed a lone figure in their midst, wearing a black leather coat, black shoes and a silver mask. I swallowed and pulled my coat around me. This time I was determined to stay focussed. I walked on, keeping to busier passages. I suspected he or she must follow me from Veronica's house. I had planned to disguise myself after, so I could emerge in my new skin and merge chameleon-like into a crowd. When I saw the silver masked man was out of sight, I turned quickly into a crowded shop. I put my mask on, removed my hat and reversed my coat. I hurried out of the shop and blended back into a herd of people wandering the street.

I saw the same man ahead of me walking away looking in shops. I turned off the street and sped up towards another bridge. It felt like a game of cat and mouse or hide and seek. I began to hope I had lost him and explored a new route home. As I crossed the bridge I stood and took in the view to calm myself. A long stretch of still water, crumbling walls of cream and pink plaster, street lamps creating pools of light and long shadows. I could see a curved red brick and stone bridge next to mine. As I watched I saw a figure walk onto the bridge opposite with a black hat, silver mask and leather coat. He looked away from me and then slowly turned to me. He looked straight at me. I panicked and ran. Tears welled up and I started to drown in fear. My street led to another bridge and as I clambered across I looked to my right and saw him jogging over the parallel bridge. I staggered, panting hard, into a busy square. I cursed that my fear had given away my disguise.

I hid behind a stall and watched as he entered the square he stopped looked around, walked across to the opposite street and loped out of sight. I crossed the square and walked alongside the canal on a different path. I began to catch my breath again. It seemed like a long tortuous walk home. I walked passed my gate and turned into the following street. I waited for nearly a minute before looking round. I could not see anyone in black or acting suspiciously so I ran back and let myself in quickly.

Back in the relative safety of my apartment I called Dorothy. I explained what had happened.

"Would it put you at ease if Henry came to stay with you?"

I hesitated. There was only one bedroom, although the living room had a sofa bed. I liked my solitude here and I did not feel like having to entertain Henry, but it would be so much better to be able to enjoy Venice without being on the run.

"Yes, I would feel more secure."

"Good, I will call you shortly."

Dorothy phoned an hour later to tell me that Henry would arrive tomorrow in the early afternoon and that I was to wait for him at the apartment. I told my aunt that I felt a bit disappointed that Veronica had not revealed anything helpful.

"Oh, but she has, my dear. Small steps. The link to Barcelona may prove invaluable and now we know to look in Argentina for his past, not Spain. Next time, do ask Veronica for the name of that bar in Barcelona."

"She said she hated Mathew and I when we married."

"'Mathew and me,' dear. Just as you would say 'hated me' if you were not including Mathew. Well, that's understandable. Perhaps she felt hurt and rejected."

"Claudia asks such strange questions about the police."

"Well, you might do a little research. See if you can find out more about her. Try to obtain her last name."

"How can I do that? I can't just ask her."

"I think I would look for a letter or envelop. Is there a haberdashery near you? I found the most delightful wool on my first visit to Venice."

"No, it's mostly tourist shops. Masks, clothes, art, convenience items, that sort of thing."

When we finished talking my paranoia subsided. I drank a cup of camomile tea making a point of listening to the sound of pouring the tea, watching the steam mix with the air currents of the room, feeling the warmth of the cup, smelling the aroma and tasting the tea to keep me in the moment and in my senses. Once I finished the tea I closed my eyes and as Dorothy had taught me felt the impression of the tea in my sinuses, throat and stomach. I felt complete.

I took out my knitting and sat by the window feeling the wool with my fingers and listening to the clickety click of the needles. I had knitted enough to begin to see the mix of colours that reminded Dorothy of the Scottish highlands.

During the night I woke from a bizarre dream. A masked man found me in a dark street. Instead of running from him I stood and let him come up to me. He led me by the hand into a deserted warehouse. I knew he was going to kill me but I did not care. I felt almost serene as he took me to a barred window. I stood looking out over the murky water. The room was dark, damp and musky. There was sand on the ground. I stood looking out over the water feeling quite content to leave my body and move on. I became aware that I was standing naked, feeling the grains under my feet and a cool breeze across my back and legs. As I became absorbed in the sensation of living, I forgot the masked man and he ceased to exist. The sun came out and I felt the warmth on my abdomen. I was in a field, feeling the long grass brush against the bare skin of my legs. I fell and looked up to see a single purple flower in front of my nose. The grass tickled my back. I surrendered and my emptiness filled with beauty.

I got up for a glass of water. I drank it looking out of my bedroom window. The thought occurred to me that if I faced the worst possibility, what was there left to fear? If death held no great threat for me and I was prepared to die, then every new day would be a blessing. I wondered how I would live each day if it was my last. What would I do tomorrow?

After some thought I realised it was not so much about what I would do and the content of the day but more how I wanted to be. Could I create those loving feelings, might I unwrap my soul a bit more, would I be able to connect with the world around me? I snuggled back into the warmth of my bed, pulling the duvet around tight. In a way it was the interplay between fear and trust that seemed to define how I stood in this world.

CHAPTER 18

Henry arrived early afternoon, travelling with a black backpack. He gave me a hug and kiss on each cheek. I smelt lemon.

"Mrs H sent me over, said you're in trouble."

"Dorothy Hope asked me to fly to Venice. She said you were frightened," I corrected him, imitating my aunt.

We both laughed. I prepared some soup for us, whilst Henry unpacked. I wanted to take Henry out and show him some of the places I had enjoyed most. After we ate, I showed Henry my trick with the hand mirror and put on my mask for him to see. I suddenly felt bouncy, energised and enthusiastic.

We strode out into the street and walked round to St Mark's Square.

"Your aunt insisted I take you for tea at this place she recommended. She even gave me the euros."

We sat in sumptuous chairs listening to musicians playing "Spring" from Vivaldi's *Four Seasons*, as we looked out over the square. Our teas and cakes arrived on a silver tray.

I told Henry about Veronica, Claudia and the chases. Henry seemed preoccupied with his pastries and made inane comments like "wow," "scary" and "cool" before taking another bite of his cake. When I finished, I felt a rush of anger. I gripped the arms of my chair and stared at Henry.

"Wow, this is some cool place. Just look at the mirror behind you. Looks hundreds of years old. Isn't it neat how they put the trays on the table, and then to clear up they just take the tray away again."

"Don't you care?"

Henry looked up from pouring his tea with surprise.

"I could have been killed by that masked madman."

Henry pointed to his mouth. He was still chewing. I took the opportunity to talk at him.

"I'm sorry, Henry, but after all I have been through I just wanted a little more than half-hearted, one-word expressions."

I felt my anger rise again. But what did I expect? I wanted more sympathy and at the very least to be heard. Henry wiped chocolate from his lips with a napkin.

"No problem, I understand. Sorry, I'm just a bit overwhelmed by Venice. You're safe now. This cake is something. How's yours?"

Dorothy's voice interrupted. *Expectations, my dear, expectations. Enjoy Henry as he is.*

"Fiddlesticks," I mumbled under my breath.

Henry broke my thoughts.

"You know in Chinese medicine, fear is associated with the kidneys, so you may be deficient there. I brought some needles and can give you a treatment later. You also seem a bit angry since we came here. Could be an excess of liver chi."

He paused and looked at me with concern before adding.

"Don't worry. When he sees us together, he'll back off."

Having my feelings summed up in terms of the energetic state of my organs did not really help but I was now calm enough to realise that I was reacting to something from within me. Why was I expecting so much of Henry?

We walked through the narrow streets until evening and found a small restaurant for our dinner. I realised I knew very little about Henry.

"So, tell me all about yourself, young man."

Henry paused from dipping his bread in olive oil.

"What's to tell? I grew up in southeast London. Mum and Dad were kind of ordinary, nurse and teacher. I went to the local school and did okay but nothing special. Then I bummed around working on building sites and a golf course. I saved some money and went travelling with a friend to Thailand. I liked all the massage and healing. I found I could go to China and study acupuncture, so I signed up. Back in London I did some more studies and started working in a natural health clinic."

I was intrigued at the way Henry managed to flatten his life out into a dull trudge along an inevitable path.

"And what about romance, love and excitement?"

"Oh, I've been in a couple of long-term relationships. Just finished with Vanessa. She's moved back to Scotland. That was a bit of a gut churner, but I'm better now."

"And what organ did that relate to?" I said smiling.

Henry put down his wine and laughed.

"That would be the lungs. I suffered lots of grief over her. Don't worry I'm over it."

I felt Henry was not over it. Her name still seemed to be an emotional trigger for him.

"Did acupuncture help?"

Henry had moved on to his spaghetti and his face reddened slightly as he wound another mouthful onto his fork.

"I tried some therapy and your aunt helped some too."

Now I became more interested and looked up from my green salad.

"Really? How did Dorothy help?"

"She helped me see life more as a journey along a path. Vanessa was a friend who travelled with me for a while and then went off on another path. I sat down feeling sad and lonely for a while, but now I am walking again and exploring new territories and enjoying the process. Kind of got me out of so much thinking and letting it build up in my head. She got me to be in the moment more and showed me this cool meditation."

We took a detour home so that Henry could see more sights. When we got home I felt a slight anxiety about where each of us would sleep. I told Henry I would sleep on the sofa bed.

"No way, you stay in your bed. I'll be fine here."

After sorting out his sheets and duvet, I went into the bathroom to get ready for bed. When I came out Henry was lying on the sofa bed listening to his iPod. He was reading a novel. I hovered for a moment wanting to say goodnight.

Henry looked up. He put his book down and took off his headphones. Henry stood up and gave me a hug. I felt slightly exposed in my pyjamas.

"Thank you for a great day, Amanda. I really enjoyed it."

Then Henry kissed me on each cheek before giving me a brief squeeze. I wished him a good sleep and went to my bed. I lay down and thought of Henry for a while. He seemed goofy and superficial, but generally kind. I caught myself being judgemental and reminded myself to be curious and interested. *Just describe, Amanda.*

In the morning I phoned Claudia and arranged to see Veronica again. Henry was keen to go out. We walked through the narrow streets, Henry bought a mask, we stopped for coffees, ate lunch, went to an art exhibition and then arrived at Veronica's. Henry said he would wait in the café down the road and read his book.

Claudia let me in and this time I looked for post on the hall side table. I saw a magazine in a clear plastic envelop with a white address sticker across the front. Claudia ushered me forward. I met Veronica in the sunny lounge room. She seemed lighter today. Veronica asked if she could put on some music. Claudia played "Nefeli" by Ludovico Einaudi, a hypnotic piano piece. She put it on repeat so I heard it about ten times. Veronica lay down as though we had developed a familiar routine. I found it easier to get into my meditative state this time and Veronica seemed more at ease. There were moments when I experienced an incredible stillness. After, I sat quietly in the chair opposite. Veronica slowly opened her eyes and stared at the ceiling. After a few minutes she spoke very slowly.

"Did Mathew like healing?"

"I never tried it with him. I only discovered it after his death. My aunt has been helping me."

We fell into silence. Then I remembered the bar.

"Veronica, do you remember the name of the bar Mathew worked in?"

"Bar Fornos, old part."

"Do you want me to come tomorrow?"

Veronica nodded and shut her eyes.

Claudia escorted me to the door.

As we passed the hall table I picked up the magazine.

"Oh, is this any good? I am always interested in Italian fashion," I said staring at the name on the label.

My voice sounded contrived and false. I felt sure Claudia would see through my clumsy manoeuvre. She snatched the magazine from my hand and held it behind her back as she opened the entrance door.

"Take good care." I felt a hint of menace in her tone.

I walked out into the cold air. I found Henry in the café. I found a pen and wrote *Tagliabue* on a napkin. If Claudia really knew my discovery I felt sure she would plan some kind of revenge.

I walked through the now familiar streets with Henry at my side. Sometimes Henry's legs would seem too long for him and he would sway slightly, bumping into me or brushing against my shoulder. I checked a few times but could not see any suspicious characters dressed in black following us. I convinced myself there was nothing to worry about.

Over dinner we chatted about Dorothy for a while. I told Henry about the various conversations at the meetings.

"I understand the bit about having an open mind, Amanda, but surely it's going too far to say nothing exists. I mean what about this table, the plate, my spaghetti?"

"I think they would say that we all experience them differently and therefore we interpret them differently, even if we agree on their labels."

I touched the table and said "table", touched Henry's hand and said "hand" and pointed at his spaghetti and said "spaghetti", in a childlike voice.

Henry laughed.

"Okay, I get the point, but I still think we agree on the colours, shapes and textures even if we might see them differently in very subtle ways."

I paused, wishing Herr Huber was here. Then a thought occurred to me.

"Could it be that by accepting that we might subtly perceive things differently, we give other people greater freedom to view life how they want, without imposing our view on them?"

I liked that thought and considered what I had just said whilst Henry finished chewing a large mouthful of spaghetti and pesto sauce. Then another thought came to my mind.

"Perhaps it is not so much the content of what is or is not, but more the way we experience our world. Rather than me getting caught up in arguments over whether this is a table or not I can take a more open, accepting approach, and if it is something else to you then that is fine, and maybe it will be something else for me one day. What do you think?"

Henry nodded and wiped his mouth. I was surprised by my own words. Suddenly they seemed so philosophical and inspiring. I was feeling a high. Was I connecting to my universe, or was I regurgitating ideas from Dorothy's meetings?

"Yeah, it would reduce the number of arguments."

Henry smiled thinking about it.

"And what about people, Henry? If we could find a way to stop judging people, making assumptions about them, analysing them and maybe just train ourselves to love them as they are, what then?"

Henry laughed whilst winding another large portion of spaghetti onto his fork.

"What are you on tonight, Amanda? I guess we would have a great, big hippie movement, where everybody loves each other."

"Sounds like more fun than a bunch of people competing, criticising, stereotyping each other, pushing each other out of the way to get their heads in the trough."

Henry held up his fork.

"Yeah, especially when the trough is full of cheap, processed, junk food."

Henry dropped his fork. The spaghetti he carefully loaded ready for an open mouth fell across his lap.

"Oh no, look at that. I've got pesto all over my trousers."

I laughed.

"Remember it is all in your head. Just your perception, Henry."

Henry smiled.

"Yeah, right."

On the way home I felt closer to Henry. I enjoyed dinner and noticed that I had started touching his arm when I started to say something. Now I tugged at his arm as we walked between the red-bricked church and the dark green canal water.

"Slow down, Henry, I'm only little."

Henry put his hand on my lower back and pushed me along faster. I gave him a mock slap across the chest. He pulled me towards him and gave me a squeeze.

I saw the shadow first and then a figure quickly rounded the end of the church walking fast towards us. It was the same person, dressed in black with a silver mask across his face. It was definitely a man. He barged between us throwing me to one side and simultaneously swinging his shoulder jolting Henry backwards. Henry half recovered his balance by throwing out a long arm and grabbing hold of the collar of the man's black jacket. He pulled the man towards him. The man lashed out with a punch that just glanced Henry's head. Henry caught his wrist with his free hand and shot his other hand up to grab the leather-covered elbow and started to twist him round. The man swung at Henry with his free fist but missed. He then kicked out, catching Henry on the shin. Henry jumped back to avoid another blow letting go of the man. They circled each other. It looked like a duel between a spider and a beetle.

I screamed out. My legs were shaking and my voice quavered.

"Help, someone help us, please."

I heard the clicking steps of shoe leather against stone and an elderly man and woman walked into our street. The attacker turned and ran.

Henry had a trickle of blood running down the side of his face from a cut at the end of his eyebrow. The elderly couple spoke to us in Italian. We assured them we were alright and walked on. I did not want to spend the rest of the evening in a police station filling out forms. Henry limped slightly as we crossed the canal on a small arched stone bridge.

"Who was that?"

"It was the same man who followed me. I think it was the same person who attacked me in Covent Garden."

"Could it be that guy we met in your house?"

"Edward? Possibly. Why would he want to harm me? A few weeks ago he was telling me he loved me."

"Maybe he saw us together and assumed we were in a relationship and lost it."

That thought did make sense to me. I wished I had managed to rip his mask off and end all this speculation and mystery. On impulse I turned and gave Henry a hug.

"Thank you so much for protecting me. I really appreciate it."

Henry returned my hug and kissed my forehead.

"That's why I'm here."

I found a tissue and dabbed at the blood. There was a small open wound that was still weeping. I slipped my hand into his as we walked home. If it was Edward and if he was trying to separate us, he had miscalculated. I felt much closer to Henry. Then I thought about Claudia.

"I should also tell you that I think I was caught taking the surname of the woman looking after Veronica. She is kind of scary. Another possibility is that she arranged someone to attack us."

"Wow, you are like a secret agent. Amanda Super Spy. What's your next mission?"

Once we returned to our apartment I found a bandage for Henry's wound. Henry pulled up his trouser leg to expose a large, dark blue bruise and mild grazing below his knee. Henry lay down on the sofa and I sat beside him. I rested my hand on his chest and head whilst we meditated. I felt his breathing slow and calm. Then when he felt peaceful I slowly removed my hands. Henry lay with his eyes closed. I got up slowly and had a shower. After I put on my blue flannel pyjamas and sat on my bed. My mind kept spinning back to Edward and the various attacks. I tried to focus on the mouth of our attacker and Edward's. I could not be sure it was the same man.

I wandered back into the living room and found Henry listening to his iPod and reading. He looked round and took off his headphones.

"I think I'll get an early night."

"Sure."

Henry stood up and gave me a hug. I turned my head slightly so that our lips touched. Henry moved a hand up to behind my head. We kissed each other's lips a few times and then I felt Henry's tongue on my upper lip. I parted my lips slightly and his tongue slipped past. Our tongues touched. I pulled Henry closer to me. Henry slid a hand down to my bottom. Then I pulled away.

"Henry, I am going to bed now. You're welcome to join me if we can just snuggle up to each other. I am not sure I am ready for anything else tonight."

"Sure."

I lay in bed flitting between rerunning a film of the latest attack in my head and trying to be in the moment. Henry wandered in wearing black boxers. He sat heavily on the side of the bed and then swung his legs in. He reached up for the light switch and we lay next to each other in the dark. He felt cautious and aloof, lying stiffly on his back. I put an arm around him and he stroked my forearm few times. It felt weird being in bed with someone after all this time, and even stranger that it was not Mathew. I expected Henry to follow Mathew's routine. I anticipated him rolling onto his side, kissing me goodnight, and then turning over, so I could cuddle up to his back and feel his hand on my thigh as I stroked his abdomen. Instead I felt each of Henry's long breaths for a while and fell asleep.

The next days I lived in that watery, faded, majestic bubble of Venice. Henry and I held hands, kissed and hugged. Henry did not attempt to take our intimacy any further. I did not reassure him further advances would be welcome either. I wondered whether he still had open wounds from his relationship with Vanessa.

We walked and talked, ate together and saw a lot of art. The silver masked man did not materialise again or intrude upon our romantic journey. Although the threat of another appearance lurked in the shadows, keeping us in our roles of the protector and the vulnerable.

I braved the stern glare from Claudia and gave Veronica a further healing. I anticipated another attack if she thought I had taken her last name but nothing happened. At the end there were no warm goodbyes or feeling that we were becoming friends, just a terse acknowledgement that I was leaving. I left feeling unsettled and held Henry close as we walked away.

CHAPTER 19

I felt sad on the plane home. I had developed a happy rhythm to my days in Venice. It felt like an escape from solicitors, police interviews, bank managers, building society debt collectors and preservation. I felt myself deflate. I tried to focus on seeing Dorothy to lift my spirits.

Dorothy appeared ecstatic when she welcomed us. I felt a warm connection, coming home to the person who was now my new family. She wanted to hear all about Venice. She seemed particularly concerned as to whether the same cafés and restaurants she had visited were still there. She even enquired whether a large lady with dark, curly hair still sold vegetables in the market.

"I found out Claudia's last name."

I handed the napkin to Dorothy.

"'Tagliabue.' I think that would be 'Butcher' in English."

We told her about the masked man and his fight with Henry.

"And was that the last time you saw him?"

We nodded. Dorothy looked perplexed.

"How very odd. At the same time you were attacked in Venice another letter came in the post. I hope you do not mind dear, but I opened it to be sure. The postmark was from London."

"Could he have arranged for it to be sent once he was in Venice?"

Dorothy started clearing the teacups away ignoring Henry's question.

"Well, what a mystery."

I got up to help her.

"What did it say?"

"Another picture of you and a masked man saying, 'I have the rest of my life to get my revenge.' It was similar to before, with very poor grammar and spelling. You can see it for yourself if you like. On another subject, my dear, Martin would like to meet with you. He has had a response from the building society."

That familiar friend, anxiety, flooded my heart as I considered that there must be two people trying to harm me. One followed me to Venice to physically attack me, whilst the other composed and sent threatening messages. Henry left for work.

My mood did not improve and out of it I started to complain to Dorothy that Veronica showed no positive reaction to my treatments.

"Oh, my dear, if you give a treatment fishing for compliments, it becomes about you, and that is the energy of your interaction. Healing means being in service to another human, to humble yourself and offer a connection where you lose yourself."

I grunted, grumpily, annoyed that my aunt was being wise rather than indulging my self-pity.

That night I noticed in the mirror how much of the Venetian cuisine I had brought home with me. I examined myself from different angles. My tummy, bottom and thighs had all acquired new rounder shapes.

Henry escorted me to the solicitor's office two days later. Since our return to London we gave each other greeting and parting hugs and kisses on the cheeks but all other physical contact had stopped. I wanted to ask Henry how he saw our relationship developing but could not bring myself to voice the words. We sat in the waiting room talking about everything except us.

Mr Ledbetter invited me into his office.

"Good morning, Mrs Blake. I have some news. Your building society would like to resolve this dispute and have offered to waive all debts. In return you would surrender the deeds to your home. This would still leave you disadvantaged as you will have forfeited the equity you enjoyed in your home up until Mr Blake started taking out fraudulent loans. After some negotiation we have agreed that the society and you will each accept half the debt incurred by your late husband. This would leave you with a surplus of just over ninety eight thousand pounds, if you agree to relinquish your home at its current value to the society."

After a brief discussion I agreed to accept his proposal. I had known for some time that I would not live there again. This was a much better situation than a few weeks ago. I felt a wave of relief wash over me. When I returned to the waiting room, Henry stood up and I transferred my exuberance into a big kiss and hug. Henry stood stiffly looking surprised.

"I'm going to take you and Dorothy out for dinner."

We went to a Japanese restaurant in Hampstead that Henry knew. Henry ordered a large range of dishes to share. We tried sushi, natto, grilled quail eggs, wakame salad, hiziki and carrots, grilled mackerel, vegetable tempura and miso soup.

I told Dorothy of my and Henry's discussion in Venice about what is real. She picked up on a point.

"Yes, if we want to feel as one with the world sometimes, it might help to free ourselves of our labels and focus more on our interactions. What do you think, Henry?"

Henry had just loaded his mouth with fish, so he nodded and gave Dorothy a thumbs up. I experienced a flash of anger. He seemed uncouth and irreverent. Dorothy smiled.

"There, you see, we are closer together again, although I sense Amanda has now constructed a temporary barrier."

Dorothy looked at me quizzically.

"It's just that sometimes Henry makes these silly gestures when I would like him to be a bit deeper."

Dorothy laughed.

"But Amanda, dear, judgements and expectations lead to separation. How can you understand Henry if you are disconnected from him?"

I felt my face flush as the anger returned. I tried to suppress it. Henry had moved onto gobbling a large piece of tempura.

"Surely part of being in the moment is being emotional and expressing those emotions," I stated louder than intended.

"True, and we can also explore what is fuelling those emotions?"

I shrugged my shoulders. It was a sullen response I used as a child when I felt cornered by my mother. It became a familiar gesture during the later years with Mathew. Dorothy touched my hand.

"You know how much I love you and enjoy the times we feel connected. Sometimes it can be interesting to ask ourselves why we choose to disconnect."

I looked at Henry. He popped a quail egg into his mouth. Henry seemed oblivious to my expectations of him. Perhaps he was the one in the moment, just enjoying the taste, smells and texture of his food. Perhaps our conversation was incidental.

Dorothy turned to Henry.

"Perhaps I can summarise it by saying: I am the universe and the universe is me. It is when I need to make distinctions that I become a separate observer."

This time Henry was between mouthfuls.

"Wow, cool, Mrs H. You are kind of mind blowing. Five minutes with you and my horizons expand to infinity and beyond."

"I think 'and beyond' might be redundant in that sentence, Henry."

I caught Henry's eye and we laughed.

"Amanda, when I woke this morning it occurred to me that you might enjoy writing some morning pages."

"What are those?"

"Do you remember I suggested before that you try writing from your heart?"

"Oh, yes. I did write about a dream I had in Venice."

Dorothy smiled.

"Before you go to sleep, play with different questions in your mind."

"You mean like, 'Why do I have so many expectations of men I feel close to?'"

"Yes, that is a very good example. Then whilst you sleep you will continue to explore that question. When you wake up, take a blank sheet of paper and just write freely. Simply express whatever comes to your mind. Write as though no one will ever read it."

"So not on Facebook or Twitter," Henry laughed at his own joke.

Dorothy looked perplexed.

"Ignore him, Aunty. They are places you can write to lots of virtual friends on your computer."

"Oh, you mean like imaginary friends."

Henry laughed again.

"Yes, exactly that."

CHAPTER 20

Sergeant Smiley telephoned to arrange to meet me. He came round later in the day. Once he was settled, Dorothy came in with the tea. I smelt stale nicotine. Smiley rubbed his right eye wearily. It looked slightly bloodshot.

"I would like to apologise on behalf of the Hertfordshire Constabulary for the treatment you received from Inspector Pride. As you know, she has been suspended pending further investigation."

"Thank you."

"Have you got any further with the investigation?" asked Dorothy softly, whilst pouring the fresh bay leaf and lemon rind tea.

"We have interviewed Mr Edwards again but as yet do not have any evidence to convict him."

"So you think it was Edward who attacked Amanda in Covent Garden?"

"He's a suspect."

"Did Amanda tell you that she was attacked in Venice?"

Smiley looked at me expectantly.

"Someone followed me and chased me through the back streets."

"Did he harm you?"

"No, but my aunt sent Henry to look after me and this man punched and kicked him."

"I see. Can you give me a description?"

"He wore a hat and mask. About five-ten with broad shoulders. After that I did not see him again."

As Smiley made notes of the dates I was followed, and of the fight with Henry, Dorothy leant forward. Smiley stopped writing and held his pencil as though it was a cigarette.

"The strange thing is that on the same day this masked man attacked Henry, another letter was sent to this address."

"May I see it?"

My aunt went through to her room and brought back a clear plastic bag with the letter and envelope inside. The sergeant examined it.

"You see, it is postmarked London."

Smiley nodded.

"I think I will be having another chat with Mr Edwards. I will keep Detective Inspector Williams informed on these developments. He may wish to interview you as well. I would like to take a statement from you and the man you were with in Venice."

With Smiley's help I dictated the statement. Smiley wrote it out on his form. He then painstakingly drew a line through every gap in the statement and asked me to initial each line. After I signed the statement I called Henry.

I wanted to tell Smiley about Claudia, but what could I say?

That night I lay in bed loosely thinking about what I wanted to do with the rest of my life. I imagined being a healer, setting myself up as a private investigator with Dorothy, running a herb tea café or going back to teaching. I tried to just play with the images and resist the temptation to dismiss something like teaching immediately. I was serving customers with one of Dorothy's cakes in my own café when I fell asleep.

In the morning I sat down with a blank piece of paper and ballpoint pen and tried to just write. Nothing seemed to come to me. I heard Dorothy in the hall. I shouted out.

"Dorothy, nothing is happening. I don't know what to write!"

Dorothy opened the door gently.

"That is what you write."

I looked back blankly.

"Write exactly what you said to me."

I wrote, *Nothing is happening. I don't know what to write.*

"There, now you have got started. How are you feeling?"

"I'm irritated about the writing."

"Write it down. Why are you irritated?"

"Because I can't think of anything to say."

"And why would that irritate you?"

"I thought it would be easier."

"Write it down."

Dorothy sat on a chair whilst I wrote.

"Feel the pen, be aware of the texture of the paper, be sensitive of the muscles you are using."

The sensations must have triggered a distant memory of writing a poem at primary school and I started to describe my school desk. Then I wrote about Amy who was sitting next to me. I tried to detail the image of Mrs Blenkinsopp standing next to the blackboard in her blue tartan skirt and cream cardigan. I remembered my desire to please her with my poem.

When I got to the bottom of the page I realised I had not written anything about the careers I thought about last night. I turned to Dorothy. She had her eyes closed.

"I'm just resting my eyes, dear. Have you finished?"

"Yes, but I did not write anything about the things I thought of last night."

"And what did you think about."

I described the options I had entertained with my sleepy mind.

"And what did you write about?"

"When I was a child at school."

"Could it be that teaching, describing your school and teacher are connected?"

It was not a connection I was hoping for but there it was.

"Try not to preconceive or judge, dear. Just let it flow. It does not mean anything. There is no need to analyse or give it meaning. Your writing simply reflects you in this moment. Tomorrow it will be different."

After Venice, I felt slightly bored. I wanted more purpose to my life. I hoped Dorothy would have another meeting soon. I devoted more time to my knitting. Later in the morning, she must have sensed my slight agitation.

"Why don't you telephone that friend of yours? What is her name? Emerald? You could invite her round if you like."

I phoned Ruby. She was in a terrible state. I must have phoned during an argument with Bill. We had a brief schizophrenic conversation, during which she said something rational to me and then yelled obscenities at Bill. I listened to a long out pouring of abuse in which she accused Bill of being a bloated snake who vainly tried to seduce young sluts to resuscitate his limp, impotent excuse of manhood. I heard Bill suggest she talk to Zoe, who was more than satisfied.

"Ruby, Ruby, just come round here. You can talk to me."

Ten minutes later I guided Ruby to our door via her mobile phone.

Ruby stomped into the hall, slightly out of breath and looking bloated. Her cheeks were flushed from the cold and the stairs. Ruby had left without brushing her hair and her lipstick looked like it had been applied on the run. I was shocked to see her so dishevelled. I led her to the living room and introduced her to Dorothy.

"I think I'll put on a soothing cup of tea for you both. Please relax on the sofa, my dear."

Ruby dropped onto the sofa as though she had been shot. Her pink skirt rode up her right leg and her sweater twisted round her abdomen. She made no effort to correct her ungainly look. I found myself compensating by adjusting the position of my sleeves. I listened as she told me how she had discovered Bill was having an affair with a younger woman called Zoe, in his office.

"He is such a pathetic cliché. That should be his epitaph: 'Bill, absent father, unloving husband and useless cliché, RIP.' I was relieved when he stopped pestering me for sex and now I realise why. That sycophantic whore was all too ready to open her legs for him. What could she see in him?"

"Hey ho, life—"

I caught myself quickly and managed to stop the sentence in a way that made some sense, and before any mention of chocolate.

Dorothy came back with the tea and set it on the low table between us.

"I felt like some orange and coconut tea today. Last time it felt so clean and refreshing."

Dorothy continued talking as she poured the tea. Then she sat down and looked at Ruby, who was still crumpled up on the sofa.

"You remind me a little of Rosemary's niece, Alison. She was a beautiful woman, very talented and quite vivacious. I think she was a portrait photographer. She married the editor of a magazine. Now what was it? It was a glossy woman's journal. I think they worked together for a while. They married and then after a few years she fell out of love with herself."

"Don't you mean with her husband?" Ruby said flatly.

"No, with herself," Dorothy replied firmly.

We sat in silence for a while. Then I could see Ruby's eye movement speed up.

"What happened?" she asked impatiently.

"I think she became quite miserable. I only met her once but I remember it occurred to me at the time that perhaps without love, something inside her died and she could only carry on living by attaching herself to whatever happened around her. Of course, she chose to perceive everything around her with the most appalling interpretations she could imagine. I suspect she had a very vivid imagination."

I waited for Ruby to explode. I watched her face redden, I saw her hand tighten around the strap of her handbag, I witnessed her lips tighten. Then the emotion passed and she softened. I felt sure if I was saying those things Ruby would have erupted but perhaps because she did not know Dorothy, or possibly because of Dorothy's age, Ruby seemed to find greater self-control. Then it occurred to me that Dorothy's message might have touched Ruby more deeply than if it had come from me. There was something so loving and caring in the way Dorothy expressed herself. She had a childlike honesty.

We fell into another long silence until Ruby looked up.

"And did she ever find love again?"

"Rosemary has not mentioned any resurrection."

"Once it has died, that must be the end."

"Oh no, dear. It is a choice you can make whenever you like. You could be self-loving right now by simply letting Amanda care for you."

"What do you mean?"

"Trust Amanda to give you a helping hand. Be close to her love in a way that you can begin to heal yourself. Why not let Amanda help you with some healing right now."

I could see Ruby shut down at the mention of the word healing.

"Maybe another time. I do have to get back."

"Try your tea first."

We all picked up our cups and sipped the hot tea. Dorothy closed her eyes. When she opened them she described a feeling of warmth across her cheeks and contentment in her stomach. She asked me how I felt.

"I feel slightly anxious because I want to help Ruby but I don't know how and I can see she is unhappy."

Dorothy turned to Ruby and raised her eyebrows.

"I don't feel anything. The tea tastes alright."

After another pause Dorothy turned to Ruby.

"If you can trust yourself to say no, you can trust yourself to lie down and let Amanda help, knowing you can get up whenever you like. Amanda will not feel hurt, will you dear?"

"No, of course not."

"I'll try a few minutes and then I must go."

We set up the massage table. I spread a hot towel on the couch and helped Ruby lie on her front. I covered her with another warm towel. Dorothy sat in the corner and picked up her knitting.

"You could start by teaching Ruby your meditation, if you feel like it. Then, when you feel connected, let your heart guide you."

I felt slightly nervous with my aunt watching me. I began resting my arms on Ruby's back. I glanced at Dorothy to see if she approved. She was looking down as she unravelled a ball of mauve wool.

When I felt ready, I helped Ruby turn onto her back. I tried to make every move with the same care I so enjoyed when I received my healing treatment. I tucked Ruby in with a motherly love and affection.

After I finished it took Ruby a long time to open her eyes. She stared at the ceiling for a while and then turned to me. I helped Ruby up and folded the towels whilst Ruby went to the bathroom.

When she returned I was interested to see that she had composed her clothing more neatly and must have arranged her hair with her hands.

"Thank you, Amanda. Really. Now I must rush."

Dorothy spoke quietly.

"Before you start rushing, sit for a moment."

Ruby sat in the nearest chair.

"Take a moment to really connect to yourself. How do you feel?"

"Very relaxed, warm, glowing." Ruby moved her shoulders. "Freer."

"How do you feel emotionally?"

"Um, interesting question. Calmer and strangely content."

"And your mind?"

"Oh, quite peaceful, I would say."

"You chose to be self-loving and this is the result."

"Yes, I guess I did. You are a very interesting woman."

"You can choose to be like this all the time. Why choose unhappiness when you can choose love?"

"Easy to say. Life does not seem to work like that."

"It begins inside you. Think of it as the birth of a feeling you are going to nourish. Care for it every day and it will grow from within. Amanda will help you if you let her."

Ruby gave me an affectionate hug as she left.

Over dinner Dorothy inquired whether I would visit Barcelona. I had not been to Barcelona before and I wanted to see the famous Gaudi buildings, but I certainly did not want to expose myself to more attacks and I was not sure how I felt about involving Henry in another trip. Dorothy suggested I wait to see if the police could find evidence that Edward had been to Venice.

In the morning I found myself writing about the time I stayed with the Edwards. I wrote about Edward's declaration of love and my feelings as I remembered them. After, I had a desire to phone Edwina.

"Hello Edwina, it's Amanda."

There was a short silence and then a frosty hello.

"I wanted to see how you are and thank you for being so kind to me after Mathew died."

"It's a shame your gratitude did not stop you from trying to implicate Edward as the murderer."

"Edwina, I can assure you I have never implicated anyone. I have been threatened, attacked and followed, and all I have done is report each incident to the police. Edward was only implicated because I was meeting him in Covent Garden when I was attacked."

"At your insistence."

"What do you mean?"

"Edward told me that you have been pursuing him since the time you stayed with us."

I had no desire to cause Edwina any distress. I resisted the temptation to tell her about Edward's advances towards me.

"Edwina, I have absolutely no desire to seduce Edward. You both were very helpful to me and I like you both, but that is all. Until recently I have not felt like being in a relationship with anyone. Then a couple of weeks ago I did feel close to someone here. Even now I am not sure I am ready. I can assure you I have never had any kind of relationship with Edward or tried to start one."

Neither of us spoke. Then I broke the silence.

"How is Edward?"

"He is very stressed, as you can imagine. First he was interrogated over Mathew's murder, then accused of attacking you. I can't imagine what next."

I swallowed and felt a slight pain in my chest as I wondered whether to mention Sergeant Smiley's imminent interview.

"Um, yes. How was he between Mathew's murder and me being attacked?"

"Not himself. I think Mathew's murder must have affected him deeply. He seemed quite withdrawn. Then, since your attack and all the harassment from the police, he has been quite ill with stress."

I wanted to ask if he had been away, but I thought it better to leave that to Smiley.

"I am very, very sorry that being my neighbour has brought all this on you both."

That afternoon Edwina phoned.

"How could you? How could you phone me like that and pretend to be all nice when you knew the police were coming round?"

"They are just doing their job. Surely Edward has nothing to worry about."

"They've arrested him and taken his computer. I have policemen in my home searching every room. Are you satisfied now?"

"Why did they arrest him?"

"What do you care?"

"The last time I saw the police it was to report being attacked in Venice and being sent another threatening letter. What else would you want me to do, pretend it didn't happen, just in case they start asking questions?"

"Oh God, what is happening? They arrested Eddie because he flew to Venice recently."

"Are you sure?"

"Yes, he said it was for business but why would he go to Venice for business? His company have no offices there. What is going on, Amanda? If you know something, please tell me."

"I don't know who it was who attacked me, and perhaps it wasn't Edward. I suppose him being there at the same time makes him a suspect, but that's all."

"Something very strange is happening. This isn't the Eddie I married. He's been aloof, snappy and disinterested for some time. I thought it was his work, my mother said it was just a phase, my friends said not to worry, all marriages lose the romance after a while, but I have this awful fear that it is much worse than that."

"Edwina, the truth is we just don't know, and there's no point speculating. Please don't put yourself through all this. I really hope it isn't Edward and this is all a terrible mistake. I'm sure the truth will come out in the end. I know it sounds trite but try to live your life one minute at a time and do something each day for yourself."

I heard Edwina cry and then the phone disconnected.

Sometimes my morning writing initiated my day, sometimes it gave me a sense of direction and other times it became a means to reflect on the past. Today I wrote about my childhood. I thought of photographs of my parents and that led to visualising photographs of Mathew. I pictured the images of us from the stolen album. I had a desire to see them again and found the album on my computer. Dorothy wandered past and asked me what I was doing. I explained how I once thought one of the photographs might have held a clue or pointed to someone who might have killed Mathew.

"Oh, how exciting. Shall we have another look?"

I went back to the images that included other people in the background. As we stared at each picture, I zoomed into people in the background. There was a photograph of us having a picnic in Hampstead Heath with several people in the distant background. We peered at children, a mother and push chair, two men holding hands and then a sole woman. I felt goose bumps across my skin as I noticed a resemblance to Claudia. The enlarged picture was unfocussed and slightly pixelated.

"What is it, dear?"

"This woman looks quite like Claudia. I'll try to make the image clearer."

I adjusted the contrast, exposure, definition and sharpness until I could see her face better. I felt Dorothy's breath on my neck as she peered over my shoulder at the screen.

"I'm sure that's her."

"Well, she does have a very distinctive face. When was this picture taken?"

I clicked to see the information on the photograph.

"It was taken in May, just before Mathew made up our anniversary album and about four months before he was killed."

The woman was standing next to a tree staring towards us.

"Perhaps this is something for the police to look into."

"They're coming today, anyway."

Sergeant Smiley came round in the morning. Dorothy had left to see a friend so we were alone. He fidgeted with a broken biro as he spoke. His nicotine stained fingers pulled at the cracked end of the clear plastic until the piece broke off. Some thick blue ink had been laying inside the tube. As he caught the broken section it smeared a trail of blue ink across his hand. He tried to wipe it off, painting blotches of blue across both hands. All this time he explained that Edward had been arrested. He admitted following me to Venice. Edward claimed he was following me to protect me. He told the police that when he saw me with Henry, he felt jealous and pushed past us, but that Henry had struck him and he responded to that. Edward still denies murdering Mathew and attacking me in Covent Garden.

I suggested Smiley use the cloakroom to wash his hands and showed him to the hallway. I held up a bin for the broken pen. The sergeant left the door open and carried on talking over the hiss of running water.

"We examined his computer and found that he had been logging into your email account. Did you ever give him your password?"

"No."

"It was from your emails that he could trace you here and know your plans to stay in Venice."

"That explains a lot. He even tracked me down in Oxford Street." I shivered at the thought of him reading all my private messages. "What now?"

Smiley turned off the tap and stood in the doorway drying his hands.

"We had to release him. It is not a crime to follow you to Venice and we have no hard evidence linking to the murder and attack yet. You could take out a restraining order to stop him following you. Now that he knows that both you and we know who he is, and what he has been doing, he may come to his senses."

"What about the fight with Henry?"

"That would be for the Italian police."

Smiley's phone rang. He dropped the towel trying to find the phone in his pocket. I picked it up for him. Smiley looked at the screen and let his phone ring onto voice message.

"There's something else I want to show you."

I explained how I had met with Mathew's ex-wife Veronica and that her girlfriend Claudia had been hostile. Then I showed him the photograph and described when and where it was taken.

"I must caution you against interfering with our work and putting yourself at danger."

"No one was following it up. Now I may have found a new suspect."

Smiley sighed and made a note of her full name and address and promised to contact the Venice police to find out more. His deadpan expression made it hard to tell if he was taking this new information seriously.

"I have to also tell you that we can no longer give you protection. Now Mr Edwards knows we are onto him, and if you change your email password, you should be safe. At the same time, please call immediately if something suspicious happens."

The phone rang again and this time Smiley took the call. He hardly spoke after his initial terse greeting and as he snapped his phone shut he mumbled that he had to go and left abruptly.

I could understand that the police could not keep someone in a car outside my home. I did feel vulnerable again, and yet I also trusted in myself.

I went to the café and changed my email password.

CHAPTER 21

Dorothy announced that we would have one of our meetings that evening. I was now familiar with the routine of arranging the room. I joined in with Dorothy's desire to be in the moment and just act out of our senses. I felt excited to spend the evening with the people that had become my temporary guides in life and smiled of the thought of how I reacted the first time.

We followed much the same introductory routine and, once we were settled, Dorothy invited me to relate my experience in Venice. Reminiscent of my first meeting they just sat there silently when I finished. There were no "how terrible" kind of comments I would have once expected. This time I felt content that I had been heard. I no longer needed them to instil their reactions in me. Sandy spoke first.

"That dream was quite a revelation. How amazing that sleep can bring forth such a profound and life changing realisation. Is the dream still with you?"

"I have felt different about my situation since. Some of the fear has melted away."

I looked to my left to see Herr Huber. Part of me craved his opinion. He spoke in his low voice.

"We seem to be wired to slip into our most primal emotion of fear. Fear can leave its anxious imprints rippling through so many of our actions. Sometimes fear floods our lives to the extent we drown in it. I congratulate you on being able to free yourself from that ocean of fear."

As I listened I did feel myself radiate warmth. I basked in his words. I looked up at Dorothy. She smiled. All of a sudden I felt a tide of emotions well up inside me. I swallowed and felt my eyes moisten. No one spoke for some time. Then Nirmal spoke very slowly.

"How do you feel, Amanda, now that you are out in the open?"

I turned to face Nirmal. Sandy passed me a tissue and I dried my eyes.

"I think I have finally started to understand what you all keep trying to tell me about living from within, instead of losing myself in the external distractions of life."

I felt I had somehow been initiated. Nothing had been said, no certificates, rituals, badges or pieces of paper. It had come from inside me. I had felt it myself. It came from an impulse within, rather than anyone's external judgement or approval.

Henrique began talking.

"I brought in a piece of text that made a great impression on me when I read it last week and I thought we could explore it together. It is from *A Portrait of Dorian Gray* by Oscar Wilde."

I remembered reading the book in my twenties. Herr Huber passed round a photocopied page of text he wanted us to read. Henrique cleared his throat.

"It is a part of the story where Dorian Gray, a young man, is having his portrait painted by Basil. The painter's friend, Lord Henry, comes to observe. Lord Henry voices most of the dialogue. Do you mind if I read the lines that influenced me most aloud?"

We agreed and Henrique cleared his throat.

"*There is no such thing as a good influence, Mr Gray. All influence is immoral. Because to influence a person is to give him one's own soul. He does not think his natural thoughts, or burn with his natural passions. His virtues are not real to him. His sin, if there are such things as sins, are borrowed.*"

Henrique looked up before continuing.

"*He becomes an echo of someone else's music, an actor of a part that has not been written for him. The aim of life is self-development. To realise one's nature perfectly.*"

We sat still for moment. The words from the last three sentences reverberated in my head. I certainly had been living as an echo of Mathew's music and perhaps I even acted out a part written for me by my parents. Then the disturbing thought occurred to me that I might become a new echo of Dorothy and her friends.

"Please continue, Henrique," Dorothy urged.

Henrique looked down the page to find the next passage.

"*I believe that if one man were to live out his life fully and completely, were to give form to every feeling, expression to every thought, reality to every dream – I believe that the world would gain such a fresh impulse of joy that we would forget all the maladies of medievalism, and return to the Hellenic ideal.*"

I was enjoying this. It felt like being back in college. I read it through again silently. I looked up and noticed Dorothy was looking at Herr Huber with a very soft gaze. Henrique spoke slowly.

"*It has been said that the great events of the world take place in the brain. It is in the brain, and the brain only, that the great sins of the world take place also…*"

Sandy spoke.

"It reminds me of a line that appears at the end of one of my favourite films, *Being There*. 'Life is a state of mind.'"

These passages kept reverberating around my skull for a long time after everyone left.

That night I stitched all the parts of my knitting together and finished my sweater. I tried it on and liked the way I looked cuddly in it. The wool felt so soft and the gentle colours blended into each other to create a sense of harmony with my hair. I modelled it for Dorothy.

CHAPTER 22

I woke early and decided to start my writing. I found myself describing an old stone wall in detail. I could see an image of the wall in my mind.

> *The stone has a light colour and looks porous. When I run my fingers across it I feel the scratches, chips and grooves worn into her over the years. There is a vine growing up the wall. Its roots are embedded into the hot, dusty mud below.*
>
> *I play with the ants crawling along their path at the foot of the wall. I let them run over my little hand. I place a warm stone on the path and watched the ants run around, creating a new track.*
>
> *I hear a woman call out. I look up. A man with darkish skin stands next to me. I am in his shadow. His sandals almost touch my bare feet. He kneels and puts his hands on my ribs. I look into his eyes. They are dark, a little watery and large. When I see right into his deep eyes I look into a well of love.*
>
> *I reach out and touch his cheeks and then his wavy hair. I let my small hand slowly curl around his ear, pulling it gently. Then he lifts me and holds me to his side.*

I read through my text twice, wondering where the words came from. It was as though a distant memory had fuelled a vision that I had been able to describe freely, without really trying.

I wore my new wool sweater and set about my preparations for my big day. I was going to my old home to get rid of everything I did not want. I felt ready to shed the load for the journey ahead, to enter the new phase in my life unburdened.

Since my dream of dying, I had the feeling that whatever happens I would know what to do in that moment. I thought about asking Henry to accompany me, but then decided it was time to risk being on my own.

I hired a car, loaded it with empty boxes and drove north. I stopped on the way to buy fresh flowers. I parked in my drive and I stole a quick glance towards Edward and Edwina's home. All looked quiet.

Once in my home, I lay the flowers over the carpet where Mathew once lay dead. After a moments reverence, I decided to sort everything into three groups. One for things I no longer wanted, which would be in the garage, a second for everything I was keeping, in the living room and a third for the things I was not sure about, in the dining room.

I felt purposeful and motivated. The physical exertion felt good. I started on the ground floor moving items from one room to another. I had decided I would not keep any furniture so I lifted and dragged chairs and tables to the garage. I would need help with the sofa, big chairs and dining room table. By early afternoon I had finished the ground floor. As I sat on the sofa chewing on my packed lunch, the front door swung open.

"Hello? Hello, Amanda?"

It was Edward's voice. I reached for my phone. Edward walked into the living room. He had his hands raised as though he was surrendering to me.

"I thought I saw you arrive earlier. Do you mind if we have a quick chat? You know, seize the moment."

"I don't feel comfortable here alone with you."

"That's understandable. Let's talk alfresco." Henry motioned to the door.

"Where's Edwina?"

"She's shopping. I would have come earlier but I wanted to wait until the coast was clear."

"I would prefer the three of us talk when she gets back."

Edward seemed unsure of what to say next. He adjusted his glasses.

"Um, to be perfectly frank, I wanted it to be just the two of us."

"That sounds creepy."

"Wouldn't you feel safe out in the fresh air?"

I agreed and waited for Edward to walk out of my front door first. It occurred to me that I could slam the door shut and lock him out. Deeper inside I felt surprisingly calm and perhaps I did have more of that trust building up inside. Besides, I wanted to hear his version. I stood in the doorway whilst Edward turned to face me a couple of metres away.

"Okay, Amanda, I know it looks bad. Yes, I did follow you in Oxford Street. Yes, I was on my way to meet you in Covent Garden. Yes, I did log into your email account and check your messages. And yes, I did follow you to Venice, but I did not kill Mathew or attack you in that truck. You've got to believe me, Amanda. I'll swear on my mother's life if it helps."

Edward held his hands out in a pleading manner.

"Are you going to leave me alone now?"

"I still have a place for you in my heart. I have only had your best interests. I just want to protect you from all the horror."

"Did you send me the notes?"

"No, I did not send you any notes."

I tried to keep an open mind, to hear him, without feeling the need to believe or disbelieve.

"How are you and Edwina getting on?"

"We are friends, but no more."

At that moment Edwina walked round the corner. Edward could not see her.

"Is that how you feel about me?" Edwina shrieked.

Edward jumped and immediately adjusted his glasses.

"I thought you had gone shopping."

"You were so insistent I go on my own, I thought I would park the car round the corner to see what your little secret is. And here you are, pleading with Amanda."

"It's not like that."

Edwina walked up to Edward and slapped him hard across the cheek. Edward's glasses lay askew across his face. Her palm crashed against his ear. His glasses fell off. She grabbed a fistful of hair. Edward grabbed both her hands.

"You little creep. After all I have done for you. This is how you repay me."

She kicked his ankle. Edward hobbled. I felt I had to intervene. I placed my hand very gently on Edwina's back.

"Edwina, come inside with me."

"Do you need any help?"

I recognised Mrs Pottersby's voice floating over the tall hedge.

"I think we'll be fine, thanks," I called back.

Edwina mustered all her strength. She fought to free her arms but Edward held her rigidly. She spat in Edward's face and lashed out with her right foot. Then I felt her weaken and tried again.

"I really want to hear you, I want you to tell me what is happening. Please, let's talk."

"I'll tell you what this bastard's been doing, I'll tell you, I'll…"

Tears started well up in Edwina's eyes. I watched the first drops find their path down her dry cheeks.

"Let go of her, Edward."

Edward let go of her wrists, took a step back and affected a karate pose before picking up his glasses. I held Edwina tight. As her sobbing increased in intensity, her body started to tremble. I had to support her weight, as her legs gave up. She started wailing.

"It's all over, isn't it? All those years I have given you for nothing. I invested so much of myself in you and now it's all gone."

I led her to my kitchen and onto one of the Shaker-style chairs. Edwina slumped forwards onto the table with her head in her hands. I handed her a square of paper from the kitchen roll. Edwina dabbed the napkin over her now blotchy face. Edwina lifted her head and turned to me.

"What's the point anymore? I can't conceive, I'm just a dried up, fat, middle-aged woman."

Edwina started sobbing and pulled a chair close to her. I put my arm round Edwina and held her tight. After a while the tremors subsided and the shaking in her breath dissolved. I experienced a flashback to when I felt so hysterical that first evening at Dorothy's home and how she comforted me. I whispered into Edwina's ear.

"When I felt so unhappy and I could not imagine anything else, my aunt and her friends talked about finding all the love I could ever want inside me, that my soul is full of love and light and that all I had to do was unwrap it. At the time I dismissed it, as you might now, but I just want you to know that later I found it. It exists and you can find it too, when you are ready."

I moved away slightly so I could see her. Edwina's eyes were closed. She looked softer and more peaceful. The blotchiness had subsided. I marvelled at how beautiful she looked.

"Do you want to stay here for a while? Or you can help me sort through all this junk, if you feel up to it."

"Just give me a few minutes."

I started working through the smaller items in the bedroom. After a while Edwina came up and helped me bring objects downstairs. It was much quicker with two of us. By the evening I had got everything except the big furniture into three piles. I packed the items I wanted to take back to London.

"You should have a big garage sale for all the things you want to get rid of. You could sell stuff through the Internet too," Edwina suggested.

I was back to my old home within a few days. I found someone to collect and store the things I wanted to keep. Save for the furniture the living room was now empty. Edwina and I laid out the rest in preparation for our garage sale. She had put notices up and an advert in the local classified. I felt we were like two children playing at shop keeping.

As Edwina passed me a book on ancient Saxon history, a card spiralled to the floor. It had a picture of snow-covered mountains in front of a bright blue sky. I picked it up. Inside there was blue writing. The writing had a flourish with big loops. I read it through.

Hello Darling,

I hope you are well. I miss you more than ever. My bed feels so empty without you. I am so looking forward to our first Christmas together.

All my love,

Cristelle x

The card had been printed in Switzerland. There was no stamp. Perhaps it had been sent in an envelope. I turned it over to see the picture and then read it again.

"What is it?" Edwina asked.

"I don't know. I've not seen it before. Could be a card sent to Matthew. It has occurred to me that he stashed all our money away somewhere. Perhaps it is in Switzerland with Cristelle."

"Oh no, how terrible. Do you think Mathew could have done something like that?"

"Not a while ago but now anything is possible. The sender doesn't mention Mathew's name and there is no address, so who knows."

I put the card in my bag.

The garage sale was fun. I saw lots of my old acquaintances and it gave me an opportunity to say goodbye to everyone. We sold about half of everything. I had also managed to sell some items on eBay and arranged for them to be collected that day. Edwina said she would take some of the leftovers to a charity shop and the rest would just remain in the house for the building society.

Back in London I showed Dorothy the card.

"Have you thought any more of visiting Barcelona?"

"I did think about it when I woke today. I think I am ready to book my ticket."

"It might be helpful to have a change of scene now you have let go of your home."

Later that day I went to the café and booked my ticket.

I happily told Martin Ledbetter that as far as I was concerned the house was empty and gave him the keys. I felt relieved, freer and lighter to escape the emotional burden my old home had come to represent.

In the morning I started my writing in a very sleepy state. I rolled out of bed and sat with my clean sheet of paper, with my eyes half open.

I sit on the dry, powdery earth, my back resting against the rough bark of a tree trunk. A warm breeze blows wisps of my long hair across my face. Every now and then a sweet smelling gust ripples the fabric of my dress, cooling my legs. Each time the wind stirs the leaves of the tree, I see the shadows flutter and shimmy across my bare legs and feet. The moving shadows create the impression that my skin, the earth and the fabric of my clothes merge into one.

I look up at the source of this light and see the sun shining through the branches of the tree. I squint and lift my little hand to shade my eyes. The sun seems to be feeding everything on the surface with his shimmering light and heat.

I watch the men working in the field. I see their hoes rise wearily and then fall into the ground. I see the rippling bare backs and arms work the soil, turning its flat hard surface to a darker, rough texture. I watch the women with their wide fawn hats carry wicker baskets of seeds. Their free hands move in a wide sweep and they scatter the seeds into the freshly exposed earth.

The seeds need Mother Earth and later the sun for their bright green shoots, just like I needed my mother and later my father. I hear the soft rhythm of leather soles clapping between stony soil and calloused flesh. He sits down next to me and puts his long arm around me. I look up. When I see his eyes I smile. He looks into my eyes and I see his twinkle. I put my arms around him and squeeze him as hard as I can.

He unwraps his cloth and takes out flat bread and breaks off a piece for me. We have olives, carrots, a walnut and an apple each. I save the walnut to the end. When I finish I lay my head on his lap and close my eyes. His salty scent fills my nostrils. I feel his hot hands stroke my hair and then rest on my back. If I squint my eyes everything blurs and merges into each other and becomes a sea of moving colour, somewhere between the earth and sun.

I left the writing, showered and dressed. After I read it slowly. I showed it to my aunt. She read through twice and put it down.

"Where do you think this is coming from? I have no knowledge of living through this scene. It seems to come from another time."

"I experience it as a beautiful expression of a little girl, sitting under a tree, whilst her father works in the field and then they have lunch together. Tomorrow I might read something else into it. You might interpret it differently altogether; perhaps a message about the relationship between the earth and sun, mother and father. It could even be a missive on polarity; the power of opposites and the movement of life between. It does not matter where the text comes from or why, we could speculate endlessly on that, all that matters is what it conveys to each of us now."

Dorothy smiled and got up to brew a pot of tea. When she came back I changed to a new topic that had been playing on my mind.

"I want to see the footage of the man walking to and from the van where I was attacked."

"Have you thought of something new?"

"I notice that Edward continually fiddles with his glasses, particularly when he is nervous. If that was Edward I am sure I would recognise the way he adjusts his glasses."

"That man wore sunglasses. Does Edward have a pair of dark spectacles he uses for the sun?"

"I'll ask Edwina."

Edwina confirmed Edward did have a pair of black framed sunglasses with long sighted lenses. I phone Detective Inspector David Williams and arranged to go to the police station for a viewing of the footage.

"Whilst you are there you might ask if they have any more information on the woman in that photograph. What was her name?"

"Oh yes, Claudia."

Sergeant Gough met me in the reception area and led me through to a viewing room. A constable then played me the CCTV footage. It started with the man on the train platform, walking through the ticket hall, walking along streets, then running away into a crowd, walking fast back to the tube station and back through the ticket hall. In all that time I did not see the man touch his sunglasses.

"That's all we have," Gough informed me.

"I don't think it is Edward."

"Why?" the sergeant looked surprised.

"I have observed Edward closely and I've noticed he compulsively fidgets with his glasses. Adjusts them, cleans them, takes them off, puts them back on. You know what I mean. This man does not touch his."

"Constable, can you get me the interview footage."

Janet brought us cups of tea whilst we waited. The acrid black liquid in a plastic cup was revolting. I put mine to one side. How my tastes had changed. We looked at the images of Edward looking frightened as Williams grilled him with questions. We both saw Edward unable to leave his glasses alone.

"It's not conclusive, but it certainly adds weight to the view that we need to keep looking for another suspect. I'll pass this on to Sergeant Smiley."

"Talking of another suspect, I showed Sergeant Smiley a photo where the girlfriend of Mathew's ex-wife appears to be spying on us. He said he would look into it."

"Yes, I think I remember her name. Sergeant Smiley sent me an email about her. Let me see."

Janet Gough opened her laptop.

"Here we are. According to the Italian police she was convicted of grievous bodily harm and assault, I think twelve years ago, and her brother is currently serving a sentence for murder. The whole family was caught up in organised crime. However, Miss Tagliabue has been out of trouble since. I've never been to Venice. I think I will arrange to interview her."

On the way home I phoned Ruby and arranged to meet her at our café. What had become our preferred table was free and we sat surveying the menus. After we ordered I looked at Ruby. She looked up.

"What?"

"Nothing, just looking."

I smiled and Ruby laughed.

"And what do you see with those magical eyes?"

"The most beautiful green eyes. The window to your glowing soul."

"Oh God, you've turned into a happy-clappy religious nut. Now you'll stare into people's eyes wearing that insane grin, dishing out salvation."

I laughed.

"Well, it beats fretting about being attacked, resenting Mathew and thinking myself into an early grave."

"Whatever makes you happy, you poor deluded fool," Ruby quipped, as she put her hand on mine. "You know I'll still love you."

"So how's life?"

"Hey, one day at a time. That's your mantra, isn't it?"

"Sure is."

"Today is going well and I'm having fun with you."

"Would you like another treatment this afternoon?"

"Now, that would spoil it!"

We laughed. After Ruby left, I packed for my early flight to Barcelona.

CHAPTER 23

The flight to Spain gave me time to think. My motivation was to find out more about Mathew's past and see if this led me to his killer and the person sending me threatening letters. I dozed listening to "Nothing Compares 2 U" by Sinéad O'Conner.

I felt the warm, Spanish spring air blow my hair as I stepped out of the plane door. I wheeled my luggage to the waiting bus and stood near the door hanging onto the overhead rail. It felt good to bend my knees and stretch my shoulders.

I checked into the small hotel I had booked on the Internet. The bedroom was basic but functional for my needs. I showered, changed and set out for a sightseeing tour. Every now and then I stopped to read the street names and reorient myself on my map. I organised my trip to pass Bar Fornos. The bar was set in the old part of Barcelona, about halfway along a busy narrow street full of small shops. Washing lines crossed the street above. Brightly coloured towels, sheets and clothes blowing in the wind against the bright blue background, created the appearance of vivid banners waving from the sky. I looked down and watched their shadows ripple across the cobbles. The walls of the old buildings were a mix of browns, yellows and beige, making a more neutral backdrop for the mass of colourful people in the street.

I went into Bar Fornos and sat near the street. I ordered a bottle of sparkling mineral water. I looked around. The bar had blue and cream tiled walls with a white tiled floor. The floor looked as though it had been recently laid. The small tables and chairs were made of dark wood. The long, mahogany bar ran down the right side of the room. The wall behind the bar supported shelves holding a colourful array of bottles of alcohol. Behind the glass bottles were mirrors, creating the illusion that the room was much wider than it was. Below there was an espresso machine and rows of glasses and cups on the counter. There was a large screen at the back showing a football match.

My stomach fluttered with a nervous anticipation. Did I really want to know about Mathew's history? I tried to imagine Mathew standing behind the bar and waiting on tables. Did he wear a black apron and white shirt? I wondered whether he ever was a buyer for a clothing store. Was it all a lie? Was our relationship an even bigger lie? My mind returned to the Swiss postcard. I could feel myself getting upset, so I paid and left.

I walked back towards the centre to look at some of Gaudi's architecture. I took lots of photographs and marvelled at the beauty of the curves and free flowing façades that blended into the cubic forms so harmoniously. I found the tiny shops charming. Some were only the width of two doors. I passed a tiny wool shop. I went in and bought deep reds, orange, brown and fawn shades, reflecting the colours of the city. Then I chose a variety of blue and cream balls of wool for Dorothy. I found a pattern that looked simple enough for me and purchased it with a pair of knitting needles.

In the early evening I tried various restaurants, but nothing opened for another two hours. Finally I passed a Japanese restaurant with signs of life inside and sat down to eat sushi. I smiled at the thought of coming all this way and eating foreign cuisine. In the evening I sat in my room listening to music.

I woke feeling rested. My morning started in a nearby café. I surveyed the street. This was Mathew's city for a while. *What would you have recommended, Mathew? What would have been your historical tour? Which cultural centres would you have taken me to?* Then I wondered about the other women he must have been with here. Would he have taken them on picnics like he used to with me?

I set off along the same route as the previous day. I arrived at Bar Fornos around midmorning. It looked quiet. This time I felt calmer and stronger inside. I walked to the bar and asked the young man behind if I could speak to the owner.

"Sure, you can speak to him, but I don't think he can speak to you."

"Why's that?"

"He doesn't speak English," the man said, laughing.

I smiled and instantly warmed to his friendly face.

He turned and shouted out, "Josep."

A stout, middle-aged man came through the doorway at the rear. He wiped his hands on a white linen cloth that was tucked into his waistband. "*Qué pasa?*" he cried out impatiently.

The young man turned to me smiling. "He says, 'What happens.'"

I took a photograph of Mathew out of my bag.

"Could you please ask him if he knows this man? He may have worked here."

The barman shouted out to the owner and pointed at the photograph. The owner marched over to the bar and took a pair of glasses out of his shirt pocket. He looked at the photograph, then at me and then spoke rapidly to the younger man. I became slightly defensive, drawing my emotions deeper inside me. The young man spoke to me.

"He wants to know who you are and how you know this man."

The older man stared at me intently. I swallowed and stammered slightly.

"My name is Amanda. I used to be his wife."

Josep looked startled as he listened to the translation of this news. He said something to the younger man and then looked at me. He raised his hands, clicked his tongue and looked down. Then he motioned me to a table by the wall.

"*Señora, por favor.*"

I sat down and put my bag on my lap. Josep walked over, followed by the younger man. Josep looked as though he had spent too much time in his own bar. His abdomen protruded and hung over the waist of his trousers. He had bags under his eyes and his round cheeks sagged slightly. Josep did have an impressive full head of black hair. He spoke to the young man.

"Josep Fornos asks, do you mind if I join you and translate?'"

In contrast the young man was tall and slim. He wore a white cotton shirt and black trousers. He had black curly hair, a thin moustache and goatee.

"No, I really appreciate your help."

He held out his hand.

"I am Francesc."

We clasped each other's hand for a moment. Francesc's palms were hot and dry. He sat down. Josep called out to the back of the bar and a girl came to our table. Josep insisted I had something to drink and eat. I ordered mint tea and an apple. Francesc laughed.

"This is very strange for us. We like coffee."

The girl left. I smiled. Josep spoke abruptly in Catalan and Francesc snapped into a more serious stance.

"Josep is asking why you are here."

"My husband, Mathew Blake, or I suppose Ramon Vilanova, as he was called here, was murdered last autumn."

Francesc translated. I listened to the urgent whine of a coffee grinder and smelt the roasted beans. Then Josep looked at me.

"*Si, ya lo sabir. Mi mas sentido pesame.*"

"He offers you his deepest condolences. We know of this. Ramon was Josep's cousin. Friends in London told us. Ramon used to work here. We are all sad about it."

Francesc had to raise his voice over the espresso machine. It felt weird calling Mathew 'Ramon,' but I persevered.

"Since Ramon was shot, I have been receiving threatening letters. I thought I would try and find out more about Mathew's – I mean Ramon's – past. See if it helps catch his killer and the person chasing me."

As Francesc translated, a dark shadow of tension crossed Josep's face. He then spoke to the young man. Francesc said something back, gesticulating with big, open movements of his hands.

"Josep says, 'Ramon is family. We have friends in London who can make enquiries. We did not know about these threats. Have you been harmed?'"

The coffees and my tea arrived.

"Yes, I was attacked in London. The man hit me, sexually assaulted me and stole my money. He had a gun and shot it at me. The same gun that killed my husband."

I felt a tightness in my chest as I described the attack again. As Francesc translated, Josep started rubbing his temples as if a headache was coming on. I could hear the sound of the Spanish football commentator in the background. Josep drank a shot of espresso and spoke briefly to Francesc who translated.

"What did the man who attacked you look like?"

"About a head taller than me, broader shoulders, smelt of alcohol. I could not see much he was behind me and it was dark in the van. He had a black wool hat, sunglasses and gloves."

Before translating, Francesc asked me the man's age.

"Hard to tell. Somewhere between twenty and forty."

Josep and Francesc then had a fairly long conversation. I wish I had studied Spanish or Catalan. As they went back and forth, Josep became agitated. Francesc seemed to be trying to reason with him. With his sweeping hand gestures Francesc seemed to expand to twice his size. Josep looked constrained. Josep finished his coffee and slammed the cup onto the table. Francesc put his hand on Josep's upper arm as if to reassure him, but Josep pushed him away. The commentator was shouting and then screamed "Goal" at the top of his voice. Josep turned to face the television. Someone had scored a goal and slow motion replays showed the ball being passed diagonally across the goalmouth, and a player wearing a dark purple top and black shorts run and chip the ball over the keeper. Three men sitting near the screen broke into excited conversation pointing to something they had seen. Francesc touched my arm.

"It is a repeat. If this was live, the bar would be full and exploded. I am sorry about Josep. He is a family man and your news upsets him."

Josep turned back. He looked calmer as he spoke to Francesc.

"Okay, Josep wants to know how long will you be here in Barcelona."

"I return to London in three days."

I wondered whether I had just given out too much information. After a brief conversation, Francesc turned to me.

"Josep will phone family in London and see if he can find out about this man who is hurting you. He says he wants you to come back tomorrow at this time so he can talk again. Maybe he has some news."

It sounded like dialogue from a mafia film. Josep, the bar and the turn in the conversation were so distant from the sophisticated, cultured Mathew I knew. I tried to imagine him hanging out here, watching football with Josep. It did not fit.

"Excuse me, Francesc. Can Josep tell me more about Ramon? I only know him from England. I know nothing of his past. I was hoping he could tell me a little about his life in Argentina and here."

This provoked another long conversation. I wondered how one simple translation could turn into such a big discussion. The espresso machine was busy again and I focussed on the smell of coffee whilst I waited for them to finish.

"Josep says he will try to answer your questions tomorrow. He is sorry, but he must leave."

Josep stood up, shook my hand curtly, looked into my eyes and walked to the door at the rear. I turned to Francesc.

"Did you know Ramon?"

"Yes, but I was only nine. I think I remember him at the bar here. My mother said he was a good dancer. He played music here sometimes. We did not hear from him for a long time and people say he is snobbish. He does not even see our friends in London." Francesc put his finger under his nose and pushed it up as he said 'snobbish.' Then he looked embarrassed. "I am sorry, I should not have said that."

I remembered Mathew complaining that my friend, Sophie, had the cultural sophistication of a footballer. I smiled.

"How are you related?"

"From a long way. My mother's sister married Josep's brother. We are not blood brothers but here we like big families, so any connection is good."

"Your English is excellent."

"Thank you. I live in London for two years. I only came back recently."

Francesc stood up and I gathered my things. When I had everything, he clasped my hand, shot me a big smile and I left. As I walked along the narrow street under the colourful washing drying in the sun, I felt disorientated, as though my insides had been jumbled up. Somehow my past didn't make sense. I looked round suddenly to check I was not being followed. There was something sinister about these friends in London. Perhaps I would have been more comfortable if they had names, or if they had explained how they are connected. I walked to a park and found a bench in the sun. I phoned Dorothy and told her of my encounter.

"Goodness Amanda, this opens a whole new avenue. Try to find out some of the names of the relations living in London. And how are you feeling, my dear?"

I tried to describe my feelings.

"I think I would find a homely café, enjoy a cup of tea," Dorothy confided.

"I do have my knitting with me."

"Treat yourself to a relaxing afternoon, dear, and enjoy Barcelona."

I told her about the wool shop. After we finished talking I walked towards the harbour and found a seafood restaurant for lunch. Then I walked for a while and followed my aunt's advice. I found a small café and looked at my knitting pattern as I prepared my wool and needles, a woman at the next table smiled. She leant across felt a ball of wool and said something. I told her I did not speak Spanish.

"No Spanish. Catalan," she corrected me.

The woman came round and sat next to me. With a broad smile she took the knitting needles from my hands and showed me the stitch on the pattern. She kept pointing to the pattern and then very slowly knitted a row. She passed the knitting back to me and I tried. With a little help I found the rhythm of the new stitch. The Catalan woman watched me smiling as I sped up a little.

"*Si, si*," she said encouragingly.

I thought how women used to have activities that could unite us and even without a common language bring us together. I imagined we might have cooked together, made pickles in groups, taken our children to play together and here we were with knitting as our common currency. Modern life could be very cold and lonely.

I returned to Bar Fornos the next day taking the now familiar route from my hotel. As I approached the bar I made a conscious effort to feel every step and each breath. I wanted to remain centred this time.

I greeted Francesc at the bar. He took my hand. Francesc summoned Josep and we sat at the same table. Where Francesc was warm and friendly, Josep played a gruff, austere role. A line from Wilde's writing flashed through my mind and I wondered what echo of someone else's music Josep might be expressing. Was he still acting out a poorly written part? If I peeled off enough layers would I find a joyful, natural expression of love inside? When they finished talking, Francesc turned to me.

"Josep is still waiting for a reply. He has asked my uncle to make enquiries with our Catalan friends. People talk, yes, and maybe we will found out more about your husband. He has asked my aunt to come and talk to you about Ramon."

"*Muchas gracias*," I said to Josep. He nodded and got up slowly. He spoke to Francesc and walked to the bar.

"Josep would like you to have a drink and food," Francesc said smiling. "Do you want your mint tea and apple?"

"Yes, please."

Francesc returned after a few minutes, also bringing a coffee for himself.

"Maybe Josep did not like Ramon. I think he finds it difficult to talk about him. Also my aunt speaks English."

Francesc stood up as his aunt arrived. They embraced and kissed each other on the cheeks. Francesc went to get his aunt a coffee and water. I stood and we shook hands.

"Hello, I am Rosa. You want to talk about Ramon?"

Her hand seemed to hug my smaller hand. Rosa smiled at me warmly. She looked to be about fifty and had a motherly air.

Francesc returned, gave his aunt her drink and sat sipping his espresso. Rosa turned and said something and he got up, said goodbye, and took up his place behind the bar. Rosa had a large round face with full rosy cheeks. Her long black hair was tied back.

"What do you want to know?"

"I only know about Ramon from the time he met Veronica here at the bar and went to England. I want to know more about his life from before."

"This is good. I only know Ramon until he met Veronica. Together we can make his history. Where do I start?"

"Please go back as far as you can."

"His parents were from here in Barcelona. They moved to Buenos Aries and Ramon was born. He grew up in Argentina. He married when he was young and later had a son."

My heart leapt. A son! Why had Mathew never mentioned this? Rosa continued.

"Then his marriage did not work and he came here. He did not talk about it, so I only hear gossip. When he came to Barcelona he lived with, Josep's brother, Carles."

Rosa looked at me.

"Are you fine?"

"No, it is the first time I heard Mathew had a son. I am a bit shocked."

"He did not say?"

"No, nothing. Please continue. I am sure there will be more surprises."

"Then he worked here. He was a good worker and good with the women."

I felt myself flush. Rosa put her hand on my forearm.

"I am sorry. I am sure you do not want to hear this."

"No, please tell me everything."

Rosa drank some of her coffee and knocked it back with some water.

"One night each week he comes here to play his guitar. Some Spanish style, sometimes jazz and he liked to sing some blues. He is also a good dancer. Many women like him. Then he is with Josep's best friend's youngest sister, Montserrat. When I see them together

I think they are much in love. Maybe Montserrat thinks they will marry. Ramon rents an apartment and they make a home together. I am thinking, when will they marry? Ramon is waiting to get a better job, more money."

Rosa paused and took a sip of coffee and shot of water. I took a bite of my apple. Rosa looked at me quizzically.

"Why do you have this tea and apple? Are you sick?"

"No, I like the taste and I do feel better when I eat like this. I have not had coffee for so long, it would probably send my head spinning off into a distant orbit."

Rosa looked at me for a moment, smiled sympathetically and then continued.

"Then something is wrong. Montserrat has a big depression. She does not talk to anyone. After a few days Ramon leaves with an English woman."

Rosa pauses and looks at me.

"I am not sure how much to say."

"Please don't worry. Tell me everything."

"This is just my mind, okay?"

I nodded.

"I think Ramon likes money. Josep say his parents in Argentina has many difficulties with money. Maybe a child with little money need it too much when a man. I am saying this because Montserrat did not have money and the English woman did."

"I have met Veronica, she lives in Venice. She is recovering from a stroke. Mathew – I mean Ramon – left her after a few years."

"Yes, we heard from Enric in London. So, Ramon leave Barcelona with Veronica for England after five years with us, and we do not hear from him again. He leaves very quickly. I don't know if he is running away or running to his new love. Montserrat is really, really upset, she cannot say what happens. Josep is angry, and we think, why? We welcome him into our family, support him, give him work, introduced him to friends and then nothing."

I felt heavy. Mathew had a history of dumping women when it suited him. My suspicions were confirmed again. It added to the feeling that, after five years of marriage, he was getting ready to leave me. Was it all for my money? The little nest egg that I inherited bought him a lifestyle he seemed to aspire to. Then I thought of his expeditions to the blues club.

"Ramon used to go to play his guitar and sing at a club in London."

"Did you go with him?"

"No, not my scene."

Rosa pursed her lips and shook her head slightly. I guessed she thought Mathew was meeting new women there. She asked me if we had children and I told her that Mathew kept finding excuses. Her facial expression gave away her suspicion that Mathew was looking for something else. I looked into Rosa's eyes for a moment. I hesitated but then said it anyway.

"Since Ramon was murdered, I have had threatening letters from someone who says he wants to kill me. I have also been attacked. Do you think any of the people who Ramon upset would still have such bad feeling towards him?"

Rosa eyes flared and her face reddened slightly with indignation.

"We are not murderers."

"I'm very sorry. I did not mean to upset you. I just want all this to stop."

Rosa let out a long audible sigh. I noticed her shoulder drop slightly.

"Josep say Enric will ask in London. But why would anyone hurt you? It is not your fault Ramon was the way he was. I do not understand why anybody kills Ramon after all this time. We are not that kind of people."

I smiled and put my hand on hers.

Rosa asked me lots of questions about our life in England. My tales of Mathew running a shop and all our travels fascinated her.

After, I walked towards the sea feeling slightly depressed. Inspector Pride's claim that I might have upset someone by starting my relationship with Mathew rung an alarm in my head. Most of all I was finding it hard to come to accept that Mathew had a son.

This information stirred up a deep recurring sadness in my heart, taking me back to that question of why he had not wanted to have a child with me. At the same time I was astonished that he had never mentioned his son, and as far as I knew, had no contact with him.

My legs felt tired, there was a feeling of anxiety in my stomach and my mind felt fuzzy. When I reached the beach I looked out across the water. That great expanse of open sea in front of me felt uplifting. No barriers, limitations or restrictions. A cool breeze blew gently across my face. I wondered whether people living by the ocean had a bigger vision of life compared to communities living in the woods. I took off my socks and shoes and walked across the damp sand to the still sea. I stood in the cold water and felt the sand shifting under the soles of my feet.

I wasted the rest of the day in a state of limbo. Part of me wanted to go back to the hotel and curl up in bed, and another to enjoy and explore Barcelona. I had lost my appetite and ended up wandering aimlessly for a while, then went back to my hotel and fell asleep in the late afternoon. I did not wake until early evening. Now I was hungry. I shook off my drowsiness and walked out into the evening air. I went back to the Japanese restaurant and sat in the corner watching the chef assemble his sushi.

In the morning I packed and checked out. I left my bag in the hotel luggage room. Then I followed my usual routine and arrived at Bar Fornos. Francesc came out from behind the bar to greet me. He kissed me on each cheek and ushered me to the same table. Without asking he brought me a mint tea and apple. He sat down with his espresso and bread.

"Josep say he is sorry. He is not here today. Did Rosa help?"

"Yes, thank you. I learnt a lot more about Ramon. Not particularly good things, but I think I understand better."

"Maybe he makes mistakes, but he was also fun, musical and athletic. You say half full or half empty glass."

I laughed.

"Yes, we do. Sorry, I'm just feeling a bit low."

"Josep asked me to tell you something."

Francesc looked at me and I smiled.

"He say, my uncle Enric will find this man and then we will tell you. He say, until then be safe. Maybe you take a holiday or go to live with friends for while."

My heart jumped slightly as I felt fear spread from my stomach to my chest.

"What do you mean?"

"We will find the man who hurts you and then you will be safe."

"But how will you find him? Do you know who he is?"

Francesc leant back in his chair.

"I can only say what Josep tell me. I don't know who he is. Maybe Enric know, or maybe he know who to ask."

"And what will you do when you find him?"

Francesc shrugged.

"I think we talk and say we know who he is and he must stop."

The way Francesc spoke it all sounded so innocent. To find the man who had shot Mathew, sent me all those threats, physically attacked me, and say I know who you are and now you must stop, and for him to then peacefully accept that ultimatum, sounded naive. Perhaps I had seen too many violent films not to imagine their plan included some kind of threat or violence should they ever find Mathew's killer.

Francesc changed the subject before I could ask more questions. We talked about London. He told me about the clubs he liked, his love of Indian food and how much money his friend in London earned working for a bank. I asked him where his uncle lived. He became slightly guarded.

"Near Ealing. It is not important."

"How will I know when your uncle has found the man?"

"You will give me your email and phone and I will contact you."

"What's your uncle's last name?"

Francesc became more assertive.

"He is a busy man. You talk to me. I give you my email."

We exchanged email addresses and phone numbers. I was beginning to feel hot and beads of sweat ran down my sides. I had to remind myself of my conversation with Rosa, to feel safer. Francesc stood up and kissed me on each cheek. I felt uneasy and slightly queasy. I walked out in a kind of daze. Images of Catalan gangsters roaming London filled my mind. I was glad to get back out into the fresh air. It took me a moment to adjust to the sunlight. Then I looked up at the sky and took in some deep breaths. I tried to focus on Rosa and her claim that they were not murderers, not that kind of people.

I walked back letting the conversations in Bar Fornos spin around my head. Francesc's suggestion that I should take a holiday sounded ominous. What did they know that I didn't? I wondered whether the police could track Enric down and question him? In reality I had nothing concrete to tell the police. The conversations in the bar expressed no more than an intention to find out who was threatening me and warn him off - hardly illegal.

I collected my bag from the hotel and made my way to the airport. I still could not find my happy state of contentment on the flight home. Each time I tried to meditate my imagination pushed its way back into my mind.

I returned home in the early evening and felt very happy to see Dorothy. We hugged and I didn't want to let go. I felt so relieved to be home again.

"What is it, dear?"

I started to explain about Mathew and his son, but jumped into the middle of the story, so it made little sense.

"Sit down and relax, Amanda. Just start at the beginning."

I told her about the bar conversations. Then, when I finally stopped talking, Dorothy spoke.

"I'll make us a warm, relaxing dinner and then we can talk more."

Dorothy made us a vegetable soup, a bean dish with brown rice, stir fried vegetables and a salad. We sat and ate. Dorothy wanted to know all about my excursions around Barcelona and my impression of the Gaudi architecture. I showed her my knitting and gave her the wool I had bought for her.

After dinner Dorothy asked me to repeat all the conversations again. She sat with her eyes closed and her head leant back against the cushion. Then she asked me to say it all again one more time. When I finished we sat in silence for a few minutes.

"If you don't mind I will now go to sleep on that and see how I feel tomorrow. I suggest you try the same."

Sleep did not come easily. I couldn't calm my mind. My feet felt too hot, my lower back too cold. Then my ankles itched incessantly. I cried out, "Fiddlesticks," as I rolled onto my other side again, an image of my father trying to start the lawnmower flooded my mind. There he was pulling a white rope with a plastic handle repeatedly. Every now and again he stopped to fiddle with the settings on the carburettor. Then he would start his frantic snatching at the handled rope. I remembered sitting in our car with him once when it would not start. I experienced a fatal sinking feeling, as I knew the car battery had lost too much energy to turn the engine. I sat listening to the churning sound of the starter motor slow to a feeble grunt, not daring to look at my father. The old television would lose its signal, sending my father scurrying up to the loft to adjust the aerial. The soundtrack to all these events was fiddlesticks. Sometimes my father would say it under his breath, other time out loud and when things got really bad he would scream it out with the worst expletive he could conjure up as a prefix.

Was I now really saying fiddlesticks of my own volition, or was my father saying it through me, having implanted the seed of that expression during my childhood? Who was saying it me or him?

After a while I got up and tried writing. The best I could do was to write a list of the people I met at the bar with a brief description of what each said.

CHAPTER 24

Dorothy and I sat in the kitchen for breakfast.

"You know, dear, I did have a thought this morning. It occurred to me that we might be looking for a young relation of Mathew's. Did you say he had a son in Argentina?"

"Yes, Rosa said he left his wife and son in Buenos Aries."

"I wonder..." Dorothy went back to her porridge.

Later, when we sat in the living room with our knitting Dorothy returned to the subject.

"It might explain the style of the letters, the way you were attacked, and why the family in Barcelona were so concerned to help. Perhaps they were worried about a wayward son. How old would Mathew's son be now do you think?"

"Rosa told me he married young, so if his son was born when Mathew was twenty-five, he would now be twenty-three."

"For me, a son would better explain why the killer took his watch and the photographs. If you wanted a memento of your father, what would you take?"

"But why come here after all those years? Mathew must have left Argentina over seventeen years ago."

"Yes, there is still much to ponder on," Dorothy mused.

I had a message to call Inspector Williams. He wanted me to meet him at the station, as he had more news.

"I followed up your suspicions of Miss Tagliabue and interviewed her. She eventually admitted to being in England and following you both when the picture was taken. She claimed she had bad feelings towards you after you took Mr Blake away from her friend, and hated Mr Blake for taking her friend's money. She met up with your husband and demanded the money back. She admits she may have made threats but denies murder and sending you the letters."

"But don't you see, this fits exactly. Was she here when Mathew was murdered?"

"Yes, she was in London on a shopping trip staying with a friend. However, she was in Italy when you were attacked in Covent Garden. Given the gun used then was the same as the one that killed your husband I think it is unlikely she killed your husband, unless there was another person involved."

"Doesn't she come from a violent family?"

"Don't worry, we will explore those avenues. Have you received any more threatening letters?"

"Not since Venice. Do you think I need protection again?"

"I think we have narrowed down your attacker to Edward or Claudia, and both of them know that. They may now feel that further action is not worth the risk. I suggest you take reasonable precautions and call me if you notice anything suspicious."

I rushed home to tell Dorothy. Once I finished she let her head rest against the back of her chair and closed her eyes before speaking.

"So are we to surmise that Claudia and another came here to get revenge and claim back money from Mathew, and he then took out loans against your house? Fearing the wrath of a violent family, he gave them £10,000 a week in cash and then they killed him anyway. After which, still wanting to take revenge on you for having a relationship with Mathew, they sent you letters and attacked you."

"And now want to kill me as they murdered Mathew," I said with a shaky voice.

"And yet Claudia was not here when you were attacked and the same gun fired. Did she give the gun to someone else who disliked you?"

I waited as Dorothy sat still.

"Well, you met Claudia. Do you think she was so upset and resentful that she would go to all these lengths for retribution? Why didn't she kill you when she had you on her doorstep?"

"Veronica did say she hated Mathew and I getting together. What if she complained so much to Claudia about it that one day Claudia snapped and decided to put an end to it all?"

"We humans are mysterious creatures, so it is possible."

The next day I had arranged to meet Edwina in Welwyn Garden City for lunch. I wanted to travel early and spend an hour or two retracing my steps through the shops that formed such a big part of my old retail life. I caught the train from King's Cross and enjoyed a compilation of all my shopping highlights. Once I was satiated, I met Edwina at an Italian restaurant she recommended.

She described her life living with Edward.

"I think Edward is still obsessed with you. He has a folder full of your pictures. I found him looking at your Facebook page yesterday. It's creepy. The man has lost it, he needs therapy."

Ironically it was Edwina who was getting the therapy. We talked about therapy until our food arrived. My curiosity had been piqued by her description of Edward. When I felt ready I steered the conversation back to him.

"He still goes to work. Now his feelings towards me are out in the open, he treats me like a friend. He is civil and polite in the home. He sleeps in another bedroom. He has hired a lawyer to helps us divorce. I would say he is very methodical. After twelve years together, he has no emotions. Just follows his plan as though he is selling off a subsidiary. He probably thinks of it as getting back to his core business – himself. Perhaps I am sinking stock he needs to quietly dispose of."

"Do you feel he is dangerous?"

"I don't know. Obsessive, yes. He even has a file on an acupuncturist called Henry, who he thinks you like."

I shuddered. I found myself looking round the restaurant just to make sure he had not followed us.

"I found a list of characteristics he thought you might like about him and those you didn't."

"Oh no, that sounds so awful."

I wondered what they were but stopped myself from asking. By the time we finished lunch, Edward was back at the top of my list of suspects. After waving goodbye to Edwina, I phoned Dorothy and told her.

"We only have Edwina's version. Is it possible that she told you what she wants you to think?"

"Oh my God, Inspector Pride is walking straight towards me. I'll call you back."

The Inspector was pounding towards me in black trousers and a billowing blue top. I put my phone in my pocket and turned to look into the nearest shop window. I cringed at the thought of meeting her again.

"Amanda Blake?"

I turned and looked up.

"Oh hello, Inspector."

Pride walked right up to me. She was too close, sandwiching me between her abdomen and the shop front. I smelt her familiar rose scent. I became slightly claustrophobic and panicked. I stepped to one side, suppressing an impulse to turn and run.

"It's just Joan Pride now. I'm glad to bump into you here. I have felt bad about what happened and wanted to talk to you. Can I buy you a tea?"

Joan smiled. A memory of her sitting on my bed, consoling me flashed across my mind. I looked into her eyes for a moment. The aggression that frightened me, had been replaced with a vulnerability I had not seen in her before.

I nodded and followed Pride to a patisserie. We found a table to the rear. She squeezed between two tables pushing one across the floor with a loud juddering sound. We sat down. Pride ordered a cake and cappuccino. I remembered the various teas with biscuits or cakes we had shared. I ordered a herb tea and scones. Although the thought of this encounter had induced so much fear, I now felt relaxed.

"You're no longer an inspector?"

"I was made an irresistible offer to leave and a very resistible option should I stay. So I retired and now work for charity."

As Joan talked about her charity work, a couple of teenagers behind her distracted me. They were standing by the counter and clearly arguing. The girl in a stretchy top and skirt was pleading with the boy. He stood sullenly looking back at her with a look of resignation. She was making big movements with her arms and shuffling her feet slightly. He stood like a rock.

Pride explained how she allocated funds to single mothers. I flitted between Joan's description of raising money from government agencies to watching the teenagers.

I imagined the girl realised she was not being heard and that the boy could not hear her because it was too painful for him. They both looked so unhappy. I had an urge to gather them up in my arms. The girl started crying and wiping her eyes with her hands. Perhaps they both realised they could not connect and understand each other.

Pride was asking me where I was living.

"Oh, up in London. I think I will stay there."

The girl sat at a table at the far corner. The boy stood by the counter looking lost. I re-engaged with Pride and blurted out the question that had been in my head for so long.

"What happened? Were you going to arrest me?"

"It was a fishing expedition. I wanted to get you back to the station and interrogate you more forcefully. You know, see whether you would break down under pressure, make mistakes, contradict yourself."

"What about trying to run me off the road by the woods?"

"I think I just panicked. I still don't really know what happened that day. The police psychiatrist thought I had a nervous breakdown. I was a mess. When I got back to the station I started screaming at the team before bursting into tears. I was out of control. And so goodbye career, hello medication."

"I'm sorry."

"How English of you to apologise. It's not your fault and I didn't really enjoy the job. Far too much stress."

I saw the boy walk over to the table with two cups.

I remembered James saying that she had been promoted because of a relationship. Perhaps it was too much too soon.

"So how are you, Amanda? Did you sort everything out? You're still alive, obviously."

"No, still chasing shadows, or should I say still looking to see who is hiding in the shadows. There is something else I want to ask you. Do you remember you became quite aggressive over the possibility that my starting a relationship with Mathew could have upset someone? For a while I wondered whether you had feelings for Mathew in the past."

Joan burst out laughing.

"That you cannot accuse me of. My friend, Clare, met Mathew on a double date. Her sister was in a relationship with your friend James and they set Clare up with Mathew. They went out a few times and she became besotted with Mathew. She thought Mathew had feelings for her. After a few months you turned up and Clare's phone calls went unanswered. Clare died of breast cancer during the investigation, and I supposed I reacted to that."

"I think Mathew broke a lot of women's hearts. I'm sure he was leaving me and stashing our funds out of my reach."

"James wasn't any better. I tried to convict him of repeatedly assaulting Clare's sister, Jane, but Jane withdrew her testimony at the last minute. Those poor women really suffered."

"So who was your main suspect?"

"I suppose now I am no longer involved, I can tell you that my gut instinct told me it was Mr Edwards. He had the motive, opportunity and means. I would have liked it to have been James but that didn't fly. I looked forward to having him squirming in the interview room again. I heard they arrested Edwards but didn't have enough hard evidence."

"That was after he followed me and attacked my friend in Venice. He was reading my emails."

I watched the teenagers leave. She walked out first pushing the door hard and the boy followed with his head down. I wondered if this would be their pattern in life if they stayed together. Do our early relationships set up behaviours that become lifelong automatic responses? Did Mathew trap himself in only being able to have a series of short-term relationships that focussed on him bettering himself? Perhaps he could only keep up appearances for a few years before starting again with a new woman. Am I caught up in repeatedly trying to find intelligent men to love me, like a moth flying into the candlelight? Joan broke my speculation.

"I have to say that you were a strong suspect. You would have had the motive, assuming you knew of his deceit, and opportunity. The mind can play extraordinary tricks and I did wonder whether you could have blanked it all out."

I shuddered along my spine as I reconnected with that old paranoia. Did I send myself the grotesque letters? Had Edward unwittingly become entangled in my own insanity and become the suspect? My eye started to twitch so strongly I had to press my hand over it. Pride looked at me with an expression of surprise. I realised this must make me look guilty, as though she had literally touched a nerve.

I forced myself out of that pattern of thought by consciously taking a sip of tea and trying to sense it in as much detail as I could. My eye started to calm and I removed my hand.

"I don't know why that happens," I complained weakly.

Then Pride made an excuse and got up to leave.

"I hope it works out. Bye."

I thought about James and Pride's claim that he was violent. Then I thought about his last conversation with Mathew as I sat alone in the patisserie. I took a deep breath in and plucked up the courage to walk round to Stiletto. I could see James talking to one of the staff behind the counter. I stood outside wondering what to do. Surely I would be safe with people around.

I walked into Mathew's old shop. Nothing had changed. I was struck by a memory of Mathew behind the till, talking to customers. James looked up and said something to his assistant.

"Amanda, how wonderful. Finally you have come out of hiding."

"I really need to talk to you."

"Sure, let's go to my office."

The office was a messy corner in the stock room next to the toilet. James offered me a seat but I chose to stand.

"James, I want you to be honest with me. I know you remember Mathew's last conversation. It would help me to know what was happening in those last hours of his life."

"I can assure you it has nothing to do with his murder or your situation. You must know me well enough to be sure I would tell you and the police if that was the case."

"The more you resist telling me, the more important and mysterious it becomes to me."

James looked down and fidgeted with a pen, flicking the ball point in and out of the housing.

"Okay, I will tell you, but this must remain confidential. Absolutely no mention of it to the police. Can I trust you?"

I nodded.

"Mathew wanted out. He knew I could not buy his shares. Why would I? The business was not worth anything. So he came up with a plan to stage a burglary of the cash and stock. Basically, he would steal a van, reverse it into the shop window at night, and we would throw the entire stock into the back of the van. Mathew would then drive off and dump it with a contact he had found. He would keep the proceeds of the burglary and I would get the insurance money."

My legs felt weak and I sat down squeezing the plastic office chair armrest with my hands. Inevitably the nerves below my eye started to twitch, forcing me to rub my eye.

"Why? He had already taken so much from me. What could the stock be worth?"

"We were overstocked, so he thought he would get £30,000 or more. I don't know why he was so desperate for the money. Perhaps he could not face walking away from the shop after all the time and effort he put in. Maybe he hated the idea that I would get his shares for free. I was glad to be rid of him. I made it clear that if he left, I would run the shop my way. He would just be a shareholder and taken off the payroll. He wasn't much use anymore. He had begun to disappear regularly without telling me. Suddenly he was full of mystery and secrets. So he became desperate to find a way out in which he would give up his shares for some form of payment."

"Where was he going?"

"I don't know. He was very secretive. I thought it had something to do with a girl, but I cannot be sure."

"So, is that what the phone conversation was about?"

"He said he would be ready for Saturday night."

"I just don't recognise this version of Mathew."

"He was different with you. He took on this persona of the cultured, English gentleman but when cornered he reverted to a nasty, aggressive, greedy conman."

I swallowed hard and felt very hot. How could I have not seen this side to Mathew?

"So now you have heard it all, does it help?"

I shrugged my shoulders. I felt shaken, disturbed and revolted by the depths Mathew would sink to, just to grab even more of other people's money. I left feeling nauseous. I had to keep my mind focussed on each footstep, just to make it to the station.

CHAPTER 25

I excitedly told Dorothy of the day's events and the new information. She listened to my theories intently.

"Could Claudia have tricked Mathew into believing she is in love with him, lured him away from me, shown him how to take my money and then when she has it, kills Mathew before returning to Veronica?"

"I suppose you think Claudia was the author of that card, using Cristelle as her pseudonym."

"Yes."

"It certainly does bring lots of strands together. It works logically. Now you would have to feel into Claudia, Mathew and Veronica as to whether they would have been capable of all this. You knew Mathew, and you have met Claudia and Veronica. I would sleep on it."

"I am not sure I did know Mathew anymore," I responded despondently.

"I imagine he has left his imprints inside you and those imprints may carry the DNA of the real Mathew."

In the morning I walked across Primrose Hill and Regent's Park into central London. The fresh air, nature and exercise helped clear my mind. I wanted to stop thinking about suspects.

I walked toward Oxford Circus feeling thirsty. As I started to look for a café I literally bumped into Henrique on the corner of Oxford Street and Regent Street. I was walking past a shop window looking at boots and he was reading a message on his phone.

Neither of us was in a hurry so we found a juice bar and sat down together. Once we had ordered and chatted for a while Henrique asked me if he could read something to me.

Henrique slid some folded pieces of paper from his coat pocket. He laid them out on the table pressing out the creases with the palm of his hand and began to read.

"Does having a brain made up of two opposing hemispheres mean we are destined to observe our world in digital, black and white terms of opposites? Do having two hands and walking on two feet reinforce this? We see our world with two eyes, hear it with two ears, feel the wind with two cheeks."

I reminded myself he was reading his notes and not looking for any answers.

"Does our anatomy predicate us to seeing our world dualistically, blinding us to other possibilities? It seems that science, religion and new age thinking keeps coming back to a dualistic, relative world built on good and bad, right and wrong and separation."

Henrique looked up and smiled. I was having to concentrate to follow him.

"Even our language holds us to certain ways of thinking. Words primarily distinguish, separate and define. They explore how we perceive things as different, rather than the same. As we often think in language, does our thinking reinforce a dualistic perception of life?"

Henrique made eye contact. I felt compelled to respond.

"We do seem primed to argue and disagree."

Henrique nodded and continued.

"To use the analogy of a computer, it is as though our hardware, in other words mind and body, combined with our software, or language, to keep us in a dualistic mindset."

Herr Huber took a sip of his juice and looked down at his notes.

"I find it fascinating that in quantum physics our universe can only be described through maths, not language."

"Really?"

Henrique nodded.

"Atoms exist in mathematical formula but not language. So do we need another way of thinking to begin to appreciate new possibilities?"

"I have read that people who speak different languages, have slightly different ways of thinking."

Henrique smiled and nodded.

"Yes, and here's the important part. At the same time we are the universe. Inside us are the particles, rhythms, cycles, energies that we seek to define on the outside. In that sense we know everything there is to know, as we are it."

"How do you mean?"

"Well, the water inside our bodies is made up of particles that could have passed through oceans, clouds, stream, rivers and ponds. Those same particles may have been through plants, all kinds of creatures and other people."

I felt a superficial shiver of excitement as I considered that all that water inside me had been around the planet.

"Similarly the air particles that enter my lungs may have been through plants, animals and people. Our boundaries may be much more permeable than we think. Just in terms of the water and air we are constantly exchanging particles with the world we inhabit."

"Wow, that is kind of mind blowing."

"Perhaps even more extraordinary is that we also absorb photons from the sun and from distant stars. If we can see a distant star some of its energy will be inside us."

"That is amazing."

Henrique smiled in a shy, boyish way. It was the first time I had seen that expression on his large face.

"What if the water and air entering your body brought with it some kind of imprint of the places it had been? Could connecting with the particles washing through us allow us to pick up on those imprints? Is it possible that photons from the sun and stars can provide us with information from the inside that is light years away?"

I made a mental note to go out at night and be receptive to those photons finding their way to our planet. I thought about Dorothy's suggestion that Mathew had left his imprints inside me. Then I had a thought of my own.

"If the universe is moving through us, is anything really ours? Where is this self we get so upset about?"

My head felt like it was expanding, reaching out into the universe. Then another thought appeared.

"Perhaps it is only when we are really still that we begin to hear some of these imprints."

Henrique nodded and then spoke.

"The challenge we have is to go beyond dualism, rather than be limited to a thinking that may represent a tiny view of everything there is to understand. Ultimately it suggests being open, curious and not judging."

"Yes, and when we experience moments of knowing from within, we may have to accept they may be beyond language," I added excitedly.

After we parted, I walked along Oxford Street with my head spinning with ideas and then caught a bus home. I sat at the front on the upper deck, looking out onto the London streets. Henrique's extraordinary ideas were deeper than anything my father or Mathew had said and yet I had not felt in awe of him or wanted to be in a relationship with him. Something had changed.

I was excited to tell Dorothy everything when I sat down with her in the living room. Dorothy listened attentively.

"I agree, and yet in all this let us consider that all these ideas are flashes of inspiration that will come and go, be proved and then disproved, and one day become obsolete. They serve us well for our own reflection and to inspire us to delve deeper into our self-discoveries, as long as we do not get distracted from this, by the theories themselves.

Dorothy spoke more about the mystery of Mathew's murder over dinner.

"I have let your idea drift around my head, and the idea of Claudia killing Mathew does not feel right. It works and would certainly make a good storyline for a film, and yet it feels a little too contrived. I think there is a huge outpouring of emotion in the killing of your husband, the notes and your attack in Covent Garden."

"So what do you think?"

"Who would be that emotional about Mathew? Veronica possibly, but she is incapacitated, and I doubt she could transfer that emotional intensity to Claudia."

"Who then?"

"It would have to be someone who is so emotionally entangled in the things Mathew has done to be willing to wreak this level of emotional havoc on himself. Remember how you described the attack in Covent Garden. He really hated you. The letters are full of hate."

I shivered at the memory. Dorothy continued.

"I've been looking at the letters again. I think we are looking for his son, someone young who can barely speak English. When I look at the wording there is an immaturity, his actions are reckless and he seems inconsistent. You have not heard anything since Venice."

I nodded.

"Don't worry, Amanda, we will resolve this. I feel we are much closer."

CHAPTER 26

I arranged to stay a few days with a friend and colleague from school, for a change of scene, but after the third day her mother was taken ill, and she left for Manchester. I took the train back to London.

As I approached Dorothy's building, my mind turned to a cup of mint and lemon tea. A plastic shopping bag had blown up against the steps. I picked it up and put it in the bin. I climbed the steps and fumbled through my bag for keys. I pushed the door open hearing the familiar sound of the draft strip brushing across the stone tiles.

The post was scattered across the black and white hall floor. I put my case by the stairs and squatted down to scoop up the assortment of envelopes. I started to sort them out. Dorothy had several letters. They looked like junk and bills.

I looked round at the sound of footsteps. I saw a young man bound up the stairs. I thought he was from one of the other flats and stood to the side to let him through. Then I noticed he had a nasty cut on his lower lip, black eye and graze across his forehead. The blood looked fresh.

"Are you alright?" I said.

He did not reply. Instead he walked up to me, grabbed my arm and violently twisted it behind my back. I felt a sharp pain in my wrist and shoulder. I felt him kick out at the front door and heard it slam shut. The youth pushed me forward, towards the stairs. I tried to resist but he gave my arm an aggressive jerk, sending a shrieking pain into my shoulder. I screamed out. I became paralysed with fear.

"No, please, let me go, please."

"Be quiet."

As he said this, he pushed the barrel of a gun against my neck and twisted it so it burnt my skin.

My body was wracked with adrenalin and fear.

"We go to your flat," he said in a Spanish accent.

I smelt whiskey. A memory from being pinned to the floor in Covent Garden hit my conscious mind. He relaxed his grip slightly as we walked up stairs. My terror hit a new peak as I thought of Dorothy, innocently knitting in the living room.

"Please, my aunt will be here. Can we talk somewhere else?"

"Open door."

For emphasis he twisted my arm so a new spike of pain drilled through my limb. I found my keys with one hand, but I was trembling so much I dropped them. The man hit me across the back of my head. He relaxed his grip so I could pick them up, before snatching them from my hand and turning the lock. He kicked the door so it flung open and pushed me hard, so I stumbled and crashed into the wall opposite. I heard the door shut. I turned and stood up. He motioned me into the living room with the barrel of his pistol. My eyes locked onto the weapon. Was this to be the instrument of my death?

I walked into the empty living room and stood at the far side facing him.

"Do you know who I am?" His voice sounded shaky.

"I think so. You are Mathew's son. I mean, Ramon's son."

"You very clever. You know why I here?"

"No, no I don't"

"I want to see the woman that Ramon left my mother for."

A drop of blood ran down his chin and he wiped it off with the back of his hand.

"Do you want me to help you with those cuts?"

He ignored my question.

"Now I see you, you are nothing."

He spat on the floor. I tried to calm myself with a conscious breath. I felt the cool air in my nose. I felt my heart and the inner me. I felt the nerve below my eye tighten.

"My mother was a princess, a beauty. Had more love in her finger than you will taste in a lifetime. Why? Why would he leave her for someone like you?"

"He had a few relationships before he met me," I blurted out, hoping it would absolve me. I was in the external world.

His eyes glazed over. Then a new thought seemed to excite him.

"Take your clothes off!"

A new shot of adrenaline kicked in. Fear tightened around my heart.

"What? No! Please!"

"I want to see. Maybe you are so beautiful he could not resist."

"But there were others before."

I used the pause before his response to feel a breath. I looked at the beauty of the daffodils in the vase on the table. I felt a slight softening inside.

"He could have come back. My mother waited every day, every hour for him to return. But instead he was with a whore like you."

He swiped his hand across the table top next to him, sending the vase of daffodils smashing to the floor. He looked up violently, searching for something else to vent his rage on. Then his eyes focussed on me. He pointed the gun at my head. I felt nauseous. The tide of calm I had been slowly cultivating drained away, like a wave receding back to the sea. I was left with a feeling of naked fear. My muscles trembled, my skin tightened and felt the blood drain from my face.

"Take off, now."

I unbuttoned my red coat. I slid it off my shoulders and draped it on the end of the sofa next to me. I bent down and unlaced my black boots. I sat down to pull them off. Mathew's son appeared a little calmer. I tried to feel every detail, the laces, the soft leather, the eyelets.

"And socks."

I felt the skin of my feet as I rolled my socks over the white of my heels. I felt the calloused skin to the side of my heel and the soft skin in the arch of my foot. My breathing slowed and I felt a breath. The outside receded and I was back with my internal self. I felt calmer and safer. I started to trust that I would know what to do.

"Please, let's talk about this. Perhaps I can help."

"Get up," he shouted. The anger was returning.

A wave of fear washed back up my body. My legs shook and I used the sofa to help myself up. My eye was twitching badly.

He looked round and picked up a tall glass with white chrysanthemums. A surge of frustration flooded his face. He tipped the flowers and water onto the floor and then threw the glass at my face. It glanced my ear and smashed against the wall behind me.

"Take off!"

I pulled my knitted sweater over my head and laid it on my coat. I wore a cream vest. The son pointed his gun at my legs.

"*Desnudate*."

I unhooked my belt and unbuttoned my jeans. I slowly wriggled out of them. They clung to my thighs. I fought to get back into the moment. I let my trousers fall to the floor and stepped out of them.

"Ugly. You not close to my mother. Why?"

I didn't know what to say. I felt anything I could say would inflame him further. For a moment I felt myself connect with the inner me again. I sensed my heartbeat and breathing. Some of the anxiety dissolved into an emerging pool of peace. Then the external silence became unbearable.

"I'm very sorry," I stammered.

He lowered his gun and I saw his shoulders drop. Then he shook his head. A drop of blood fell from his eyebrow. He raised his gun again and glared at me.

"Take off," he said quietly this time. He motioned his gun towards my breasts. I lifted my vest over my head and gently laid it over my sweater. I felt exposed and highly vulnerable in my underwear. I felt very aware of my hips. I was back in my bedroom getting undressed, aware of Mathew's critical stare. Now his son had the same expression. I thought about my choice of underwear. My bra was cream, and apart from lacing along the top of the cups it was quite plain. My pink knickers were large and only decorated with white lace. Both were thankfully modest. My eyes settled on his. I tried to see into them.

"I'm sure your mother was much more beautiful than I am. Please, can I dress now?"

"No, turn."

He flicked the barrel of his gun at me. He seemed resigned. The anger had evaporated. Panic seeped back inside me. This is the end, I thought. He's going to shoot me in the back of my head.

"Please, let me talk to you. I think I can explain everything."

His face contorted into dry cracks and creases. Blood dribbled from his lip.

"Turn!" he bellowed.

I turned my back to him. I thought he would ask me to kneel next. I had seen footage of kidnap victims being executed by terrorists. I remembered that Mathew had been shot kneeling. I summoned all my energy to take a conscious breath. I felt the dry carpet under my bare feet. I remembered my dream in Venice. I tried to recapture that feeling that death held no fear for me.

"Take off."

"What?"

"*Todo*. Everything!"

I reached behind, pulled my bra strap down a little and unhooked the clasp. I leant forward slightly and slid the straps down my arms. I put my bra on my vest. Then I slid my knickers down my upper legs and let them fall to my feet.

"Turn."

I turned to face him. Instinctively I put my right arm across my breasts and left hand over my pubic bone. I could feel my skin crawl with goose bumps. My breasts felt soft and fluid against my arm. All my muscles seemed to be shaking.

"Why? I not understand. You nothing."

My eyes watered and I felt a tear slip down my cheek. I willed another conscious breath to wash over me, but I couldn't focus. I felt lost.

"Oh, you cry now, but where were you all those years I heard my mother cry herself to sleep? She died because of you." He spat out those last words, with a deep anguish. "I want to smash you. Why should my mother die poor and you have everything? Why do you have his love and my mother nothing? Because you are a whore."

"He was leaving me and tried to take all our money," I shouted in desperation.

Mathew's son looked at the ground shaking his head. I thought he had heard me this time. I looked into his eyes, I focussed on another breath and tried to return to that ocean of love inside me. I was rocking from one foot to another, like a boat rolling on a stormy sea. Then I took control of myself. I steadied myself and centred myself between my feet. I spread my toes and gripped the carpet, I bent my knees slightly. I began to immerse myself in a warm, pool of light. I could feel strength float up from the depths of my pelvis. The trust returned.

"You are a whore. I treat you like a whore. Lie down."

Mathew's son walked over to me quickly and hit me hard across the side of my face with an open hand. I nearly fell but managed to regain my balance. The side of my face felt numb.

My heart missed a beat. More tears traced the wet streams on my face. My lips quivered. I tried to plead with him but I could not mouth the words. I cried out in my mind, *Lord, why have you forsaken me?*

I felt myself slip emotionally and sobbed as a sense of hopelessness enveloped me. He slapped me on my bottom. I felt the sting. Then he put his hand round my neck. His face screwed up into an insane expression of wrath. I saw him look down at my breasts. Then he pulled me off balance towards him. I thought his face was going to hit mine, but he pushed me back violently sending me sprawling to the floor next to the sofa. I tried to catch my breath. My skin felt wet and clammy.

The man put his gun in his mouth and held it there with his teeth as he released his belt and unzipped his trousers. I tried a desperate lunge at him, hoping to snatch the gun from his mouth. He caught my arm and bent my wrist so I arched in pain. I let my arm go limp and he released it.

I struggled to get back to my right brain. I became aware of the soft, dry carpet under my back and bottom. I moved my fingers gently across the tufts of wool feeling the direction of the pile.

I looked at the ceiling. My eyes focussed on the ceiling rose. I tried to examine every detail of the petal pattern in the moulding. A very slow and faint feeling of warmth soaked up into my heart, like water to a sponge.

The realisation came that whatever I said he could not hear it, he was too attached to his mother's suffering.

I felt him lift my left leg and I looked down. He was kneeling by my feet. He had taken his top off. His trousers and boxers were pulled down. I noticed two large bruises across his ribs. There was a graze across his arm. Then I felt him lying on top of me. His legs were between mine. He rested on his right elbow, leaning against the sofa. My husband's son kept the barrel of his gun against my neck. I could feel him stimulate himself with his other hand. If anyone ever asked me what my worst nightmare was, it was this, being raped.

A feeling of complete resignation flooded over me. My muscles felt limp and heavy. I was drowning in despair, sinking into the depths of hopelessness. Deep inside me was a growing sensation of nothingness, a kind of deep, black void. I felt compelled to the emptiness. Its stillness invited me to embrace it. As the stillness spread I felt empty. The fighting, the resistance, the hope that I could somehow talk him out of it, had dissolved into a sea of acceptance.

Without realising it I had put my hand on my son-in-law's heart. I moved my hand in almost imperceptible circles. I then I reached up and put my other hand behind his head. I tried to feel every short black hair. I felt him enter me with an aggressive thrust.

A tiny spark of light appeared somewhere close to my heart. It grew, shimmering its rays through the blackness that had consumed me, like the sun shining through to the depths of the ocean.

"This is not how you make love," I was surprised to hear the whisper of my own voice. I stroked the back of his head gently. I looked into his watery eyes. Our eyes met. We connected, glimpsing each other's soul. His body became still.

Then he lent down and pressed his lips against mine, forcing his tongue into my mouth, as though he was trying get back to the aggression and violence. I tasted his blood and smelt alcohol.

He lifted his head and looked down at my naked body. "This is not making love," I repeated softly.

He tried moving again. I felt him slip out of me. He reached down.

"This is not how you feel love."

Mathew's child looked into my eyes again. I felt the soft skin of his back with my fingers. My palms felt very hot. I saw tears well up in his eyes and then felt drops splashing on my face. He let go of the gun, brought his hand up and laid it on my breast. Then, the man with so much sadness in his eyes, crumpled and rested his head between my breasts. I held him. I felt connected to myself and to Mathew's little boy. I felt him quietly sobbing. I felt the tears streak across my chest and down the sides of my neck. I felt tears from my own eyes run across my temples.

Between sobs he kept repeating "*Madre, perdóname por favor.*"

We lay in each other's arms crying. I was crying for life, love and salvation. Somehow, I knew he was crying for his mother, the father who abandoned him, the anger, frustration and rage that had become his life. With that realisation my own sobs strengthened. Slowly that natural tide of sadness washed up the beach and then back, leaving us feeling the warmth of each other.

Mathew's child moved so he lay beside me with his arm around my tummy. One of my arms was underneath his neck. His head rested on my shoulder. I bent my elbow so I could rest my hand on his long back. My other hand lay on the arm that embraced me. It could have looked as though we were a pair of lovers that had just finished an intense and satisfying afternoon of lovemaking. Except we weren't. We had been on an extreme, emotional journey together.

I felt paralysed. I could not move or speak. I felt myself tremble as ripples of shock echoed through my body, like the tremors after an earthquake. It was as though my blood sugar had crashed. My peripheral vision flickered. I tried breathing deeply. Time did not exist, I had no idea how much passed before I heard him speak.

"I was not coming here."

"Mmm," was all I could muster.

"I want to hurt you but then think no, I must go home."

"Uh."

"I was watching the house from the bus stop. An old woman came and talked to me."

I felt my attention crystallise.

"Oh."

"I throw my ball against the wall. She talk about the weather and ask me where I go. So I say Highgate. I am not sure but I think bus goes there. Then bus comes and she ask me to help her in so I must get on. She sit next to me. She talk very much. She say she get off and walk back across Hampstead Heath. Did I want to walk with her? I feel good with her, so I say yes."

I felt a spark of life returning.

"Dorothy?"

"*Si*, Dorothy. You know her?"

"My aunt."

Mathew's son shifted his position. He lifted his head from my shoulder and pulled a big cushion off the sofa and put it under my head. He lay next to me with his head on a second cushion. He looked at my chest.

"Sorry, I put blood on you."

I smeared the blood away with the palm of my hand. I reached up to the sofa and pulled the blanket off so I could cover myself. He continued.

"We are walking. She show me plants and talk about a magic hill. We look at her best tree. Then she tell me a long story about a friend, I think Margaret, who had a son. He is named William. The father left when he small. William grew up hating his father. Then he is very angry. His whole life is full of anger. He is so angry at his father when William marries and has a son, he is very angry with his wife and son. She say, William leaves them just like his father did. She ask me if I think William son will grow up to hate his father."

"Then what happened?" I asked softly.

"I thought this is amazing. This old woman comes from nowhere and tell me a story that is me. It was like a message from heaven.

So I think I must go back to Argentina. I want to have my own son one day and love him. She was very kind. When we go to Hampstead she buy me a tea and cake. I think she is like an angel."

"Why did you come back here?" I asked frowning.

"I go to my room. Two friends of Ramon relatives are waiting. At first they are friendly. They give me whiskey. We drink together. They say I must leave UK and go to Spain or Argentina. They say they help me. I say why? I do not like these men. I hate Ramon and his family. I say no, I want to stay. They say they will hurt me if I stay. Now they are rude. I say I leave when I want. The men tell me they will kill me if don't do what they say. We are drinking more and I get mad. They call my mother a peasant. I hit one and they beat me. They laugh and say go home. I am crazy. They say Ramon better with you. You make him happy. They are strong. I cannot get up. One rips my photo of my mother and throw pieces at me. They kick and hit me. Nothing hurts as much as ripping photo. After I get my gun but they gone. I so angry, I come back here and…" a tear tipped over his eyelid. "I very sorry now. I am a very bad person. I kill Ramon and now I hurt you very much, I think."

I turned onto my side to face him.

"What is your name?"

"Mateo."

"Did you send me the letters?"

"*Si.*"

I heard the sound of a key in the door. Mateo tensed. I recognised the sound of Dorothy entering the hall and the gentle closing of the front door. I instinctively covered his body with the blanket. I felt Mateo's muscles tighten.

"It's Dorothy," I tried to reassure him.

Mateo looked mortified. Dorothy walked in.

"Oh, I am sorry. Do you mind if I just go through to the kitchen? I didn't think you would be back yet."

"This is not quite what it must seem. Dorothy, this is Mathew's son, Mateo." My voice sounded shaky.

I noticed Mateo nudge his gun under the sofa.

"Oh yes, we have already met. Would you like some tea?"

All Mateo could say was "Sorry." He kept repeating the word. Whilst Dorothy was in the kitchen we hurriedly dressed as though ashamed of our bodies. I ran over to the daffodils and put them into a third vase. Mateo picked up pieces of broken glass by the wall and put them into a waste paper basket. I felt irrationally guilty. I don't think either of us wanted Dorothy to see the evidence of what had just happened. I don't think we did either. I found the pieces of china from the broken vase and laid them in the bin with the glass shards.

My hands and legs started shaking again. I looked at Mateo. The tension, fear and intensity were back on his face. For a split second I saw an impression of Mateo as a middle-aged man. The resemblance to Mathew was striking.

"Sit here, Mateo."

"I must go."

"Please sit. My aunt is making you tea. You like her."

Mateo looked at me then back at the sofa. I assumed he was wondering whether to take his gun. Dorothy came back in.

"Ah, that is better. Why don't you sit here," Dorothy ushered Mateo to a chair. "And Amanda and I can sit on the sofa."

I could see it was too late for Mateo to leave. His manners obliged him to sit down. He sat rigid on the edge of the chair. Dorothy poured out the tea. She passed the first cup to Mateo.

"Would you like a slice of walnut and banana cake? I made it yesterday."

Mateo opened his mouth but no words came out. He gave a nod. Dorothy sliced the cake, laid it on a plate and passed it to him. Mateo placed in on the table beside him. She served me and then herself. Once the tea ritual was complete she looked Mateo in the eye.

"Now, Mateo, how are you feeling?"

"What you mean?" he said defensively.

"Can you describe how you feel inside?"

"No, I don't feel."

"Are you feeling warm?"

"*Si*, a little."

"Do you feel comfortable?"

Mateo seemed to think Dorothy was talking about the chair and he sat back it bit.

"Yes, it is nice."

Mateo reached into his trouser pocket and pulled out a small yellow ball. He tossed it from one hand to another. It seemed to relax him.

"Are you still feeling angry?"

"Yes, no," and then after a pause. "I not sure."

"How are you feeling about your father?"

"He is a bad man. But same as your story, I am bad too."

"You feel guilty?"

Mateo nodded.

"I have sinned. I ashamed. I feel very much shame for my mother. I do not know if her spirit can forgive."

"She loved your father. Did she forgive him?"

"*Si*. She always love and forgive. I think too much forgive."

"You liked her love?"

"*Si*, very much."

"Better than if she had been angry and bitter and hateful?"

"*Si*, of course."

"Why don't you be loving too?"

Mateo looked down.

"Surely you don't want to spend your life full of hate."

"How do I love?"

"We will show you. For now tell me about the tea."

Dorothy helped Mateo experience the tea and then describe its smell and taste. When he finished his tea she suggested I move, so Mateo could lie on the sofa. She left the room and then came back with her first aid box. I watched her gently dress his wounds. After, she sat next to him and placed her hands on his heart and forehead. Dorothy encouraged him to feel each breath. She closed her eyes and I saw Mateo slowly let go. The tension in his face dissolved and he let his eyelids drop. I remembered Dorothy once saying that there were many ways we could bring about a healing when talking about the person sending me those threats. Although this was not at all the way I would have ever imagined, here she was slowly introducing that possibility to Mateo.

After a while I felt I had to leave the room. I went out into the kitchen. Out of habit I opened the fridge and got out some ingredients for dinner. My mind was well aware of the absurdity of the situation. I had been assaulted and raped by a violent man, and here I was cooking supper for him, whilst he lay with his feet up on the sofa. A flash of anger and indignation inflamed me.

During the attack, I oscillated between my head and heart, the external and internal; now something similar continued whilst I looked through the cupboards for culinary inspiration.

My head told me this is all wrong, we were harbouring a murderer and rapist, his gun was lying under the sofa, I should call the police: in essence do the right thing. By not taking action I was letting my sex down. Men like Mateo, needed to be punished. I was entrenched in that dualistic state Henrique described. Right and wrong, good and bad, separation from Mateo.

My heart felt an emotional bond between us. A bond through which I felt I shared some of the pain, sadness and rage he had lived with for so long. I felt I had touched him in a way that filled me with optimism. He could heal himself, just as I had done. Mateo was so young.

Were my feelings confused by his black hair, deep brown eyes and long nose that so reminded me of Mathew? Was a tiny part of me hoping the man I loved all those years had been resurrected in the form of his son and that we could start with a clean sheet?

Then my mind kicked in again and I thought of all the letters, the attack in Covent Garden, his enthusiasm for violence and I felt unsure. Perhaps it would be better to encourage him to leave and then call the police. Give him a chance to escape. Was my mind just playing out an abstract and taught morality? I heard Henrique reading Wilde's prose. *His sin, if there are such things as sins, are borrowed.* Was I hearing an echo of all those utterances, voiced so definitely and absolutely, by people reading lines about subjects they had never experienced for themselves? What was left if I took all the words out? Right now, it felt like all that would be left, would be changing and confused feelings. What were those feelings? I felt sadness, insecurity and anxiety, mixed up with relief and an appreciation that I was still alive. I also sensed the ebb and flow of feelings of compassion and empathy. Muddled into all this were the subtle and distant hints of love and affection, delicately dyeing my water with their beautiful imprints.

Dorothy walked in and closed the door quietly behind her.

"He is sleeping. Are you alright, Amanda? What happened?"

We sat on her wooden kitchen chairs. In my telling of the events, emotions returned and I started crying again. My body sagged. Dorothy comforted me whilst I rested and then I continued. When I finished Dorothy looked pale and shocked. I had not seen her like that before.

"I just don't understand it. When I left him in Hampstead, he seemed so peaceful. Today I went to have lunch with Henrique and then on impulse we went to the Royal Academy of Art. I wished I had come home straight away. How stupid of me."

"I think it was just as well you didn't. He was so angry, so out of control, anything could have happened."

I told her how Mathew's relatives attacked him and how their threats enraged him to defy them. I explained how, fuelled with alcohol, Mateo went back to his original plan. I noticed how my telling of it was almost apologetic for Mateo. I was giving him some kind of justification for what he did. Did I blame myself for going to Barcelona and getting Mathew's relations involve?

"What would you like to do?"

I told Dorothy about the way my feelings kept changing. We agreed to wait and see how I felt after dinner.

"You know, my dear, there might be an opportunity for you to find a much deeper healing for yourself here. You might find a new understanding of Mathew. You might free yourself of some of your feelings about your marriage."

Dorothy helped me for a while and then went back into the living room to sit with Mateo. When I went in to tell them dinner was ready, Dorothy was sitting in a chair knitting, whilst Mateo slept. Dorothy woke him gently. He looked startled and I could see him take some time to orientate himself.

We sat around the kitchen table and ate our food. Dorothy complimented me on the meal. Mateo joined in awkwardly. After some small talk Dorothy turned to Mateo.

"Why after all this time did you now decide to come to England to find your father?"

"My mother die of cancer in the summer. I am very sad. I become very angry. I say she die of broken heart. She always missed Ramon. She say he will come back before she die. But no, he doesn't. I say I will revenge her death. I will kill the man who did this. So I borrow money for ticket. When I arrive I meet a friend from my mother's family. It take me a long time to find a gun. With my gun I go to Ramon and shoot him."

"And you wanted his watch and photographs as some kind of memento?" my aunt enquired.

"*Si*, I want to take and put on mother's grave, to bring him back to her. But when I look at photographs all I see is new wife. Every picture. Nothing of me, my mother, nothing."

"It was an album Mathew made especially for our wedding anniversary," I mumbled. "But you are right, I never saw any pictures of you or your mother. He did not mention you and it was only when I went to Barcelona that I found out you existed."

Mateo winced slightly when I mentioned Barcelona.

"You saw his family?"

"Yes, we knew he met Veronica in Bar Fornos in Barcelona."

"And why did you send Amanda those letters?"

Mateo looked up at me.

"I am sorry now. I felt very angry. I see you happy with Ramon. I see you wearing nice dresses, going to expensive places, and laughing together. My poor mother died with nothing but debts. So now I could not hurt Ramon anymore, I want to hurt you."

With Dorothy's questioning we discovered that Mateo worked at a stall in Camden Lock market and shared a room in Kentish town.

After dinner we cleared up and took cups of camomile tea into the living room. We took up the same seats. Dorothy wanted to know why he stopped sending the threats.

"I was sad for a time. Later I feel better. I have job and a room. I meet this girl. We have a good time together. I like her and I think she likes me. She is quite short and very funny. We laugh a lot. So I think I must stop following you."

"What happened to her?"

"She left me."

"How did you follow me?"

"I took one of your cards by the door. Then I try your email address at Hotmail. I knew Ramon changed his name to Mathew so I tried 'mathew' as the password and it worked first time. Easy. Then I check your emails."

"So that is how you knew Amanda would be in Covent Garden."

"*Si*."

"Why did you attack her?"

"When I read the email it was nearly too late. I had to run to the station. I don't know what I do but I want to be there. I want to see Edward. I think you are a…" Mateo looked down. "Is not important. I have a small bottle of whiskey my friend give me in my pocket. I drink on train. I know you have cameras everywhere. So I put on black hat and sunglasses. I see big coat in pub and take it. Now camera does not see me."

"Why so violent?" Dorothy asked.

Mateo turned to me.

"I think I will make you very scared. I not mean to shoot. That is accident. Once I start I get crazy. I so sorry. After I worry my mother spirit will know and feel shame."

Dorothy put down her knitting and looked up.

"Well, we must consider what to do next. You can leave and we may call the police or you can stay the night and we can explore this more tomorrow. I think it needs to be Amanda's choice. She must feel comfortable with whatever we agree on."

They both looked at me. I could see fear in Mateo's wide eyes. Dorothy's eyes looked gentle and kind. I focussed on my senses for a moment. My thoughts receded.

"I would be comfortable with you staying tonight, Mateo. You will have to sleep on the sofa. There is more I would like to know from you. When you are ready, I want to hear more about life in Argentina and what you can remember of your father before he left. You will need to give Dorothy your gun."

After a long shower, I lay in my bed, rested my head on my clean white cotton pillow and closed my eyes. I though how I did not want to be a victim. I wanted to continue my journey forwards in life. I could feel a pull towards helplessness; needing sympathy, compassion and condolences from the outside. It felt like an old addiction that might return. I wondered what it would be like going to court. How would I cope with a smart lawyer accusing me of enticing Mateo, of inviting him in, undressing in front of him or whatever his defence counsel would conjure up to discredit me.

I considered Mathew. His own son had murdered him. The correct action would be to hand Mateo over to the law. What would Mathew want? Did Mathew feel any shame or responsibility for his actions?

I noticed how analytical I became and meditated. After, I considered how a small part of me felt motherly towards Mateo. This led me to remember Oedipus, the Ancient Greek myth of a man who killed his father so he could make love to his mother. I hoped my scenario would play out to a happier ending. I sighed and said, "Hey ho, life's a box of chocolates," out loud. I smiled as I thought of the drama my mother would have made of my experiences. How easy it would be to slip back into the echo of her morality.

BUTTERFLY

CHAPTER 27

When the butterfly is ready to hatch out of its chrysalis, it releases hormones to soften the shell. The butterfly will push its way out of the chrysalis and cling to the chrysalis with its wings hanging down.

The butterfly will be unable to fly for several hours as it pumps fluid from its body into its crumpled wings to harden them. Then the butterfly will be ready for its first flight. The caterpillar has now turned into a butterfly.

In the morning I woke early. The house was silent and still. I turned on the bedside light, sat up in bed and picked up my writing pad. I shut my eyes and meditated until the impulse came.

I walk along a stony path, holding my father's warm hand. The clouds blow across the night sky and the moon reveals herself. She is full, bright and shining. I can see the contours across her face. I look up at my father. He is looking at her too.

We turn off the track into a meadow of fresh grass. I can feel the moist soil, soft beneath my sandals. My father stops by a small oak and touches the new shoots at the end of a branch.

I want to run, so I pull him forwards. He trots beside me. I feel his strength. We run through a small wood and then I see the flames through the trees. As we get near I can see a shower of sparks fly high into the air.

We walk into the opening and I see so many people. My father talks to a man dressed in red fabric with a long stick. I feel excited. I see my friend on the other side of the fire. Her face lights up with an orange glow. I let my hand slip from my father's and run round. She runs screaming. I chase her into the darkness.

We fall giggling. I look back at the fire. I can still see my father. He is with a group of people. He is talking. I love to watch my father when he cannot see me.

I like to run away, almost as far as I can, then run back, fast and jump so he catches me. The girl chases me round the fire and then I run up to my father and into his arms. He gives me an apple and I run to a big root. I sit and eat.

Now we are quiet. We all hold hands and stand looking up at the moon. I can feel a stone under my foot and roll it back and forth. My father stands on a fallen tree trunk and talks. People gather around him. He rests his hand on an old man. I run with my friend. We hide in the dark. We see women take food out from the ashes of the fire. We run back to feast. I like to watch and imitate. I want to dance like the woman near the twisted old tree.

We eat for a long time. Now I feel sleepy. My father makes a bed with leaves and grasses. He lays me down. Later I wake as he lifts me. I look into his eyes and he kisses me. On his shoulders I feel the rhythm of his pace. My fingers run through his hair. I kiss the top of his head. He is love.

I put the paper on my bedside table, slid down under my covers and shut my eyes. I tried to resist analysing the writing and just be aware of my emotions. There was a yearning inside me for something that was missing. Was it the love? I thought of my father and the love I felt from him. I wondered how Mateo felt growing up without that love in his life.

I could hear Dorothy padding around the flat. This was followed by the sound of her talking to Mateo. Had I forgiven him? How would I know? Was forgiveness a moral judgement or something I would feel? The more I understood Mateo the greater the empathy between us. Once I'd dressed, I walked out into the living room. I could hear Dorothy and Mateo in the kitchen. I heard Dorothy speak.

"Yes, I would like a cup of peppermint tea, please."

Then I heard Mateo repeat it twice. I smiled to myself. Dorothy would have plenty to occupy herself. I joined them for breakfast. Mateo stood up and kissed me on both cheeks. I felt slightly uncomfortable. We said "Good morning," and sat down. Dorothy looked at me.

"Did you try your writing today?"

"Yes. It was another unusual piece."

"Could you read it to us?"

I brought back the sheet of paper and read it to them. Mateo spoke.

"Did you have a father like this, Amanda?"

"Not quite."

"I want to know how life is with a father. I think woman can find father again with husband. Perhaps you find such a man."

Was that the missing piece? I felt myself blush. Mateo looked away.

After breakfast we sat in the living room and Mateo told us about his life in Argentina. He had the ball in his hand again. Sometimes he tossed it high in the air so that, without any movement, it fell into his other hand. He grew up in Buenos Aries, in a small apartment. He remembered his father playing the guitar and singing. He thinks he worked in an art gallery or museum. It was an office job but he did not know what he did. He could not remember them arguing. His memories were of an idyllic family.

Then when he was about five he came home one day and found his mother crying on her bed. She would not say why. Ramon did not return that night. After several days he still did not come home. Then Mateo noticed his guitar had gone. His mother told him his father had left. She told him not to worry and that he would be back soon.

They waited and then Mateo's mother became afraid that the military junta had taken him. She queued for information with mothers and wives at the end of the Dirty War but nothing came. Many men had disappeared. Sometimes just a rumour of being communist was enough. Every night they prayed for him.

After a year or more, Mateo came home and found his mother with her head in her hands. Next to her was a letter. He could not read many of the words, but he did recognise Barcelona. It was his favourite European football team. Later his mother told him his father was safe in Spain. He wanted to know when he would come back, but this made his mother cry again. When she calmed herself, Mateo said he wanted them to go to Barcelona. His mother said it would be too difficult. Mateo asked his mother to write a letter from him to his father but no replies came. His mother said the letter must have been lost in transit. Later she told him that Ramon was with someone else.

Mateo dreamt of living in Barcelona. Every time he had a challenge in life, the solution was to move to Barcelona. He could not believe that once they got there, that his father would not want to be with them. As he grew older he wrote so many letters pleading for his father to take them to him. He begged his mother to move there. His mother told him they did not have enough money, that they needed connections for a visa and ultimately she did not want to live in a city where her Ramon was with another woman.

When Mateo became a teenager he heard stories about his father. At first he could not believe it. His uncle on his mother's side confirmed that Ramon had an affair with a singer. He had promised his mother it was all over but the uncle never trusted Ramon. As the years passed he grew to hate his father. Then they heard he had married a rich English woman and moved to England. With this news his mother gave up. She lost weight, aged and eventually became ill with breast cancer. Mateo watched her die for seven years. She wanted to live long enough to see Mateo go to university. He studied literature and completed his military service.

Then a year ago at the beginning of spring his mother's health worsened. He nursed her through to summer until she died. Mateo swore on his mother's still-warm body that he would avenge her death. All he knew was that Ramon married Veronica Blake and moved near to London around ten years ago. He borrowed the money for a plane ticket and flew to London. He worked in cafés and kept asking people how to find a record of marriages. Finally the manager of a café in Soho steered him to the records office in Holborn. From there he found that they divorced five years later and that now his father's name was Mathew Blake. More searching revealed that Mathew Blake was now married to Amanda Birch and he traced them to a house in Tewin near Welwyn Garden City. Mateo said he took the gun but he had not decided whether to scare him or kill him.

When he knocked on his father's door in Tewin, Mathew did not recognise him. Mateo took his gun out and Mathew thought he was being robbed. He denied he had ever lived in Argentina. He swore he had no Spanish wife or any child. Mateo showed Mathew a picture of him with his wife and son shortly before leaving Buenos Aries. Mathew's face gave away his lies. That's when Mateo knew he would pull the trigger. Whilst his father knelt on the carpet pleading for his life, Mateo took a pillow from the sofa, held it in front of his gun to muffle the shot and sent his father to finally join his mother.

"It was so slow. Like slow motion film."

"Like a slow motion film," Dorothy corrected him.

"*Si*, like a slow motion film."

"So he was married to your mother all the time," Dorothy mused.

It took me a while to take in Mateo's story.

"Perhaps you could tell Mateo everything you know, Amanda."

I told him about Ramon living in Barcelona with Montserrat and how he left her after a few years for Veronica. They came to England and married.

"He changed his name to Mathew, I suppose after you," I added looking at Mateo.

I continued, describing how Mathew divorced Veronica and had a relationship with a woman called Clare, who later died of cancer. It struck me that so many of Mathew's lovers had become ill. I told Mateo how Mathew and I met at tango classes. I described how we married and lived in Tewin. I kept my description factual and avoided describing Mathew as a husband.

I explained how after he was shot I found that he had taken out large loans against our home, whilst drawing out cash every Monday.

"Where is this money?" Mateo asked.

"It is all missing. I think he was about to leave me and had secretly moved the money so that he would not have to split it with me. It was essentially my money. I had inherited it after my mother died."

"Why don't you find it?" Mateo asked.

"I got some of it back from the building society and I'm not sure I really care anymore."

Mateo looked surprised.

"But it is your money."

"I wouldn't know where to start."

Dorothy put her knitting down.

"You have the name on that card you found. If I was looking, I think I would try the blues club he played at. From your description of what Rosa told you in Barcelona, that might be where he would meet someone new."

After breakfast we walked across Hampstead Heath to Kenwood House. Mateo demonstrated an impressive ability to throw his ball against a tree trunk in a way that it bounced back into his waiting open hand. Dorothy continued her theme, speaking softly.

"I wonder what would have happened if you had tried to understand your father rather than judge him."

"He do same things anyway."

"He might. The difference would be your reaction to him. You may not agree with his actions, or support them, but if you can try to understand them I suspect you would feel different. Maybe you would be better able to enjoy some aspects of your father rather than be so upset with the qualities you don't like."

"When I see what he does to my mother, this is not easy."

Dorothy stopped and put her hand on Mateo's shoulder.

"In my limited experience, we can only live our own lives. Your mother lived hers in a certain way. She chose to marry your father. She found qualities in him she could love. As you say she forgave many things. And ultimately she chose to wait for your father to return. Did she ask you to kill him when she died?"

"No."

I could see Mateo's face redden, his lower lip quiver and tears start to roll down his cheek.

"You can only live your life, Mateo. In your life you can choose. You can choose to judge or understand, you can choose to love or hate, you can choose to embrace or separate."

"So, maybe I try to understand my father?"

"I would not say you should. All I am saying is that your life may be different if you do. You may develop yourself differently through the challenge of trying to understand your father and out of that you will be different."

"You think I made big mistake. Maybe you are right."

Mateo wiped the tears from his face.

"It does not matter what I think. There are two things you can think about for yourself. The first is that we are creatures of habit. If you spent all this time hating your father and feeling resentful, then out of habit there is a risk that you will transfer that behaviour onto someone else; like you did with Amanda. Like poor William did with his family."

"*Si*, I understand."

Mateo threw his ball hard against a silver birch and was ready for the rebound with his hand held high above his head.

"The second thought is that it is not too late. You can still try to understand your father. You can still learn about him. You can talk to Amanda, Veronica and his relations in Barcelona. You can appreciate the whole man. Some things you might admire and respect, others not. Rather than focus on a few parts, embrace him as a complete person. Remember he was a baby once, strived for his mother's attention, went through all his childhood challenges, coped with the struggles of becoming a teenager and became a man. What of his failures, disappointments and regrets?"

I felt this also carried a message for me. I had recently been focussed on all the things I disliked the most about Mathew. It made it easier for me to distance myself from him and his actions.

"Mateo, we could do some of this together if you like. I have been feeling very negative about Mathew for a while."

"*Si*, I think I will need very much help. This is not easy, what you ask."

Mateo bounced his ball on the ground.

"I think I will need a lot of help. You ask me to do something that is not easy," Dorothy said emphasising the missing words.

Mateo repeated the sentence three times.

"A practical step would be to commit to resolving this peacefully, and send your gun to the police," Dorothy said.

At home, Mateo wore some yellow washing up gloves and cleaned the gun. I found the address of a police station in Manchester and Mateo posted it from a post box in a residential street at the end of the Jubilee Line, where I hoped there would be no cameras.

The three of us agreed that Mateo could stay another night. That evening he walked to his bedsit to change and bring his wash bag. I wondered whether he would return but he arrived a few hours later wearing a more colourful maroon top and beige trousers.

I decided to take one day at a time. If I felt I could develop myself and the feeling of love inside me whilst Mateo was with us, I would continue. If his presence made it harder to be myself, then I would ask him to leave. I still felt unresolved about Mathew's murder and whether I should let a judge and jury decide Mateo's fate. At the same time my desire to hand him over was weakening.

I emailed Francesc to tell him I had met up with Mateo and that everything is now fine. I thanked him for his help and said that I might bring Mateo to Barcelona one day so he could get to know more of his father's relations. Francesc replied within minutes to say he would forward my email to Josep and Rosa. I hoped this would prevent any further violence between Mateo and Mathew's relations.

Mateo wanted to pursue Dorothy's suggestion that we might find out more about Cristelle by visiting the blues club Mathew played at. I felt some resistance but accepted it would continue our understanding Mathew. I remembered the blues club was in Charlotte Street, London. I found it on the internet and noted that Wednesday was the jam night.

When the time came, Mateo and I took the tube to Goodge Street and found the club. The club had a long bar to the right with a seating area and stage at the back. There was a mezzanine floor above. Mateo wanted a lager and I ordered a sparkling water. We took our drinks upstairs and Mateo found a table at the front.

I learnt Mateo was twenty-one, fifteen years younger than me. I was just old enough to be his mother.

Different musician came and went playing a variety of blues songs. There were a few slow ballads and plenty of faster twelve-bar rhythms. Couples at the front were having fun jiving together.

I leant forward when I recognised the bearded, longhaired man who came to Mathew's funeral, get up on stage. He slung his maroon guitar over his shoulder and when the musicians were ready sung a couple of songs. As soon as they finished Mateo and I walked towards the stage. We intercepted him on his way to the bar.

"Excuse me, I'm Amanda, Mathew Blake's wife. We met at his funeral."

The man looked surprised and then smiled, as he finally recognised me.

"Can we talk?"

I introduced Mateo and bought him a beer. I led him back to our table. I asked him to describe Mathew's playing to Mateo. Jeff extolled about his style of play and his ability to improvise using a variety of scales. According to Jeff he was one of the highlights of any evening. Mateo listened intently.

"You can see Mathew on YouTube." He wrote out the words to search under and gave the paper to Mateo.

I waited until a certain level of friendship had been established and then moved onto the subject of Cristelle. I took a deep breath.

"Jeff, Mathew told me a about a friend he met here called Cristelle. I was hoping to see her here. I need to give her some information. Can you help?"

I saw Jeff retract slightly.

"Cristelle used to sing. Pretty good. She left around the summer. Does she know about Mathew's passing?"

"No, I don't think so. Do you know how I can contact her?"

Jeff shrugged.

"You could see if she is on the club's mailing list."

"Did she ever mention where she was from?"

"No, but I once heard her talk to Mathew about jazz clubs in Zurich."

Mateo fidgeted with his yellow ball.

I asked someone from the club about the mailing list. I got the answer I expected. The Data Protection Act prevented them from giving me any information. Mateo had been quiet and said very little on the way home.

In the morning I described the evening to Dorothy.

"I wonder how many jazz or blues singers there are in Zurich called Cristelle?" she asked.

Later I went with Mateo to the café and tried searching for Cristelle, jazz clubs and Zurich. Nothing specific to a person called Cristelle came up but I did find a list of jazz clubs. I wrote out their names and phone numbers. Then we found Mathew playing on YouTube and watched the five minute clip. It felt weird seeing Mathew up on stage singing. His guitar playing sounded impressive to me. I glanced across to Mateo. His face was solemn and did not reveal anything. I looked for clips using the name Cristelle but nothing came up. Our teas arrived and I put my laptop away. I looked up at Mateo.

"So, how are you feeling?"

"Bad."

"What is it?"

"I feel bad about Ramon, bad about you and I miss my mother."

"I had a really bad time after Mathew died. It just kept getting worse. I felt very frightened by your letters. After a while I did not have a home, so I went on the run and ended up at Dorothy's. Even that was not easy at first. She and her friends had some very challenging ideas. Slowly I healed myself and even after being attacked by you twice I feel stronger inside. I feel that I am now in a better place than before Mathew died."

Mateo gave me a half smile.

"Right now, you and Dorothy are all I have."

I felt a lump in my throat and felt my eyes water. I patted his hand and smiled reassuringly.

CHAPTER 28

A week had passed since Mateo attacked me. The residual trauma of being raped tempered the relief that I was no longer being hunted. The last nine months had come to a resolution and I felt free. I began to think more about what I would like to do with my life. I could now spread my wings and take off. Perhaps I had finally become that metaphorical butterfly. I mentioned it to Dorothy, whilst we were knitting.

"Nine months," she mused.

I knew to wait and see where this took her.

"Nine lunar cycles for you evolve from conception to birth. Nine lunar cycles for you to transform yourself into this beautiful, sentient being."

"It does feel like a natural cycle, Mathew died in the autumn, I suffered my biggest lows in the winter and here I am beginning to blossom in the spring."

Mateo came to visit us almost daily. He might come round after work for tea or for dinner in the evening. In a way we felt like a little family. My aunt and Mathew's son: entwined on this part of our journey together.

One day, I impulsively rented a car and drove Mateo out to the meadow where I had buried Mathew's ashes. I led him along the same path I had walked with Mathew when he was dead and alive. It was sunny and warm. Tall lush grass, daffodils and dandelions created a mottled green and yellow canvas. Bluebells grew round the oak tree.

I stood in front of the spot where I had buried Mathew's ashes and just stared. Mateo stood respectfully by my side. I suddenly realised I had taken his hand in mine. I self-consciously let go and used it to pull my hair back. I squatted down and turned to Mateo.

"This is the exact place I buried your father's ashes."

Mateo dropped to his knees next to me. His form was uncannily similar to Mathew's, the day he proposed to me in this very spot.

A bumblebee danced around the flowers and buzzed passed my ear. Then a black, orange and white red admiral butterfly fluttered its wings, passing between Mateo and me. It appeared again and rested on a daffodil.

The extraordinary thought occurred to me, that Mateo had killed the caterpillar that was my old life. Mathew's death had forced me to escape into my cocoon, Dorothy's flat, to emerge after a long and painful transformation, free from my old limitations. I thought I could see myself in that beautiful butterfly, spreading her wings, enjoying a new life that, I suppose, could never have been imagined in her previous incarnation.

I turned and looked at Mateo. He stared solemnly at the ground, with his hands on his knees. I wondered how he was coping. He had witnessed so much for someone so young. Had he come to terms with his actions? Could he transform himself? I felt a wave of compassion. I held out my hand.

"Help me up, please."

We walked back towards the car. This time I left my hand in his.

When we returned, Dorothy announced that she had arranged another meeting that evening. Mateo quickly said he was seeing a friend and left. I helped Dorothy prepare and we waited for Nirmal, Henrique and Sandy to arrive.

At the beginning Dorothy invited me to tell my story. I found it very hard. I felt exposed. Perhaps part of me felt I was being judged. That other people would think I led Mateo on or somehow attracted his attack on some kind of spiritual level. I didn't want to be tainted by that event and certainly not be remembered as the woman who was raped. I did not want to paint myself as a victim. I also recognised that I had not really talked about it.

As I spoke I felt strangely remote. It was as though I was describing a film. In fact I was disconnected from my feelings. My memory was mechanical, robotic and frozen. I think it was my way of detaching from the horror and terror I had experienced. I felt a surge of resentment towards Mateo.

After, there was a painfully long silence. I felt like leaving the room. Sandy was the first to speak.

"How do you feel now, Amanda?"

I took a deep breath.

"I feel disconnected from my body. Some parts feel very distant."

Sandy looked into my eyes for a while before speaking.

"Would it help if we talked about those distant parts? Would you like to try and reconnect?"

I nodded cautiously.

Sandy took me on a journey, where I felt each part of my body and described it to her. After a rest, Sandy helped me describe each part of the rape. This time I tried to describe how each part of my body felt. Sandy kept asking me which place felt painful and what that part needed.

In the morning I phoned the jazz clubs in Zurich. One receptionist did know of a Cristelle Tschopp. She had sung there last month. She was due to sing again on the second Wednesday in May. They would not give me her contact details. I went to the café and tried searching for her on the internet. I could only find her listed on the billing of the club I had phoned.

I told Mateo of this news when he came round for tea after his shift at the stall. He insisted we see her.

"Is this all about the money, Mateo?" I asked.

"Not all. But maybe the man who took so much from so many gives it back in death. It is your money, Amanda. Anyway don't you want to find if Ramon was leaving you for this woman?"

"I am trying to develop myself from within. I don't want to be defined by Mathew, by how much money I have lost or a sense of injustice. If I did I would have hated you and called the police. I enjoy being able to feel love when I am with you. For me that is more important than anything Mathew did or didn't do. Trying to find Cristelle may just distract us with the external."

I could see Mateo wasn't convinced. Cleverly he tried another tack.

"Why not go on a little holiday together? Dorothy can come too if she likes. I have not been to Zurich. I like jazz a little. You could teach me more about love. I can discover more about my father."

I laughed.

"Go and sort out a visa."

A few days later Sergeant Smiley phoned to say that the gun that killed Mathew and was used against me had been returned. My heart raced as I asked whether it provided any more clues.

"No, it was wiped clean and sent to a police station in Manchester. Have you had any more letters?"

"No."

"Good."

After, I realised I was not going to tell the police about Mateo. I experienced a shot of guilt. I felt ashamed and for a moment disconnected from society. I was committing a sin and breaking the law. I sat paralysed for a while. Then I felt a rush of anger towards Mateo. Dorothy padded into the living room with her knitting.

"Despite all my efforts, I feel this incredible rage against Mateo right now."

Dorothy looked at me quizzically.

"I am glad. There may be lots of suppressed emotions that will surface. Just be kind to yourself, sensitive to the emotion and kiss them on their way."

My initial reaction was to feel irritated with Dorothy. She smiled.

"Loving Mateo is not leading to any kind of prize. Do you need to set yourself up with these challenges?"

"But you said it would lead to a greater healing."

Dorothy laughed.

"Goodness, did I say that? Don't pay any attention to me, darling."

I sat with my arms folded, grumpily tapping my foot, whilst Dorothy started her knitting. After a while she looked up.

"I suppose when we are in dialogue we respond to each other. It is a dialectic process that has a life of its own, rather than be exactly what either person would have thought by themselves."

Later I told about Mateo's desire to fly to Zurich.

"I think that is a splendid idea. Yes, do travel and explore. I would be happy to help you both with the tickets."

CHAPTER 29

Henry called in the morning to ask me out for dinner. I had missed him. He came round at seven. We kissed and hugged before walking to a local Greek restaurant. I didn't feel comfortable telling Henry about Mateo attacking me, but I did tell him Mathew's son from Argentina had been staying with us.

"Cool," was Henry's response.

I told Henry about Henrique's ideas as he ate.

"What do you think?"

I waited for Henry to finish chewing. I did not have to wait long; he soon swallowed. I imagined his long neck was that of a snake gulping down a huge ball of matted chickpeas and flour. I put my hand on Henry's arm, to prevent him taking another mouthful.

"Neat. Awesome ideas. If there is no self, no choice and we are all part of the universe, what's there to worry about," he reasoned.

Whilst I thought of a response Henry filled his mouth. I felt myself become irritated. Why was Henry such a challenge for me? I tried to relax but found myself unable to restrain myself as he loaded up another slice of pita.

"Henry, just as an exercise, why don't you try to eat slowly. Savour every mouthful."

"Wow, you really have a thing about food. It seems every time we eat together, you get on my case about it."

Here I was nagging, criticising and imposing my views on Henry. Why did I have this need around him? Then a surprising thought occurred to me. Was it because I had feelings for him? Was I trying to mould him into someone that would be more attractive to me? I remembered the teenagers in the café when I was with Joan Pride. Would this be the pattern of any relationship Henry and I could have?

"I'm sorry, Henry. It's my problem. Can you forgive me?"

Henry laughed.

"Sure, it's cool."

I managed to laugh through the site of Henry forcing a whole falafel down his throat. We were, after all, simply a collection of particles and photons flowing through the universe.

"You know, Henry, I felt very close to you in Venice. I miss that."

This time Henry did stop with his fork halfway between his mouth and plate. He looked up to my eyes. I continued.

"When we slept next to each other, I felt secure. It was really weird after Mathew, and being on my own for so long, but I liked it."

Henry put his fork down and smiled. I thought he might say 'Cool' but he surprised me.

"Yes, there was a magic in Venice. I felt it too."

After dinner we walked home. Henry put his arm round me so his hand rested on my shoulder as we entered our street. I put mine around Henry's waist. I felt our bodies rubbing against each other.

When we arrived at Dorothy's door, I thanked Henry and gave him a kiss. I had to stand on my toes and pull his head down to reach his cheek. Henry put his arms round me, bent his knees, held me tight and picked me up. My cheek rubbed against his. I bent my head and kissed his neck slowly. I smelt a slightly sweet scent on his skin. Then we kissed each other on the lips. Our tongues slowly met and explored each other for a moment.

When Henry put me down, I suddenly felt flustered. I did not know what to do next. Part of me wanted to cuddle up to Henry and another wanted to be home on my own. I still felt insecure about physical contact after Mateo's attack.

"Thank you so much for such a lovely evening. I really enjoyed it. Good night," I said hurriedly.

I turned and retreated to Dorothy's flat. Later I lay on my bed still feeling the imprints of Henry's arms around me and his lips on mine.

My next social encounter was with Ruby. It was a sunny day so we arranged to walk through Primrose Hill and into Regent's Park. Ruby was in a negative mood.

"I've tried your 'living in the moment' philosophy and it doesn't work. Bill is still ruining my life however I choose to perceive it. I can't let him do this to the children. There is no use pretending everything is fine when it isn't. I'm sorry, Amanda, but I need to say it as it is."

I was just about to explain to her that she could be different when I thought about my challenge with Henry last night. If I found it so hard to accept Henry's eating habits, how would I cope with a husband and the father of my children behaving in ways I did not like?

As we walked under the trees in Regent's Park I had an urge to tell her about Mateo.

"Ruby, would it be possible to tell you something that might be shocking, and for you to just listen without making comments or creating a drama?"

"Well, now you have told me this much you must know I am intrigued, and you know what a drama queen I am. But sure, I'll try just listening."

We sat on a park bench and I told her the whole story. I found it very difficult to describe the attack, but persevered. I thought she would be appalled that I had not contacted the police, and worse, was now friendly with Mateo. I was even planning a trip to Zurich with him. I dreaded her reaction. My voice trembled as I spoke. At times I had to stop. My voice sounded thin and wavering as I told her how Mateo had shot Mathew. Eventually, tears began to fall and I could not continue.

Ruby looked at me with huge eyes and an open mouth. She put her arms around me and kept her word, she said nothing. When my weeping subsided, we got up and continued our walk.

"Talking to you was very difficult for me, but now it feels like a huge release. Despite how I seem, I feel a bit better."

"Thank you for trusting in me. You know me too well not to realise I have a zillion thoughts and questions, but I will respect your wishes and never mention it again unless you want me to."

"Oh Ruby, that was the kindest thing you could have said right now."

CHAPTER 30

Mateo's visa arrived and I booked cheap tickets to Zurich. I found a hotel near the blues club Cristelle would be singing at.

After an early flight to Zurich, Mateo and I walked through corridors, passport control, baggage claim, customs, retail and down to the train platform. I could see Mateo enjoyed the hard, flat, clean surfaces to bounce his ball. A short train journey took us to Zurich's main station.

The hotel was clean and tidy. We had rooms next to each other on the third floor. During the late afternoon, we walked through Zurich, stepping through the long shadows until we found the club. It was part of a jazz school.

We then looked for somewhere to eat. During dinner I tried to explain Herr Huber's theories to Mateo. He listened intently whilst looking a little sceptical.

"You are saying that we are made of the universe and so we know it. We just have to listen and we hear it."

"Yes, just embrace those moments of stillness. Try to be nothing for a moment."

"Maybe I will try," he said with an amused smile.

"How are you feeling about your father?"

"Suspicious. I think maybe he did want to take money and move here."

"And how do you feel about that?"

"I am angry. Sad he is a bad man. I don't want his blood."

"Dorothy's friend Nirmal thinks we each come to this world with our own soul. He told me that we live our own life and make our own choices. I hope you will live your own life and do all the things you came here for rather than get distracted by your father."

Mateo held my eyes in a soft gaze.

"I will try and do as you say."

It felt as though Mateo really heard me and that I sensed his emotions respond. In that moment I felt incredibly connected. I wanted to hold him to me. The waiter coming to take our order broke the spell.

After we had eaten we walked back to the club and found a table near the stage. Cristelle sang her set. She had a deep luxurious voice that oozed sensuality. Her body-hugging dress accentuated every move. She looked slim whilst being curvy. Her deep black, wavy hair fell around her shoulders. Each time she moved her head, her shiny hair fanned out before taking on a new shape. I imagined most men would find her attractive, including Mathew.

I tried to relax and watch Cristelle, but a restless sense of anticipation gnawed away inside me. What would I say? How would Cristelle react?

As she sung her last number, I wrote a note requesting she meet us for news about Mathew. When she took her final bow, Mateo walked to the stage and handed it to her. I watched him point me out and I gave her friendly wave. Cristelle looked back impassively.

After about twenty minutes I saw Cristelle weave her way past the tables and chairs, having changed into a black sweatshirt and jeans. She fitted in with the crowd. Her journey was interrupted to shake members of the audience's hands and exchange greetings. I noticed her flick her hair back with a jerk of her head.

When she reached our table, her smile evaporated and her face took on a colder, granite tone.

"So, you want to talk about Mathew."

"Yes, please sit down. Would you like a drink?"

Cristelle shook her head and sat.

"I am Amanda, Mathew's wife and this is Mateo, his son."

Cristelle's lips paled.

"Mathew did not mention he had a son."

"He didn't tell me either."

I gave Mateo's forearm a reassuring stroke.

"And how can I help you?"

"I assume you know he died nine months ago."

Cristelle nodded and, I thought, winced slightly.

"I understand you were close."

"We shared some very beautiful times together."

"Cristelle, we are not here to judge you, or Mathew. I am certainly not interested in accusing you of anything, but it would help us both to find out a little more about what happened to Mathew. Can you talk freely?"

Cristelle shrugged. Strands of hair became stuck to her lips. She brushed the hairs to one side.

"Let me come straight to the point. Was Mathew planning to move here?"

Cristelle's eyes gave it away. They flitted between Mateo and myself and then down. Mateo clenched his fist. I continued without waiting for a verbal answer.

"So, yes, he was leaving."

I put my hand over Mateo's fist and looked into his eyes reassuringly. Then I turned to Cristelle.

"I am very sorry it did not work out. I imagine it was very distressing for you waiting here and then finding out he died."

Cristelle looked up at my eyes.

"Murdered," she hissed.

I sensed Mateo tense and began talking immediately to cover any signals he might unwittingly give out.

"In the process of trying to find his killer, I found out a lot more about Mathew's past. I found out a lot more about the women in his life."

I thought Cristelle blushed.

"I think a lot of the women felt sad for a long time as a result of being with Mathew. Of course, it was always fun at the beginning. Maybe you feel sad too."

Cristelle stared blankly.

"Don't concern yourself with me."

I did not feel confident in asking her any more. The background music and chatter were too loud, and Cristelle seemed understandably defensive.

"Cristelle, could we meet again? I would like to talk to you a little more."

We arranged to meet her for lunch the next day.

During our walk home, Mateo asked me why I didn't interrogate her about the money.

"We need to find the right time. If she denies it then it will be very hard for her to admit she lied. Better to wait until she is ready."

In the morning Cristelle phoned and suggested she pick me up in her car. She said she would be more comfortable if I came alone. I told Mateo.

"Are you crazy? She might kill you. She think you have killed Ramon. Maybe she want to keep money."

I held Mateo by his hands. I looked into his face. He looked flushed, angry and scared at the same time.

"What is the matter Mateo? We are only going out for lunch. Try to come back into the moment."

Mateo looked down and shook his head slightly. Then he looked back into my eyes.

"I think you love people too much. Maybe you invite bad people."

"I would rather die loving people than live longer out of fear. You can have a nice time exploring Zurich. Here take this."

I handed Mateo a handful of Swiss francs.

"You are crazy!"

It occurred to me that he might have unnerved Cristelle with his clenched fist last night, but there was nothing to be gained now by saying it.

When the time came, we walked out of the hotel together. Cristelle waved from her red hatchback. Mateo looked at her suspiciously. I kissed Mateo goodbye and walked over to the car.

Cristelle started the car and we jerked forwards to the main road.

"I thought I would take you to a village in the mountains. It's less than an hour away. Great views and more relaxing."

Cristelle's driving was erratic, and I found myself holding the door handle and sometimes having to put my hand on the dashboard to steady myself. She snatched at the wheel to turn corners. Every gear change was accompanied with a revving engine, crunch of cogs and a sudden jolt forwards. We exited Zurich and after a short spell on a fast road turned off into smaller roads that wound their way into the mountains.

I tried to make conversation but my small talk was rebutted with short answers that left no room to continue the theme. Cristelle appeared tense and deep in thought. Perhaps she was nervous about our looming lunchtime conversation. I tried to remind myself that she was a beautiful human being, who had overcome all kinds of trials and tribulations to blossom into this wonderful, elegant, intelligent, emotional creature.

We drove up along the narrow road into a forest of pine trees. As the car continued to climb we drove into the bottom of a cloud. Mist swirled around making it difficult to follow the road. Cristelle slowed to a near walking pace. Then she pulled over into a slight clearing at the side of the road. I thought she must be finding the fog too thick.

"Are you alright, Cristelle? Should we go back?"

Cristelle reached down for her handbag, fumbled around for a minute and then opened her door.

"I think we should get out."

I looked round. The trees loomed eerily in the mist. Sometimes they would disappear and then reappear looking cold and pale. Cristelle walked round to my door and opened it.

"Please," she said curtly.

Her bag was open and she reached into it and pulled out a small pistol. Cristelle pointed it at my head. Oh no, not again, I thought to myself. This time I felt surprisingly calm. Cristelle did not seem violent. Perhaps I was getting used to having a gun pointed at me. I slowly eased myself out of the car seat and stood in front of her.

Cristelle looked uneasy. She fidgeted with the gun in her hand. She moved her weight from one leg to the other. Her hair blew across her face and she pulled it back with her free hand and a flick of her head.

"Give me your bag."

I reached into the car and found my bag. I handed it over to Cristelle with an outstretched arm. She snatched it from me.

"Cristelle, why are you doing this?"

"Stand over there."

I walked away from the car.

Cristelle lifted the rear hatch and took out a spade.

"You can walk along that path."

I turn and walked along the narrow path she indicated. Cristelle followed.

"Wait!"

A new thought seemed to have occurred to her. She tipped the contents of my bag onto the ground. Cristelle moved the pile of objects with her foot until she saw my passport. She picked it up with my purse.

As we walked into the woods, I felt the soft pine needles under my feet. I could feel the crunch of pinecones. It was easy to feel every step. I became aware of the wind on my face. As it changed direction I could feel the cold air cross from one cheek to the other. I put my hands deep into my coat pockets. The trees were very straight. If I scanned my eyes across my vista I saw a pattern of dark brown vertical lines against an off-white background.

I thought about Henrique and his idea about us being predicated to being dualistic. I became conscious of my two feet, my two cheeks and my two hands in their pockets. I could hear my footsteps with my two ears and see with my two eyes.

Was I part of Cristelle's dualistic world? Was I evil, bad, a threat, someone that had to be gotten rid of? She seemed lost in a world of injustice, loss and revenge.

I went on to consider how we were both, in current scientific terms, essentially a collection of atoms that came in and out of us. We were both made up of the universe and continually exchanging particles with the universe. I focussed on a breath to experience the exchange of a huge number of atoms entering and leaving. Yet, here we were, two parts of the universe marching into the woods, so one could send some atoms at high velocity, into a temporary collection of particles, I like to think of as me.

"Stop here."

I stood still and turned to face Cristelle.

"You can dig a grave for yourself."

Cristelle handed me the spade. She wobbled slightly as she took a step forward. Her green eyes blinked rapidly as they darted around nervously.

"Have you ever killed someone before?"

"No, but you have. Dig, please."

I started to press the spade into the ground. The soil was soft, but there were many roots making it hard to move the rich earth.

"Why do you say I have killed someone?"

"Because you killed my Mathew."

"When Mathew was killed, I was in the park."

"You lie to try and save yourself."

"Why would I want to kill the man I loved?"

"You knew he was leaving you for me. He told me he had spoken to you the day before he died."

Now I was surprised.

"I can assure you he never said anything to me."

Cristelle's eyes glared, her nostrils flared and her mouth contorted as she screamed out.

"Don't lie. You will not save yourself."

She stared with a look of righteous indignation. Her chin jutted forwards. Hair was stuck to the makeup on her face. She pulled it away and flicked her head so that it fell behind her shoulders. I went back to digging.

I thought about my dream in Venice. I thought how easy it would be to pass over into the next life. I did not feel any fear. I was surprisingly calm. Somehow I was enveloped in a beautiful feeling of trust. I trusted myself and I trusted in life. I had survived the rape ordeal and here I was still alive.

After a while, I began to feel hot. I stood up and unzipped my coat.

"So how did you meet Mathew? Was it at the blues club?"

Cristelle opened her mouth and then paused whilst she seemed to decide how much to tell me.

"I met him in Barcelona. I was fifteen and still at school. My father was opening a Swiss bank there. Mathew was thirty-six and working in a bar. He sang, played guitar and danced. I knew he was special straight away. He offered to teach me to play the guitar. Soon we were lovers."

"What about his girlfriend, Montserrat?"

Cristelle looked surprised for a moment. She swayed slightly before continuing.

"He used Montserrat to keep his family happy and stop people suspecting he was really with me."

"Didn't you mind?"

"I knew it would be crazy to be with him. My father would kill him with this pistol. The police would put him in jail. So we used to meet in his flat when Montserrat was out and make love. He taught me guitar and I became pretty good. It would be a reason if anyone wanted to know why we were together so much."

Cristelle's mood lifted as she talked about Mathew.

"My whole day revolved around being with him. I used to lie in bed dreaming of the time we could really be together. I used to fantasise about the house we would have together and how I would look after Ramon. I mean Mathew."

"So what happened? Why didn't your fairy tale come true?"

"We were lovers for a year and then Montserrat came home early from work. She was sick. She caught us in bed. She went crazy. Mathew had to hold her down. I left. After I could not see him. Mathew was frightened she would tell his family. She threatened to tell the police. So he said he must leave Spain. He knew an English woman and they married so he could live in England. He said he would come back for me when I was seventeen. It was only another year."

My interest had been aroused. I noticed how eager I was to hear the rest of her story.

"So what happened?"

"I waited but he did not come. He said it would be difficult for me in England. He said to wait and wait. Then my family moved back to Zurich and I met a Swiss man. We broke up five years ago, and then two years ago I found Ramon on Facebook. We had a mutual friend and Mathew's face appeared on the side of my screen like a miracle. We arranged to meet in London and it was as though nothing had changed between us."

Oh no. Mathew had been having an affair for the last year of our relationship. I felt my heart sink, I felt heavy on my feet. My shoulders dropped as my chest deflated. There was a slight pain near my heart. I had slipped out of the present into the past. I was back at home watching Mathew rushing out to go up to London with his guitar. I was back wondering if Mathew still loved me. I was back in suspicion, jealousy and hurt. Cristelle continued relentlessly.

"We met during the day when you thought he was at work. He used to come to my hotel so we could make love for the whole afternoon. In the evening, we made beautiful music together."

Cristelle sneered with a crooked smile as she spat out the next words, as though spraying her venom over my face.

"He never loved you. He always loved me and only me."

That was a turning point in my emotions. It was the line I needed to get back into the moment. Cristelle was voicing her delusions. It was her bitterness, jealousy and insecurity pouring out like blood from a gaping wound. I did not need to be a part of any of it. I felt my weight uneven over my feet and shifted slowly so that my body felt centred between my soles. I felt the cold air in my nose and throat.

Cristelle looked down at the grave. I had only dug about a foot into the ground.

"So, now I will kill you and you can rot in hell."

"Don't you think you will be caught when Mateo tells everyone you took me for lunch?"

Cristelle looked back defiantly, with a flick of her head.

"Maybe I'll shoot him too. Maybe I'll use your passport and ID to get our money out of the bank."

"Mathew took most of that money from me. I inherited it from my parents."

"So what!"

I could see Cristelle's face flush with anger. She raised the pistol with both hands to point it at my chest. She took a step forwards readying herself. I looked into her eyes.

Something extraordinary happened. I glimpsed the love that I had envisioned in my imaginary father's eyes during my free writing. It was there in her green eyes. It looked like the sun behind clouds peeking out through sky blue gaps. I could see the murky layers floating across the love in her eyes. The layers looked to be full of pain, disappointment, jealousy, pride and self-righteousness. The layers mirrored the mist, like a fog of illusions covering the pure light behind. I thought of Nirmal and unwrapping the soul.

As I looked into Cristelle's eyes, I felt a connection, I felt love well up in my heart. Cristelle flicked her head again. She shifted her weight, dropped her arms by her sides and then almost wearily brought the barrel back up to my chest. She looked at me curiously before closing one eye. I could still see the love in her remaining beautiful green eye. I was ready too.

Something flashed across my eyes, I heard a single sharp metallic crack, and then I saw the gun fall from Cristelle's hands. Cristelle turned to her left as though in slow motion. Something white and grey hit her cheek and she stumbled back. I followed her gaze. Mateo was standing about twenty paces from us raising his arm with a rock in his hand. I saw he had several stones clasped between his other hand and abdomen.

"No, Mateo, wait."

I looked back at Cristelle's eyes. Layers of fear swirled across the tiny shafts of love. Cristelle looked from me, to the gun, to Mateo. Mateo looked like a taught spring ready at the slightest twitch to fire another cold, sharp, hard rock. He did not blink, just stared transfixed on his prey. Mateo took two slow steps forwards.

Cristelle blinked nervously, blood ran down her cheek. Strands of hair stuck across the wound. I thought I saw her legs wobble.

She looked behind her and back at the gun. Could she pick up the gun before Mateo struck again? Could she run back into the fog and to her car? I could see a cloud of despair cross her face. She looked so alone, a cold solitary figure, isolated in the mist. She seemed to be slowly drowning in her own emotions. She tried another flick of her head but her hair stuck to her face. Then I saw her look back to me. Her beautiful green eyes appeared pleading. I saw the rims slowly redden and tears begin to fill the lower lid. The water in her left eye gently spilled over into a tear that slid down her cheek until it diluted the crimson blood.

I held out my hands to Cristelle and took a step forward. She shook her head, and cried out "No," but fell into my arms. I put my arms around her, gently stroking her upper back. I felt her head against my shoulder. She began to tremble. The quivering built up until savage sobs broke through her wall of suppression. Cristelle felt so heavy in my arms.

Mateo walked over softly. He stood still beside me. Then he let his arms relax, dropping the stones, one by one, next to his feet. I felt my universe slow to an eternal stillness. Cristelle's crying subsided and we stood in silence.

CHAPTER 31

Gradually we shifted positions. Relief washed over me like a warm shower. Cristelle straightened up and started to compose herself. Mateo picked up the pistol with a stick and dropped it in the trench. He covered it in earth and pressed it down with his shoe. I zipped up my jacket.

We walked slowly back along the path. The mist was lifting and I could see across the valley through a clearing in the trees. When we got to the car I bent down to collect my pile of belongings and put them into my bag. Cristelle handed me back my passport and purse. A question came to my mind. I turned to Mateo.

"How did you get here?"

"After you go in car, I take taxi and follow. We lose you in fog. But then I see car. I see you leave things on path and I follow. I hear shouting and I know where you are. I see her with a gun."

"The taxi must have cost a fortune."

"I give him the money you give me and he comes to hotel for the rest tonight."

"Thank you for caring so much about me. I'm sorry I didn't listen to you."

Mateo smiled.

I drove the car home with Cristelle giving directions. Cristelle fidgeted incessantly. She pulled at her hair, bit her lower lip, wrung her hands together. When we joined the main roads, I put my hand over hers, encouraging her to keep her hands still. She let her head fall back onto the seat rest and sighed.

It was now late afternoon and I was experiencing pangs of hunger. As we drove into Zurich, Cristelle guided us to a restaurant not far from our hotel.

"Cristelle, please join us. We can talk about what has happened and about Mathew, if you like. We might all benefit from being together for a while."

Cristelle turned her face to look out of the window and then nodded slowly.

We found a table in the corner and ordered.

"How are you now, Cristelle?"

Cristelle looked sullen. She shrugged her shoulders and looked down.

"Life will change. I hit rock bottom after Mathew died, but then I ended up with my aunt who took me on a life-changing journey. If I had not been in that place emotionally, I don't think I would have listened to her. I would have thought she was crazy, just like my parents did."

Cristelle raised her green eyes and looked into mine.

"There is something different about you. When I wanted to shoot you, there was something in your eyes, your calmness, maybe you seemed so… I don't know how to say it, kind, maybe loving."

I smiled at Cristelle and looked into her sparkling eyes. I wanted to look into Mateo's eyes to see if I could see the love in him but he looked away self-consciously. He seemed uncomfortable with our conversation.

"I don't think I could have shot you. It was a relief when he threw the stones at me."

The food arrived and we started eating. We were so hungry, we chewed in silence. After I had finished my soup and salad, I looked up. Mateo glared at me and flicked his eyes across to Cristelle.

"Cristelle, when we were in the woods you mentioned that Mathew had put our money into a bank account. Where is it?"

Cristelle wiped her mouth with a napkin. There was a bruise on her cheek forming around the cut. She brushed her hair back over her shoulders. Then she looked at Mateo and back to me. She seemed to be thinking. Perhaps clinging to a thought, exploring a way to keep the money. I could sense Mateo tense up. We waited.

"Mathew used to give me the money in London to put into the account here. I could have kept it, but I put it all in his account."

"Can you give me the account details?"

Cristelle's eyes watered slightly. A wave of defiance passed across her face. I waited. Then she softened and looked in her bag. She found a paying in book and handed it to me.

"Are you short of money?" I asked her.

"I have debts but that is not the point. It's the life I was going to have. Ramon, the apartment, a sense of security; it has been taken from me. My life is empty."

"A very loving woman once told me 'Nothing is a beautiful place to be.' From nothing, everything and anything is possible. If you can free yourself of all the layers that are holding you back, imprisoning you in these feelings, your world will become enormous. We all have Mathew to thank for that. He has given the three of us the amazing gift of being able to transform ourselves from nothing."

I reached out and held Mateo and Cristelle's hands. I felt the warmth of Mateo's palms, with the slightly leathery texture of his skin. I felt the cold clammy surface of Cristelle's hand. I felt the softness of her skin. I looked at Mateo and then Cristelle.

"We can all be loving."

I watched Cristelle take her free hand and tentatively offer it to Mateo. He responded and the three of us were connected. The image of colourful, wild flowers growing from Mathew's ashes blossomed in my mind.

CHAPTER 32

A visit to the bank revealed the extent of paperwork and form filling I would need to access my money. Phone calls and emails to Graham Parker ensured that signed copies of Mathew's death certificate, will and marriage certificate were sent over.

Whilst we were waiting, Mateo and I had more time together. Drinking smoothies in a local juice bar, we tried making a list of all the characteristics we most liked about Mathew. When I described Mathew's obsessive attention to detail around the house, Mateo began to laugh. It was the first time we laughed about Mathew together. There was something immature and innocent about Mateo that made him attractive to me.

That night we rented a film and watched it in Mateo's room. We lay on his bed eating packets of popcorn. I must have fallen asleep half way through. I woke in the early hours of the morning lying next to Mateo. He had put his duvet across me. Mateo was wearing pyjama trousers. He looked peaceful and secure in his dreams. I edged myself to the side of the bed and sat up feeling drunk on sleep. I tried to will myself to stand up and go to my room. I felt hot and uncomfortable in my clothes.

As I finally stood, Mateo cried out. He started talking in Spanish as he rolled onto his side towards me. I sat on the side of the bed and stroked his head.

"Shh, Mateo, it is just a dream. You're safe."

Mateo reached out and pulled me towards him. I lay on the duvet next to him and put my arm around him.

"Try to go back to sleep."

Mateo put his arm around me. He kissed me on the cheek.

"Please don't leave me," he said sleepily.

"I think we will always be close."

I waited until I felt him return to his dreams. I carefully eased myself off his bed and stood looking at him. He seemed so young and vulnerable lying there, tucked up in bed. On impulse I took off my sweater, socks and jeans and lay next to him.

In the morning I woke to see Mateo lying on his side facing me. His big brown eyes looked into mine.

"Hello, Amanda. You stayed. Thank you."

"How did you sleep?"

"Good."

Mateo looked away and then back at me. His eyes suggested he was troubled.

"What is it, Mateo?"

"You know when I say undress. Then I say you ugly."

"Yes."

"I am very sorry. You not ugly at all. I think you are very beautiful. You have a special beauty that comes from inside. I can see it now. Before I was too angry to see."

"Thank you."

Mateo propped himself up on his elbow and leant across and kissed me on the cheek. I instinctively put my hand on his back.

"Are you going to teach me how to make love?"

I pushed him away playfully.

"You already know. And by the way, you can make love to me with your beautiful eyes."

Mateo looked into my eyes and I could see the love.

"You know I love you very much."

"*Si.*"

"Good. Time to get up."

Later in the morning we shared lunch with Cristelle. I told her that when I had control of all the funds, I would transfer enough money into her account to pay her debts.

"Cristelle, I would like to invite you to come to London and meet Dorothy. She has really helped me and perhaps you would like someone to hold your hand as you explore how life could be different for a while."

Cristelle smiled and for the first time I saw her face relax. We exchanged contact information and parted. We collected our luggage and took the train to the airport.

Back in London I met up with Martin Ledbetter so he could inform the building society that the funds had been recovered. I also telephoned Sergeant Smiley to tell him where Mathew had put the money and explain the circumstances.

"Do you think Cristelle had anything to do with the murder?"

"You can check, but I think she was in Zurich at the time."

I put down the phone and checked my emails. There was a message from Edward, pleading to meet up. Now I knew it was not Edward who had attacked me or sent the threatening letters, I felt more kindly towards him. His declaration of love to me had brought several life-changing challenges upon himself. The curse of trying to get Amanda into bed, I thought.

We met up on Primrose Hill. The sun was shining and a brisk wind tossed my hair into the air. I stood looking across the London skyline with Edward by my side.

Feeling a little flustered, I blurted out, "How is your karate coming along?"

"I gave up karate ages ago. Too much like using a sledgehammer to crack a nut. No, tai chi is much more me."

Edward proceeded to show me the beginning of the short form he had been learning. I smiled at the memory of all those karate stances and wondered how long this would last.

Once Edward finished his flowing moves, he told me how he and Edwina had divorced. Edward had a bachelor pad, as he described it, in Soho, near his office.

"I still feel the same about you, Amanda."

"Oh, Edward, I would have thought that after all you have been through, you would run a mile from me."

"No, nothing has changed."

I think if I was the same woman I was before I started this journey I would have felt a flutter of excitement. I might have turned on my girlish charms. Now we felt so far apart.

"Edward, I don't want you to waste any time thinking of me. I really do not think I am ready for a relationship, and even if I was, my interests are so different from yours."

Edward made a gallant effort to win me round. He promised undying loyalty, financial security and love. After all my struggles, it all sounded so easy. Could Edward be my rock, as Roger was to Dorothy?

Then an image of a distraught Edwina flashed through my mind. There she was, in so much pain and Edward so detached. I remembered the way Edward dismissed me after taking me out for his romantic lunch.

"It really does have to be goodbye, Edward."

I left him with his clothes flapping in the wind.

After a few weeks I met up with Edwina in a small café in Primrose Village. The sun shone and we sat near the window.

After the small talk ran dry, I asked Edwina about her life.

"We divorced, sold the house and now I am living in Welwyn Village. It must be costing Eddie a fortune. I am finding it hard. Some days I just slump on the sofa with a gin and tonic watching daytime television. I'm comfort eating, as you can see. Still, if it doesn't kill me it just makes me stronger. Isn't that how it goes?"

I smiled. I watched three children outside. One of the boys snatched a phone out of another's hand and threw it to the third boy. They hurled the phone back and forth whilst the boy in the middle lunged one way and another to retrieve it. After a while the short boy seemed to get bored and then dropped the phone into the gutter. The child grabbed his phone and started drying it frantically. The other two children laughed and ran out of sight.

I had witnessed a scene that was hard not to judge as malicious, unkind and spiteful. And yet, I did not want to judge. Could I understand each of them? Edwina interrupted my thoughts.

"So, what has happened with you, Amanda?"

I told her about meeting Mateo and getting the money back.

"I now have enough money to buy a small flat near to Dorothy. My offer for my new home has just been accepted. I have enough left over to give Mateo money to pay off his mother's debts and look after himself."

"That's kind of you."

"I am starting a job teaching art at a comprehensive school on the other side of Hampstead Heath."

I went on to describe how I took Mateo to Barcelona to meet his relations at Bar Fornos. I told her how they made a big fuss over him and immediately took pride in his looks and physique. I remembered how at first Mateo was shy. He seemed to cling to me slightly. After the first day he and Francesc spent more time together whilst I enjoyed some sightseeing with Rosa.

"Oh, Amanda, you and Mateo seem to have such a strong bond. The way you talk about him you could easily be his mother. I think it is wonderful that even though you lost a husband, you have found a son."

On the way home I thought about the three children and the phone. Was my choice to return to teaching an opportunity to offer the children I would be guiding, other possibilities in life? I wondered if I could somehow impart my love to rowdy teenage boys. If I could keep my love through being threatened, attacked, raped and taken to the forest to be shot, why not? I smiled to myself.

DEATH OF A BUTTERFLY

CHAPTER 33

The red admiral butterfly lives for about one month, giving the males time to mate and the females to lay their eggs. After this the adults have no further role in the survival of species.

Late afternoon at Dorothy's flat I helped move the chairs and prepare for another meeting. I arranged the candles whilst Dorothy prepared the tea and snacks.

The sun shone through the west windows, casting long shadows across the room. Dorothy had bought some fresh flowers and I arranged them into a tall glass vase. I was aware of feeling calm, contented and in a way loving, as I touched the stems.

I thought back to the first time I engaged in this ritual after I arrived at Dorothy's, fearful and on the run. I remembered my confusion, scepticism and distrust. I didn't realise there was so much to discover. Just as now, I did not know the hidden possibilities of what life could be.

People arrived filling the hall with coats and shoes before taking their seats. The chatter of small talk filled the living room. Once everyone was seated Dorothy sat at the end of the room. I cast my eyes around our group observing Ruby, Henry, Cristelle and Mateo. Only Edwina had declined to join us.

Dorothy started with a meditation and asked each of us to describe our feelings. I noticed her patient, gentle probing to help each person stay in the moment, when our natural inclination to justify, analyse and refer to the past, broke through.

"You might ask why I am here and why have I invited you to my home. This journey is more fun with other people. So my invitation to you is to join me on an open ended adventure. I will support you when you ask me. I may gently challenge you, help you discover different perceptions on life, and encourage you to free your minds sometimes, as I hope you will me. Now, would anyone like some tea?"

I got up and poured the camomile and olive leaf tea. Dorothy sat back in her chair with her eyes closed. I offered each person some nuts and slices of apple. I enjoyed being in service to these beautiful humans. I felt so light, almost as though I could spread my wings and fly. I sat down and Dorothy invited us to try the tea and snacks.

The caterpillar turning to a butterfly metaphor came back to me. It was easy to see my journey as one of transformation, and yet thinking like that placed me in a new kind of dualistic thinking, as Henrique would claim. It suggested my old life was wrong, that Mathew was bad and that I had elevated myself. I enjoyed that image of me as a butterfly, the aware, evolved, spiritual woman and yet I knew I had to let it die. In a sense it had become a new hole I had dug for myself, as Nirmal might say.

I looked at the faces around me. Perhaps by being part of this group, I could experience the death of the butterfly I had created. My time as a butterfly might let me lay the eggs that would become the means for someone else's transformation. Being part of Mateo's life would help me rediscover my love for Mathew. I certainly did not want to separate myself from the people around me by taking on the airs of being more spiritual.

My attention came back to the group. I had to look away when Henry scooped up a large handful of walnuts, tipped his head back and ladled them into his gaping mouth. I had a vision of Henry munching his way through the rest of the evening. I smiled to myself. You are going to be my delicious challenge, dearest Henry.

Mateo looked guarded. His inner strength kept him sitting with an upright posture. He stared straight ahead until Ruby engaged him in conversation. Ruby was colourful, exuberant and expressive in her purple dress. I smiled as I watched Ruby making small talk to a man she knew had murdered and raped. I turned to look at Cristelle and she smiled. Her green eyes sparkled in the candlelight.

How unbelievable that two people who wanted to do me so much harm were now sitting with me and about to accompany me on a new adventure. I laughed inwardly as I thought to myself, I couldn't make it up. Hey ho!

Dorothy started talking in her distracted way.

"I wonder whether, if I perceive my world in a particular way – if my perception is partly of my own choosing – I am living in a self-constructed illusion."

There was a pause whilst Dorothy leant forwards to adjust the position of a flower in the vase in front of her.

"Perhaps we all have our special way of relating to the world we inhabit. We may each have our own understanding, even if we try align our interpretations with other people's perceptions."

Dorothy slowly picked up her cup and took a sip of tea. She leant back and closed her eyes.

"The point being that, I find it so easy to make my understanding right, to defend my perception and win those battles of opinion. And yet that reduces me to one illusion, one possible interpretation of life and one relationship with my world."

Dorothy opened her eyes and leant forward.

"Perhaps the bigger challenge is to recognise my illusions, as illusions and to be open to other people's illusions; to have the flexibility to understand people through their illusions, rather than judge them. I sense that through an appreciation of each human, as he or she is, I flow through an infinite range of perceptions that ultimately helps me connect. Those connections help me feel loving. And yet, I can I accept that even my intention to embrace all understandings is just another temporary chosen intention that will change."

Dorothy reached to her side and picked up her knitting.